YOU DON'T LIVE HERE

Also by Robyn Schneider

Invisible Ghosts

Extraordinary Means

The Beginning of Everything

Robyn Schneider

YOU DON'T LIVE HERE

KATHERINE TEGEN BOOKS
An Imprint of HarperCollins Publishers

Katherine Tegen Books is an imprint of HarperCollins Publishers.

You Don't Live Here
 For information address HarperCollins Children's Books, a division of HarperCollins Publishers, 195 Broadway, New York, NY 10007.
www.epicreads.com

Library of Congress Cataloging-in-Publication Data

Names: Schneider, Robyn, author.
Title: You don't live here / Robyn Schneider.
Other titles: You do not live here
Description: First edition. | New York : Katherine Tegen Books, [2020] | Audience: Ages 13 up. | Audience: Grades 10–12. |
Summary: "After the sudden death of her mother, Sasha moves in with her grandparents and realizes new truths about herself"—Provided by publisher.
Identifiers: LCCN 2019056127 | ISBN 9780062568113 (hardcover)
Subjects: CYAC: Photography—Fiction. | Dating (Social customs)—Fiction. | High schools—Fiction. | Schools—Fiction. | Grandparents—Fiction. | Death—Fiction. | Sexual orientation—Fiction.
Classification: LCC PZ7.S36426 You 2020 | DDC [Fic]—dc23
LC record available at https://lccn.loc.gov/2019056127

Typography by Molly Fehr
20 21 22 23 24 PC/LSCH 10 9 8 7 6 5 4 3 2 1

First Edition

To the girls who don't know yet,
and the girls who are figuring it out,
and the girls who have known forever

And I asked myself about the present; how wide it was, how deep it was, how much was mine to keep.

—*Kurt Vonnegut*

CHAPTER 1

THE APRIL THAT EELS STARTED FALLING from the sky in Alaska—the same April that we Californians hoped for much-needed rain—everyone was looking up. It was like a cosmic magic trick, how we were all gazing in exactly the wrong direction the day it happened.

It had been a brutally hot week, and the heat showed no sign of breaking. The blacktop wavered as I locked my bike outside Randall High, and the tops of cars seemed to sizzle in the dry air.

Even in the air-conditioned gift shop of the Pioneer Museum, the heat snuck in whenever someone opened the door—which was often, since it was the museum's only exit. I slouched behind the register most afternoons, ignoring the trickle of patrons who were forced to walk past me, most of them ignoring the unappealing carousel racks of stuffed animals on their way to the parking lot. Whoever decided people should exit through the gift shop had probably never worked in one.

It was a decent after-school job, though, working at the Pioneer, which was either California's forty-ninth best natural history museum or its second-to-worst, depending on your perspective. Mostly, I babysat the bins of posters that no one ever bought and actually got paid to sit around and read library books. I measured my paychecks in romances and classics, in stories about big cities and boarding schools. There was the week of Meg Wolitzer, and the month of Haruki Murakami. So it was no surprise that I was reading on the day in question.

The museum was crowded, but it was early enough in the evening that most patrons were still loitering in the air-conditioned exhibition halls, pretending to be interested in the displays.

I was absorbed in a biography of Zelda Fitzgerald, reading about Paris in the 1920s, which sounded fabulous, full of flappers and champagne, when the insistent squeak of a postcard rack brought me back to reality.

"Can I help you?" I asked with minimal enthusiasm, glancing up from my book.

Immediately, I knew I shouldn't have said anything. It was a boy, maybe nine years old, all swagger and basketball shorts. There was a yellow museum pin bunching the center of his T-shirt, which made it look like an invisible hand was grabbing a fistful of fabric.

"No," he said. Without breaking eye contact, he pocketed

a dinosaur eraser. "I'm just looking."

And then he did it again. I watched in despair as more erasers went *plonk, plonk, plonk* into his pocket.

"Those cost fifty cents each," I warned, using my babysitter voice.

"I said I'm just looking," he shot back.

Plonk went another eraser.

It was like he knew I wasn't going to do anything. Because, honestly, it wasn't worth the trouble. No one was checking inventory on the eraser bin.

The kid shot me a screw-you grin, this time pocketing a miniature geode.

Six dollars each, my brain supplied automatically. And those would be missed.

"You can't just take things," I said.

"Oh yeah? 'Cause my mom will get you fired if you tell," he threatened.

I suppressed a sigh. Shit like this was always happening to me. It was like the universe had stuck an invisible sign on my back, telling everyone to walk all over me. And the worst part was, he probably *could* get me fired. I pictured the confrontation, loud and exhausting. The kid crying until his outraged parents took down my name and threatened to write a negative Yelp review. The way that, somehow—this I knew with total certainty—everything would be my fault.

Or, I could just pretend it had never happened.

The boy was watching me. Waiting.

Well? his expression seemed to say.

My shoulders sagged.

"Um, let me know if I can help you find anything," I mumbled.

The boy smirked, and I forced my eyes back to my book, trying to ignore him. Except I couldn't concentrate. I was reading the same paragraph for at least the fourth time when the earth shook violently beneath us.

There was a rumble, and a tremendous boom. My chair rattled, and I grabbed on to the counter to keep my balance. I watched in horror as the postcard racks toppled like felled trees and the shelves shook, their contents cascading to the floor.

"Get under a table!" I yelled, ducking beneath the counter.

It's just an earthquake, I told myself, trying not to panic.

We'd done earthquake drills in school for as long as I could remember, rolling our eyes each fall as our teachers forced us to squat beneath our desks, heads down, hands protecting the backs of our necks. And every year we brought in personal emergency packs (protein bars, bandages, water pouches) that our homeroom teachers collected, and which we never saw again. Sometimes, I imagined a gigantic room in the school basement with shelves full of the things, rotting away.

Still, all of the earthquakes I'd experienced had been

tiny. At worst, a few seconds of swaying, and then it was over. Back to sleep, back to your tests, back to the mile run in gym. But as I ducked under the counter, something told me this was the reason for all those drills. It went on forever, the floor lurching and rolling, the building groaning in this deep, unsettling way. Inside the museum, I heard people shouting.

And inside the gift shop, the eraser thief let out a terrified wail.

"You okay?" I called.

"Y-y-yeah," he said shakily.

"It's going to be fine," I promised, even though I didn't know that.

At that exact moment, a light fixture crashed down on top of the cash register. Shards of glass rained to the ground, nipping against my arm. I hadn't expected an earthquake to *hurt*. I was so surprised by the pain, and by the very real possibility that it might not be fine, that my head banged against the counter, hard.

The next thing I knew, the earthquake had stopped, and my ears were ringing. No, the museum was ringing. The emergency alarm flashed from the corner, its warning shrill and insistent.

I groaned, pressing the tender place just above my ponytail. My hand came away clean, but my arm was flecked with blood. I had the overwhelming sense that something terrible had happened, but for a moment I couldn't think what. And then the ground lurched again—an aftershock—and I remembered.

The alarm blared. My head throbbed. My arm stung. The whole world seemed thick and slow. Plaster dust swirled through the air, like we were caught inside a snow globe. Not that anyone would want a snow globe of a scene like this. I'd seen the displays fall, but somehow, surveying the aftermath—the ruin—made it horribly real.

I was shaking shards of glass off my backpack when the kid crawled out from under a table with a muffled cough. He was dusted with plaster, his swagger gone. He looked stunned.

"Come on," I told him. The path to the exit was littered with fallen postcard racks and shattered geodes that were no longer worth stealing. But the neon sign still glowed above the door. Exit through the gift shop, I remembered. This was the only exit.

I started clearing the debris, kicking it aside, making a path. The kid followed behind me like a ghost, silent and trembling.

When I got to the door, I pushed against it, hard, but of course it didn't budge. I strained, pushing harder, and then I snapped at the kid to help me. He did what he was told, which honestly might have been a miracle. And between the two of us, the door popped open, the sunlight dazzling.

CHAPTER 2

TEN HOURS EARLIER, IT HAD BEEN just another late-start Wednesday. My high school had them every week, to the delight of no one. Homeroom was canceled, break was a fond memory, and each period got cut short by five minutes. Our teachers always forgot, their lessons spilling frantically into the passing bell. But the absolute worst part was not getting a bathroom break until lunch. The cafeteria line was nothing compared to the line for the girls' toilets.

Which is why, when my mom barged into my bedroom far too early that morning, I knew exactly what had gone wrong.

"Sasha!" she yelled. "School!"

"It's LATE START!" I bellowed miserably.

"Oh no." She made a face, realizing. "Wednesday."

"Wednesday," I confirmed.

"Since you're up," she said, opening the curtains with

far too much cheer, "how about breakfast at Coffee Bean?"

"Afraid to venture in there without a chaperone?" I teased.

She shot me a look, but she also didn't deny it.

I had complicated feelings about Coffee Bean. It was the only place in town to get a decent latte, but the college-age barista was completely in love with my mom. And he really wasn't subtle about it.

Sure enough, when we appeared that morning, in desperate need of caffeine, Barista Todd lit up the moment he spotted us. He lifted a hand self-consciously to his messy man-bun.

I rolled my eyes. My mom was thirty-seven and unfairly gorgeous, with long dark hair and exactly the kind of tall, thin frame that was made for vintage Levi's and gauzy blouses. Trust me, Todd wasn't the first chambray-wearing hipster to notice.

"Morning, Alice. Mini-Alice." He beamed, leaning across the counter. "What can I do you for?"

My mom reeled off our usual order with a smile.

"Awesome, I'll get started on that *dirty chai*," he purred, making it sound like she'd ordered a porno instead of an extra shot of espresso.

"You really need a new coffee order," I observed as we sat down at the table by the front window.

"Next time I'll order *Kopi Luwak*," she promised.

The fact that the world's most expensive cup of coffee

was brewed from beans pooped by a weird tree cat never ceased to amaze me.

Not like our town was the kind of place that served rare imported coffee beans. It was the kind of place where tourists driving past on their way to Palm Springs stopped to pee.

The worst part was, we weren't even the most popular bathroom pit-stop town between Los Angeles and the Coachella Valley. That honor went to Cabazon, which boasted a casino, a luxury outlet mall, and enormous concrete dinosaurs that loomed over the highway. We weren't anything—just box stores and tract homes and the occasional tumbleweed blowing through. Drive a little farther north and you'd hit the resort town of Big Bear. A little farther south and you'd pick up California's historic Mission Trail.

We'd moved here before I was old enough to remember living anyplace else. Back when my dad was still in the picture. Before he had a bullshit existential crisis and took off with his guitar and the car he was always tinkering with in the garage. The car had seemed like another of his selfish, expensive hobbies. We'd never imagined he was building an escape vehicle.

After he left, my mom and I had stayed. She said it was because she was a hairdresser and couldn't leave her clients. But really, I think the idea of starting over somewhere else scared her, even though my mom was the bravest person I knew. So we were stuck here, together, in a fractured version of what once was.

Barista Todd slid over our drinks with a dimpled smile. "How come you ladies always order to-go?" he teased. "My company that bad?"

"Actually," I mumbled, and my mom elbowed me.

"You know what they say about too much of a good thing," she replied airily.

"I'm a good thing?" Barista Todd looked hopeful.

"I meant coffee," my mom explained, her grin dazzling. Barista Todd's man-bun actually seemed to deflate, just for a second.

We took our breakfast outside and parted ways, me to school and my mom to the salon. She called over her shoulder that she'd pick up a veggie pizza for dinner.

"*Stranger Things*," I yelled back, since we had a rule that if one of us picked the pizza toppings, the other chose the entertainment.

That was the last conversation we ever had, by the way. The last time I saw her, vibrant and alive and wearing her favorite boots from that weird vintage store in Joshua Tree.

What else should I tell you? I spent lunch in the library at one of the tutoring tables, helping freshmen with their *Romeo and Juliet* essays. The yearbook crowd had waved me over, like they always did, but I'd pretended to misunderstand and just waved back without stopping. I always felt nervous sitting with them, like no one actually liked me and they only tolerated my presence because we had the same sixth period. Like they were secretly relieved on the days when I didn't show up.

That afternoon, in yearbook, I put on my headphones and sat at the back table in the computer lab, editing the pictures I'd taken for the class superlatives.

I don't even know why we had sophomore superlatives. It wasn't like, years later, anyone would reminisce about the time they got voted most athletic tenth grader. At least, I hoped not.

The list was full of the same kids who always seemed to win things, who would probably win the same awards again next year. I wondered idly if I could make everyone redo the same poses, lining the identical pictures up on the yearbook pages when we were seniors, showing how nothing had changed.

Shana Diaz and Sean Howell would always be the cutest couple. Tyrone Thompson, the star athlete. Jason Worth, the perpetual class clown. I was editing his picture, which he'd wanted to do with his eyes closed and mouth open, as though caught in mid-sneeze.

I applied a layer mask, making the midtones pop. This was why I loved photography. Because with the right angle and the right light, you could capture people exactly how they wanted to be seen instead of how they truly were. Their ugliness or sadness could be hidden, swept out of frame, until you'd never know they were anything other than the class clown or the cutest couple.

I added Jason's photo to the layout, then clicked to the next page. Immediately, I wished I hadn't. *Best Personality: Tara Angel* stared up at me. I wished it were a joke, but I'd long ago learned that the universe didn't have a sense of humor.

Tara and I used to be friends. We used to have sleepovers and marathon *The Vampire Diaries,* shrieking so loudly when Stefan took his shirt off that her mom would rush in to see what was the matter. And then, in the seventh grade, catastrophe struck.

That year, I was the first girl in our group to get a boyfriend. We were twelve, so it was adorably tame. Notes tucked into my locker. Plans to attend the Valentine's Day dance together. And then one morning I saw Tara talking to him.

He wouldn't look at me in the hall that day, and I had no idea why. "I broke up with him for you," she explained at lunch. "And now that you don't have a boyfriend anymore, sorry, but you're not cool enough to sit with us."

My friends abandoned me there, next to the vending machine, laughing like it was a silly prank. I'd stared at my reflection in the glass, trying not to cry. I couldn't tell anyone. What would I say? It was the perfect crime.

But Tara kept going. She made up rumors about me to anyone who would listen. Once, when she couldn't find her glue stick, because it had rolled onto the floor: "Sasha probably took it to get high." Another time, when I made the mistake of wearing purple socks: "You know that wearing purple means you're gay, right?" she'd said loudly, leaning across the aisle in homeroom. "Do you want everyone to know you're gay, Sasha?"

I never wore purple again. I tried to blend in. To camouflage. But Tara's campaign to take me down was a resounding success. Partnering up in class was a nightmare. Girls scooted away from me in the locker room. Offensive notes constantly turned up in my locker.

But middle school is terrible for everyone. At least, that's what my mom said when she realized I wasn't sleeping over at Tara's anymore. I didn't tell her the truth about what my former friends were doing. It was too humiliating. And anyway, it wasn't fixable.

In high school, I found ways to fake a social life. I learned photography off YouTube and volunteered to take the photos for the yearbook. That way I was always attending school events, and it didn't matter that I had no one to go with. I stood off to the side, with my camera, documenting.

Enough time passed that everyone mostly forgot about middle school. But still, whenever I saw Tara in the halls, my stomach twisted, and I found myself terrified that it could all start up again.

And I'd rather be invisible than find myself a continued target. Especially since Tara had come so close to getting a bull's-eye. So I made myself forgettable. I held the yearbook camera from an unimportant corner of the gym. I captured my classmates' best angles, their perfect moments. And in a way, their moments became mine, too: *photos by Sasha Bloom,* the captions read in six-point font.

I stared down at the quarter page of our yearbook celebrating how well liked and popular Tara was. If the headline were accurate it would read, *Worst Personality: Tara Angel.*

Actually . . . I clicked the little text box. And then, my heart pounding, I changed it. I added her picture, and for one glorious moment, everything was perfect. The caption revealed her. Her eyes seemed mean, and her smile fake in a way that it hadn't before.

There was a chance no one would catch it. And if they did, they'd never know it was me. Still, the stress of doing something wrong made me feel ill. I didn't upset the status quo—I tiptoed around it. By the time the bell rang, I'd put everything back to the way it was supposed to be.

I biked to the museum that afternoon thinking about alternate captions for the yearbook, ones that exposed a truth far deeper than best hair or most class spirit. Mentally, I sorted through my classmates, choosing who would win worst lab partner, or dirtiest gym clothes, or most desperate for Instagram likes.

I spent my afternoon sitting in the museum gift shop, reading about Zelda Fitzgerald and trying to stop eraser thieves and forget about Tara Angel.

And then, miles away, deep beneath the ground, the San Andreas Fault shifted at exactly 5:02 p.m., and with it, my entire life crumbled to pieces.

CHAPTER 3

WHILE EVERYTHING LEADING UP TO THE earthquake is as clear in my mind as a page of study notes, everything immediately after is blurry and fractured, as though, in all of the chaos, the pen slipped, leaving a smudged, illegible trail down the page.

And so I can recall very little from the rest of that day. Even now, there are only fragments: strangers exiting the museum, shaken and trying to get cell service. The eraser thief shouting "Mama! Mama!" and launching himself at some spiky-haired woman in a navy tracksuit. Sirens in the distance. Sirens getting closer. The dark plumes of smoke that signaled us from town, from my suburb, from the next suburb over. The choke of cars on the road. The five tries it took to unlock my bicycle with shaking hands.

And in the background of all of these flashes, the unbearable silence from my mom. The lack of missed calls. The way she wasn't answering her phone. The frantic stack of texts I sent, all asking the same question over and over: *Mom, where are you?*

When I'd left the apartment that afternoon, hastily changing out of my school clothes into a button-down shirt for the museum, I'd thought: turn off the lights, lock the door, did you forget anything, got your keys?

Except it turned out none of that mattered. When I finally made it home, the sky hanging dark overhead, I didn't need my keys. The large apartment building on the corner had collapsed, debris and concrete spilling into the street. A row of cars was crushed under a fallen oak tree. The houses, small one-story cottages, slanted crookedly, a collection of sagging roofs and smashed porches.

There was a surreal quality to all of it, as though I were seeing a simulation of a disaster, instead of numbly witnessing the real thing. The electricity was out, and the streetlamps should have come on by now. Without them, everything was in shadow, twisted and wrong. The neighbors, instead of going for their nightly jogs, were digging their cars out from under debris.

I called my mom again, getting her voice mail. Despairingly, I tried the salon and then considered calling the police. But what could they do? She wasn't missing. They probably had real emergencies. Car accidents. Wrecked buildings. People stuck in elevators. Any minute now, her red Civic would pull up. Any minute, my phone would ring.

I didn't know what else to do except wait, so I sat down

on the curb, feeling shaky and unglued and a little dizzy.

Living in California meant we were always teetering on the cusp of disaster. Between top forty hits on the radio, commercials urged us to earthquake proof our homes, and then to buy a season pass for Six Flags. Every few months, there was a wildfire, a landslide, a drought. Everyone knew it was just a matter of time before something like this happened. So we'd kept on living in denial, figuring that, when the big one did strike, it wouldn't hit so close to home.

It was going to be fine, I told myself. My mom's phone could be broken, or dead.

But then again, *she* could be broken, or dead.

A harsh light flooded over me, and I shielded my eyes, squinting up. An eyewitness chopper circled overhead. I imagined its camera pointed right at the breaking news, the way my classmates did at parties with their phones.

Let's go to our reporter on the scene, where a 6.0 earthquake struck the San Bernardino Valley this evening. Devastating. Just devastating. Thoughts and prayers go out to the victims as hashtag San Bernardino Quake is trending worldwide. You can text SANB to the number below to donate ten dollars to the Red Cross. How's it looking out there, Bill?

That's what all the news reports said, more or less. But of course I wouldn't know that until later, at the hospital.

Is this part important? The part between the earthquake we all experienced and the aftershock that was mine and mine alone? I don't know. When I close my eyes sometimes, I can still see bodies being pulled out of the crushed cars. I can still remember how it hurt to squint into the searchlight of the eyewitness chopper. To sit there, waiting, my unease giving way to panic, even before my phone finally rang.

An unfamiliar number flashed across my screen, but still, I scrambled to answer it.

"Hello? Mom?" I said, my voice tinged with desperation.

That was the last time I'd ever answer the phone thinking she was on the other end.

Earthquake footage was playing on every television at the hospital. It didn't feel real. But then, bad things never do, at first.

I don't remember getting to the hospital, or what they said on the phone after realizing I didn't count as an emergency contact because I was only sixteen.

I just remember the doctor in his green scrubs, his eyes shadowed, his mouth a thin line as he told me what I didn't want to hear: that my mom was in critical condition. That she was undergoing emergency surgery.

She'd been in the stockroom at the salon, mixing dye, when the earthquake had hit. The shelves had fallen, and there was damage to her lungs. The surgical team was prepping . . .

Everything became a dull roar, like the ocean was crashing into me. I sank down, down, into freezing darkness. He kept talking. It didn't matter. It didn't fix anything.

My grandparents came, driving straight from Bayport. They didn't even drop their bags off at the nearest Hilton, which is the first thing my grandmother said when she saw me, wrapping me in a hug that smelled of expensive perfume. My grandfather took one look at my mom on the ventilator, having just come out of surgery, and disappeared, his face ashen. He returned half an hour later with hot chocolate from the vending machine that no one drank.

It was tense and awful, sitting there, the news cycling over our heads, the real tragedy unfurling right in front of us. We were poised on the edge of something, together, and there wasn't a plan for what came next. I didn't know what we were waiting for, or if we even wanted to be waiting for it.

But the worst part, the absolute worst, was that, even though I'd heard the doctors warn otherwise, I still believed my mom would pull through. Even as the nurses wheeled in a bright red cart, as the doctor shouted for someone to "get them out of here." Even then, I still thought, *When she wakes up . . . After she gets better . . .*

Here's something I didn't know about hospitals until the moment it happened: They kick you out of the room when someone's dying who isn't supposed to be. You don't get to hold their hand, or say goodbye, or hear them say it's okay, and I love you, and be brave. Instead, you're shoved outside while a nurse rushes in with a cart full of emergency equipment. You watch from the hallway while a doctor runs the code, calling out numbers like she's on the bridge of the Starship *Enterprise*.

Numbers that fail to restart your mother's heart.

She says it out loud, the time of death. Not for you, sobbing in the hallway, but so she can write it down on her chart.

11:52 p.m.

I drifted, listless, through my mother's funeral. For some reason, I couldn't remember who anybody was. I looked to my left, and I didn't know who that lady was. And I looked to my right, and I didn't know who that man was, either. They were all faces I recognized, but I couldn't put the pieces together in any meaningful way.

My mom was dead, so what did it matter if the bald man who smelled of mouthwash or the plump lady with the pixie cut was a cousin or a neighbor or a coworker? What did any of it matter, when none of it would bring her back?

She was gone. The world had ended, and for some reason we were all still here. In this funeral home where the parking lot was horribly full. Standing around a beige room decorated with an enormous beaming photo of her that I'd taken six months ago, on my birthday.

The last thing I wanted to do was talk, about anything but especially my mom, and yet all people did was come up to me and start conversations about her. And when they'd had their turn telling me everything happens for a reason, or she's in a better place, or whatever, they drifted away, toward the food.

My grandmother was responsible for the spread. She'd fussed with the fan of napkins almost to the point of hysterics. There were six kinds of fancy crackers. Three flavors of brie, all with the labels cut off and placed to the side, like descriptions of paintings in a gallery. Duck liver pâté. Four varieties of French olives. Crab dip studded with little green capers. Melba toast. A jar of caviar. And the crowning glory, a bowl overflowing with everyone's spit-out olive pits, which felt, for some reason, unspeakably gross.

My mom would have loved that, I thought. We would have laughed about the olive pit spittoon as we sat in freeway traffic, leftovers resting at my feet. "Eleanor Bloom, ladies and gentlemen," my mom would say, rolling her eyes. I couldn't wait to tell her about it, or about how—I stopped. I couldn't tell her anything, ever again.

The idea that I was all alone now astonished me. My chest clenched, and my breath hitched, and I tried not to think about the dull thud her casket had made when they lowered it into the ground.

And so, I thought about the eels.

It had been all over the news, back when the news was

something that happened to other people, in other places. I'd been fascinated as the reporter explained that, up in Alaska, eels were falling from the sky. Birds scooped them out of the water and carried them off for dinner, but some of the eels got loose. They fell in fields, suburbs, a grocery store parking lot. They fell mouths first, full of sharp teeth.

But there was one thing the reporters got wrong. They all talked about eels falling from the sky as though the eels were the problem, frightening innocent people who were going about their ordinary afternoons. Except I knew the truth: The eels weren't the monsters. They were the victims. Their lives had been shaken apart by something they never saw coming. And in trying to get free from their unwanted fate, they'd only managed to make things that much worse.

CHAPTER 4

TWO DAYS AFTER MY MOTHER'S FUNERAL, I sat in the back seat of my grandfather's car, headed south to Bayport, California.

After someone dies, you're supposed to pick up the pieces and carry on with your life. Except I couldn't, because there weren't enough pieces left. So instead, I was the one who had to be picked up and carried on.

I fell asleep just past Corona, lulled by the steady hum of our tires and the white noise of the freeway. When I woke up, it was late, and we weren't on the 91 anymore. We were speeding down the Pacific Coast Highway, the ocean stretching dark and wide on our right, and the bluffs of Laguna Canyon rising tall on our left.

This wasn't the California I knew, full of dull strip malls and beige tract homes. This was a tropical, glamorous California, the one with movie stars and convertibles. The kind of place you see on TV and think it can't possibly be real, until suddenly you're driving through it, and it is.

"Well, here we are," my grandmother said.

Here we were. The *three of us*.

It had never been just the three of us before. Not even for a weekend. Not even for a day at Disneyland.

We weren't close, my grandparents and me.

I knew facts about them, but that wasn't the same as really knowing someone. I knew that my grandmother did Pilates and planned charity benefits, all in a cloud of expensive perfume and a tasteful leather jacket. I knew that my grandfather was a mildly terrifying lawyer who doted on their tiny dog in a way that was almost too pure for someone so buttoned up. Even in their vacation photos, he posed stiffly in front of the Trevi Fountain or the Acropolis in pressed khakis and tasseled loafers. You could just imagine my grandmother ordering him to stand there and smile as she counted down from three. It was a mystery where my mom had come from, and a no-brainer why she hadn't gotten along with them.

And yet, Eleanor and Joel Bloom were my guardians now. They were stuck with me, this fragile, fractured teenager. And I was stuck with them, thrust into a bizarre repeat of my mom's old life, right down to the house she'd grown up in.

"You'll recognize it in a second," my grandfather promised, as though it was the town I was having trouble picturing, and not what it would be like to live there.

The road curved, depositing us straight into the glittering sprawl of Bayport's main drag. We drove past luxe yoga studios, designer clothing boutiques, and upscale seafood restaurants, all of them closed for the evening. The dark silhouettes of palm trees thrust upward from a center divider. Occasionally, a colored spotlight cast dramatic shadows through the fronds.

After a few blocks, the shops gave way to a marina, full of ghostly white sails. A country club, lit up behind iron gates, was hosting an event, orchestral music floating down the curved driveway. And then there were the houses: overgrown foliage shielded us from peering in, but every so often, the hedges would dip, revealing a set of pillars and a gatehouse, along with the name of the subdivision.

Old Bluffs. Back Bay Estates. Pelican Crest.

The few houses that I could see, way up on the cliffs, were all glass windows and enormous balconies. It was hard to believe my laid-back mom, who padded around the house in thrifted men's flannels, had grown up here. When we drove down last Christmas, she'd muttered about rich Republicans driving Porsches and gluten-free housewives in designer yoga pants. Which, ironically enough, was a fair description of my grandparents.

We paused at a red light, and a Land Rover full of teenagers peeled out of a subdivision, windows down, music blasting. A blond boy drove, and a dark-haired boy sat in the passenger seat, grinning. The back was crammed full of laughing girls with long, wonderful hair that unfurled in the wind. They were all so beautiful, so perfect, like something out of a movie. I couldn't even imagine what it was like, being them. Their lives seemed easy and safe, unmarked by even a hint of tragedy. And then the car sped away, leaving me with the disappointing sensation of having glimpsed something that would never, ever be mine.

My grandparents' house was spotless. That was the first thing I noticed, how frighteningly clean it all was, more like a showroom than a place where people actually lived. They'd left in a hurry, I knew, shoving clothing into overnight bags, and yet, not so much as a throw pillow was out of place. I wasn't sure whether to be impressed or concerned.

The sharp tang of citrus disinfectant followed us down the white hallways, past rooms filled with pale furniture and enormous pieces of abstract art. I stopped at a table displaying framed photographs: black-and-white pictures of relatives I'd never met, my grandparents outside city hall on their wedding day, a family portrait with my mom in a pink ruffled dress. There was her high school graduation, the two of us at the beach when I was a baby, my yearbook photo from second grade with the missing front teeth.

And then there was the picture that had been blown up for her funeral. Her hair was wild and lovely, her smile genuine. She'd just bought me a portrait lens for my birthday, and she'd been a champion when I'd spent the entire weekend trying it out on her.

I realized with a start that I would never have any more pictures of her. And the force of that realization almost knocked me over. Now, she was an old photograph. A memory. This was the town she'd grown up in, the house she'd lived in, and she wasn't here. She wasn't anywhere.

I hadn't taken enough pictures. I hadn't saved enough videos, or kept enough voice mails, or known I would need things to remember her by. And now I didn't have them. I'd never have them.

I didn't realize I was shaking until my grandfather put a soft hand on my shoulder, as if to steady me.

He was carrying Pearl, their fluffy white mop of a dog, whom he'd tucked under his arm like a football. She stared at me, squirming, her little pink tongue hanging out.

Wordlessly, my grandfather handed me the dog, her body soft and warm against my chest. I cuddled my face into her fur, and she licked my arm, where my cuts from the earthquake were fading into pink welts, and didn't stop licking for a while. It sort of helped.

"I had Magda put fresh sheets on your bed," Eleanor said, pushing open the door of my mom's childhood bedroom. It had been frozen in time, from the window seat crowded with Beanie Babies to the No Doubt poster over her desk. There was a bed with a white wicker headboard. A Laura Ashley duvet. A bookshelf decorated with blown-glass figurines prancing in front of worn paperbacks. A lava lamp on the nightstand, filled with silver glitter.

A portrait of the artist as a young woman. The sorrows of young Alice. A room of no one's own.

"Oh," I said, staring.

I hadn't been expecting it. I'd figured there was a guest room, or that my mom's bedroom would have been dismantled finally, the way Eleanor was always threatening, and converted into a craft room or a gym. Of course, my grandparents had plenty of other bedrooms for that. Their house was enormous, and I couldn't imagine how big it felt with just the two of them. No wonder they'd gotten the dog.

"If you'd rather stay in the guest room—" Eleanor began doubtfully.

"No, this is good," I said. "I mean, this is great. I mean, thank you."

I wanted to be as little of an inconvenience as possible. To be a good houseguest, or whatever I was. I needed my grandparents to like the idea of having me around, because without them, I was screwed. Without them, it was Child Protective Services, which led to my dad, whose sole communications after ditching us were the emails he sent every year on my birthday. I deleted them unread.

I wasn't supposed to know that he was living in Bangkok, giving food tours, but I did. I'd found him one night on an internet deep dive, cringing with secondhand embarrassment at the pictures of him driving a *tuk-tuk* in a company T-shirt. His beard was patchy with gray, and he'd finished his tattoo sleeve. That was what he'd left us for. Not a successful music career, after all. Not even close.

It had been a relief when he hadn't flown in for the funeral. Or bothered to see how I was doing. But maybe he didn't know. Maybe he'd deleted my grandparents' email unread.

"Bathroom's just here," Eleanor went on, opening the door to what I had initially taken for a closet. "There are fresh towels in the cabinet. Shampoo, conditioner, whatever you might need. Oh, and I almost forgot the most important thing: After you use the shower, you have to squeegee the glass."

"Squeegee the glass," I echoed.

"From top to bottom," she elaborated.

She said this as though it was perfectly normal.

"There's a squeegee in the shower," my grandfather added helpfully, in case I might have worried I was expected to provide my own.

"Great," I said. "Thank you. For, um, everything."

"Well, of course, you're family," Eleanor said, moving toward me, like I was about to get some awkward hug that was all hands. Instead, she took back the dog.

After they left, I changed into my pajamas and crawled under the covers. In the cool darkness, I could hear footsteps on the stairs, the soft gurgle of pipes, the thud of a door being shut.

It was strange, realizing that these noises were unfamiliar

to me, but to my mom, they were all part of the house she'd grown up in. Was this what it had sounded like when she fell asleep at night, before my dad and I were even a speck in the distance? Or maybe even when she was pregnant with me, over some school break, before her parents figured it out and lost their minds over their perfect daughter wrecking her perfect future?

My existence had always been a burden to them. And now, staying here, I was even *more* of a burden. It wasn't fair. Any of it. So many people who had stood within shouting distance of us both got to keep on living the same lives. Or at the very least, got to keep on living.

On my classmates' Instagrams, the earthquake had already become a meme. This weird earthquake expert interviewed on the news had gone viral, and now the whole thing was an enormous internet joke. Whenever I opened Instagram, it made me want to scream.

I burrowed deeper under the covers, until I felt the edge of the bed with my toes, until the duvet was over my head, and I was breathing in my own warm breath. You could die like this. Suffocate from the carbon dioxide expelled by your own body. The idea sent a shiver through me. All I had to do was stay like this long enough and the nightmare would be over.

And then I was ashamed I'd ever had that thought.

"Mom," I whispered. "I miss you."

No one had warned me grief would be like this. I ached

so much that it felt like a vital part of me had been removed. And I didn't know how I was still living and breathing without it. Without her.

There, in the privacy of her childhood bedroom, I fell quietly to pieces, sobbing into her pillow with my jaw locked open, the tears hot and salty and never ending.

The things I was feeling didn't have words, didn't have a name.

I poked a tunnel in the covers, the cold air rushing in, clearing my head, and suddenly I was exhausted. It seemed impossible that, a week ago, I'd been concerned with nothing, with yearbook headlines and shoplifted erasers. That the chasm between one Wednesday and another could stretch so wide.

CHAPTER 5

I DROWNED IN MY GRIEF, and when I was done drowning, when I bobbed to the surface of that summer, it was already over.

The backyard pool was my refuge. I sat out there every afternoon, reading the childhood classics from my mother's bookshelf, trying to lose myself in Narnia and Xanth and Tortall.

Instead, I lost May, June, July, and the better part of August. I was sleepy all of the time, which was a new and surprising side effect of my chronic sadness. I had trouble concentrating on people, conversations, meals. And I cried at the drop of a hat. I used to be the stoic one, dry-eyed during death scenes on our favorite TV shows, making fun of my mom for needing a tissue. Now, I wept unexpectedly during breakup scenes in cheesy movies and sad songs on old playlists. I even cried over the scent of Kérastase shampoo in the shower, which my mom always brought home from the salon and had gifted to my grandmother at Christmas. No matter what I was doing, I was moments away from tears. They hovered just beneath the surface, along with the French for *Hello, my name is Sasha* and the catchy lyrics of a pop song that was getting beaten to death on the radio.

On the upside, my grandparents weren't around that much. They kept busy, too busy, which I knew was their way of coping. They filled the painful hours with trivial commitments, and I was strangely grateful for it, since it meant that having me around was less of an inconvenience.

I hid on a different floor when the maid came twice a month, and I felt impossibly awkward whenever I ran into her and she asked if I needed anything. Even after a summer together, Eleanor and Joel still felt like strangers, whose lives and habits baffled me. Once, in search of a Band-Aid, I'd caught my grandfather on the floor of their bedroom, doing push-ups in his underwear. Another time, I'd opened the freezer and found it full of my grandmother's face creams. And so I tiptoed around them in a cloud of grief, while they fluttered around me in one of cautious politeness.

It wasn't until the end of August that everything seemed to click back into focus. I brought my book out to the pool as usual, but everything felt different, clearer, like life was starting over again, the way Fitzgerald always claimed it did in the fall.

My grandmother was at Zumba, and my grandfather was at the office, doing lawyering. I had therapy later—that summer it seemed I was always in the waiting room of that unpleasantly cold medical center, pretending to be occupied on my phone while my grandmother leafed through celebrity magazines.

I made progress in the therapy sessions, googling late into the night to figure out what I should say so my grandparents didn't worry. I didn't want them to think that they were stuck with some depressing, broken person moping around their life.

That afternoon, like every other, I got out a plastic float and propped my book on my chest, squinting at it through my sunglasses.

It was incredibly peaceful, having the entire pool to myself. And then there was the view. In the bright morning sunshine, the ocean was everywhere. It was as though we were floating in it, suspended in glass. The air carried a salty tang, and seagulls screeched and swooped overhead.

This sun-bleached stretch reminded me of the book I was reading, set on the French Riviera, of the poolside parties at an Art Deco chateau. I closed my eyes and imagined I was there, a raucous 1930s soiree all around me, with glamorous actresses sipping cocktails and sad-eyed young artists memorizing every detail.

Except, the way I imagined it, I wasn't one of the gorgeous women. I was one of the artists, collecting it all. I pictured myself reaching for my camera, capturing those wild parties. Which was a good feeling, because I hadn't wanted to photograph anything in a long time. Not since the first public exhibition of my work had been my mother's funeral.

I got out of the pool to make some lunch, and Pearl trailed after me, letting out a string of insistent whines and then racing up and down the hallway. It was pretty cute.

"Um, hi," I said. "Do you want to go for a walk?"

She went crazy, taking off toward the front door.

"Guess that's a yes," I mumbled.

I could walk a dog. I was capable of that much, I told myself. So I scooped her up and clipped on her leash, letting her lead me around the neighborhood. I hadn't been outside much, hadn't left the house unless it was absolutely necessary. My mother's room—now mine—felt like enough world, and when I got restless there was always the kitchen and the backyard. Seeing just how far in every direction my new life extended, that there was an entire town full of people just beyond the walls of my grandparents' house, startled me.

A shirtless older gentleman was backing a golf cart out of his driveway, his face shadowed by a baseball cap. Long-haired blond boys played a game of street hockey at the end of a cul-de-sac. An Asian grandmother in an enormous sun visor, Darth Vader style, power-walked down the opposite side of the street.

I didn't recognize any of them. We were neighbors, I guessed, but it didn't feel like it, and I wondered if it ever would.

Eventually, Pearl dragged me back toward the house, stopping to roll around on someone's lawn. Their grass was freshly cut, and the little green shavings stuck to her white fluff like spikes. She stared up at me, panting in a way that seemed like smiling.

"You look like a tiny dragon," I said, bending down to brush her off. She whined, hating it. I wasn't sure what kind of dog she was. My grandparents had rescued her from a shelter where my grandmother did a lot of fund-raising, and their thoughts were: part Maltese, part Bichon. My thoughts were: part dandelion, part hyperactive marsh-mallow.

"Hey," someone called, startling me.

It was a boy around my age, with dark curly hair and a varsity jacket, although he didn't look like much of an athlete. He was standing on the curb, two houses down from my grandparents' place, carrying a grocery bag full of snacks. He had on a pair of neon-green wayfarers, which he pushed up into his hair, squinting at me.

I wasn't expecting him. I wasn't expecting to have to *talk* to someone, especially a boy my age. He had a Baycrest High School insignia on his ocean-blue varsity jacket. I was supposed to go there, I knew, but I'd tried not to think about it. The summer had seemed endless, until suddenly it wasn't, and ads for spiral-bound notebooks and back-to-school fashion had appeared in the local mailers.

"You're not a dog thief, are you?" he asked pleasantly.

"Only on alternate Tuesdays," I said, surprising myself with how easily the joke spilled out. But then, I was good at keeping up appearances. I always had been.

"Well, that's a relief." He grinned.

"I tell you that I steal dogs twice a month, and you're relieved?" I asked, frowning.

"Eh, I'm chaotic neutral," he replied, walking over and sticking out his hand. "Adam. I live here. In this house."

"Sasha. My grandparents live there, in that house," I said, waving toward it.

His hand was still out, so I shook it briefly, thrown by the formality. He was more eccentric-looking close up, and the script on his varsity jacket read *Academic Decathlon,* which I hadn't known it was possible to letter in.

"Have you been here all summer?" he asked.

"Um, pretty much."

"We just got back this week," he said. "School starts on Monday."

Did it? I hadn't been paying attention. Today was Thursday. No, Friday. Because therapy.

"Getting a head start on your school spirit?" I asked, gesturing at his letter jacket.

"Psh, my school spirit is perpetual," he said. "What's your excuse?"

I was confused for a moment, and then I realized I was

wearing one of my old RHS shirts. *Randall High Lion Pride,* my chest advertised.

"Oh, this?" I shrugged, keeping a straight face. "Yves Saint Laurent is having an exceptionally weird fashion moment."

"Aren't they always?" he returned, not missing a beat.

And then a low-slung white Mercedes pulled up. A gorgeous Asian girl in cat-eye sunglasses and bright red lipstick lowered the passenger side window. Françoise Hardy crooned loudly for a few moments before she turned the stereo down.

She stared at us, and I stared back, fascinated. I couldn't stop staring. She felt like someone I had conjured from the pages of my book. Even though she was around my age, I couldn't possibly imagine her sitting in a high school cafeteria with a sack lunch and a binder full of math homework. She seemed somehow better than that, and more interesting.

"Hi," she said, and it took me a moment to realize she meant me.

"Um, hi," I said, feeling self-conscious in my dog-walking clothes.

"Let's go!" she called. "Club presidents have to get there early, remember?"

"Trust me, no one's gonna care!" Adam yelled back, and then swiveled toward me with a sheepish grin. "That's my ride. See you around?"

"Sure," I said.

The girl turned the music back up as Adam climbed into the passenger seat. She said something, but I couldn't hear what. And then the car swung around, white paint gleaming in the sun and music trailing from the windows like smoke as the most beautiful girl I'd ever seen sped away.

CHAPTER 6

LIFE REALLY WAS STARTING OVER IN the fall, because my grandparents were going out on Saturday night, and they were taking me with them. To dinner. "As a family."

I let that phrase hang there, not even wanting to merit it with a response.

"Cocktail attire," my grandmother warned. "No jeans."

I didn't own any cocktail attire, seeing as how I wasn't old enough to drink one. But I knew where I could find some.

I'd gone into my mom's old closet just once, during my first few days in Bayport, when I was half out of my mind with grief. Tears had bubbled up, hot and fast, as I ran my fingers over the abandoned pieces of my mother's unfinished life. The soft college sweatshirt. The vintage prom dress. The thrift store finds she'd loved even back when she was my age. I couldn't help myself: I'd sat down at the bottom of the closet, closed the door with me inside, and bawled.

Now when I pulled open the door, my hands only shook the tiniest bit.

It's just a closet, I told myself. It's just a dress.

I almost believed it.

I took out a cream-colored sheath that looked like it might fit. The dress was a little snug, but thankfully it zipped. I stared at myself in the mirror. My hair was a lighter shade of brown than my mother's, but it had the same wave. My bangs had grown out from neglect, parting like curtains. Without them to hide behind, her face stared back at me. The barely there freckles, the wide brown eyes, the lashes that could never hold a curl.

I was a lesser version: shorter, curvier, with a rounder face and a sharper nose. A knockoff of the original.

Except not even that, because I wasn't anything like her in the ways that actually mattered. My mom was charming and brave and immediately likable. She made a great first impression, whereas people tended to forget they'd ever met me. She was forever chatting with strangers in checkout lines or singing along to the car radio or wearing enormous vintage earrings.

I was never going to be her. But I also wasn't going to snap back into being me again. And that was the part I couldn't quite wrap my head around. The earthquake and its aftermath had changed me, and I wasn't quite sure who this new person staring back at me from the mirror was, or who she was supposed to be.

"We're leaving in five," my grandfather called, his voice floating up the stairs.

"I'll be ready!" I called back.

I twisted my hair up, put on a quick swipe of winged liner, and stepped into my ballet flats. When I came downstairs, my grandparents were waiting, calm and cool and perfectly pressed as always. My grandfather in his pink Hermès tie with little elephants on it. My grandmother in a beige leather jacket and black silk pants, her hair in a French twist.

They stared at me, and I saw the pain in their eyes. I was the ghost of the daughter they'd lost.

"White?" Eleanor said, pursing her lips, her haunted expression clearing as she surveyed my dress. "It's almost Labor Day."

"Should I change?" I asked, unsure.

"It's fine," she said.

"You look beautiful," my grandfather added.

The dress had been a mistake.

I knew that as my grandfather maneuvered his car through the weekend traffic down on Ocean, the three of us sitting in awkward silence. Now, instead of just leaving the house, we'd also left the neighborhood. It was a lot. I thought wistfully of the Korean drama I'd been watching in bed, full of ridiculous fashion and even more ridiculous hair, about a girl masquerading as her twin brother to join a boy band. I'd just gotten to a good part.

The radio was turned too low, and was just that type of jazz that gets piped into waiting rooms, but my grandfather tapped along on the steering wheel anyway as he turned through the gates to the Bayport Country Club.

"This is dinner?" I asked, confused. I'd been expecting a restaurant.

"They have excellent food here," my grandfather promised. "Best dinner rolls I've ever had. Served warm. And don't even get me started on the salmon."

"Sounds great," I said, forcing myself to smile.

I stared at the massive Craftsman-style building, all exposed beams and geometric windows that overlooked the ocean. Now the whole cocktail attire thing made sense. My grandparents weren't trying to make "dinner as a family" feel special. We'd gotten dressed up because there was literally a dress code.

"Some of our friends will be here tonight," Eleanor said, studying me with a frown. She reached forward and smoothed back a loose wisp of my hair. "And some of their grandchildren. We thought it might be nice for you to make friends before school starts."

Oh god.

She went on, saying how important it was to start off on the *right* foot and know the *right* people, and I had this horrible flash of a country club version of Tara Angel sneering down her nose at my Forever 21 flats.

"What if they don't like me?" I asked weakly.

"What's not to like?" my grandmother retorted as though the notion was ridiculous.

I'd given my grandparents the impression that I had plenty of friends back home. I didn't want them to think I was weird, or that my mom had failed to equip me socially or whatever. Old people never get how brutal high school can be, how a screencap or a bathroom emergency or a vindictive friend can cause someone's permanent undoing.

"Don't worry, sweet pea," my grandfather said. "I'm sure you'll be just as popular here as you were at your old school."

I nearly choked. At least before I'd been invisible. Now I was a new student, and people paid attention to those. *What's her deal,* they'd wonder. And then they'd find out: I was the sad new girl with the dead mom. Or earthquake girl, which was even worse.

But I had a plan. A foolproof way to get through the next two years: I'd do what had worked before. I'd sign up for yearbook, sit at their lunch table, and volunteer to photograph events so it looked like I had a social life. I didn't need to make friends, I just needed to not make enemies.

Which meant that, whoever it was my grandparents wanted me to meet tonight, all I had to do was not make them hate me.

And so I took a steadying breath and followed my grandparents through a lobby and onto an oceanfront patio.

Waiters in bow ties stood at drink stations, mixing

cocktails and pouring wine. Passed hors d'oeuvres were being served. Music played, soft and inoffensive. A silent auction was set up along the back wall, where you could bid on spa packages and ski retreats. We'd had a silent auction at my high school to raise money—my mom had donated a haircut, and the woman who'd won it had angrily demanded her money back when she realized my mom wasn't a dog groomer. We'd laughed about it for days.

This was another new thing: the discovery that all of our inside jokes were buried along with her.

My grandfather disappeared instantly into a clutch of older gentlemen, who were recapping some golf game. Eleanor steered me toward a woman with short gray hair and a prominent gold cross necklace, who introduced herself as Joan, from the book club. Her nose was sort of melted, and her skin was strangely tight, and she could have been anywhere from fifty-five to seventy.

"Please tell me you'll be at the next meeting," Joan said, giving my grandmother a double air kiss.

"I'll be there," my grandmother promised.

"Thank god." Joan dropped her voice to a whisper. "I need a buffer. Annette won't stop going on about her kitchen renovation, and there's only so many times you can look at photos of marble slabs without going crazy."

My grandmother snorted.

"And this must be Sasha," Joan said, swiveling in my direction. "Has anyone ever told you that you look just like"—Don't say it, I thought—"Audrey Hepburn?"

"Never," I said, flattered, even though I didn't see it at all.

"The spitting image," she promised.

She switched gears, asking me about school. They were standard questions, easy conversational volleys that I tried to return to my grandmother's satisfaction.

"Hold on, that's my grandson," said Joan, waving over a tall, impossibly handsome blond boy. Water polo, I guessed. With a side of homecoming king. "Cole, come here! I want you to meet Sasha."

"Hey," he said, running his hand through his hair before offering it as an afterthought. "What's up?"

Did every teenage boy shake hands in this place? It was even weirder than using a shower squeegee. I clasped his hand briefly, mumbling a hello.

He was even better-looking up close, all broad shoulders and broader grin. His eyes were green, and his eyebrows thick and brooding. His hair magically stayed where he'd finger-combed it, a perfect golden swoop.

I pictured his yearbook caption easily: *Most Likely to Succeed*. He was the kind of boy who expected the whole world to fall willingly into his lap. And the kind of boy who definitely didn't talk to awkward, invisible girls like me.

And yet my grandmother was expecting it. Oh god, was *Cole* who she pictured I'd have as a friend? The idea was so absurd I almost laughed.

"Sasha will be starting at Baycrest this year," Joan said.

"Dope. So you're a freshman?" he asked.

I knew I looked young for my age—the perks of being five-one—but still. My cheeks went pink.

"A junior," I mumbled.

"Whoa, really?" Cole grinned. "Same."

"I'll be seventeen in November," I said, in case he thought I was still fourteen, but really, really smart.

"Mine's January third," Cole said mournfully. "Doesn't it suck having a birthday around the holidays?"

"Totally," I said, relieved he wanted to talk about something so normal. "It's like I'm being greedy, wanting presents early."

"At least having to celebrate yours doesn't interrupt your family's annual ski trip."

"God, how horrible," I said, deadpan. "What do they do, stick a candle in a mug of hot chocolate?"

"Shhh! Don't give anyone ideas," Cole said.

His eyes lit up when he smiled, shining bright and clear as stained glass. I couldn't remember the last time I'd had a conversation like this with a boy. Certainly never with a boy who was so attractive. Which had somehow brought down my guard. All of the clever remarks I kept locked inside my head were spilling out unprompted, and to my total surprise, they were *working.*

But it was probably only going well because I was an unknown quantity. He'd learn soon enough that I wasn't worth paying attention to. *Sasha Bloom, a disappointing mystery.* That's what he'd think, if he bothered to think of me at all.

Our grandmothers had drifted away, and I wondered why Cole was still here with me.

"I like your dress," he said, filling the pause.

"Thanks, it's my mom's." The words were out of my mouth before I could think twice, and I instantly regretted them.

"Are your parents here somewhere?" he asked pleasantly, twisting around, as though he expected a smiling mom and dad to materialize out of ocean air and insist on shaking his hand.

"Um," I said. I still wasn't used to this. To the screeching halt, followed by the swift calculation of whether to tell him the truth or spare him the awkwardness. I went with the truth. "Actually, my mom died."

"Oh. Shit." Cole made a sympathetic face. "I'm so sorry."

I'd been expecting him to react with half-terrified politeness. To cut his eyes anxiously toward the door. Not to roll with it.

"Thanks," I said. "So now I'm living with my grandparents."

"Good thing you're a freshman," he teased. "Because it would *really* suck to start over junior year."

"Oh my *god,*" I said. "For the last time—"

My grandmother interrupted then, to say that our table was ready.

"Well, nice to meet you," I told Cole.

I knew I should be relieved that I'd gotten through our little chat without making a bad impression. But to my surprise, I wished he'd stick around. He made me feel like a normal girl, and it had been a long time since anyone had made me feel like that.

"Actually, I'll join you," he said, and then turned to Joan. "If that's okay, Gran?"

"Always," she said, beaming.

"You don't have to," I said, in case he hadn't really meant it.

"My parents are over there," Cole said with zero enthusiasm, nodding toward a sleek blond woman in a pantsuit, who reminded me of a greyhound, and a bald man glued to his phone. Next to them was a taller, older, more muscled version of Cole, who seemed like he got really amped about protein shakes.

"Wow," I said. "Did he eat a Hemsworth?"

Cole snorted. "Honestly? It would explain a lot."

The six of us sat down at one of the round tables. I was between my grandfather and Cole. Another older couple joined us, introducing themselves as Dick and Annette. My grandmother looked like she'd swallowed a bug as Annette took out a hilariously outdated iPhone, showing off pictures of her ongoing kitchen remodel, with extra close-ups of the marble, which was apparently being reinstalled on Thursday and was an ongoing saga. Joan was trying not to laugh.

Cole, it turned out, did play water polo in the spring. And soccer in the fall.

"No football?" I asked, taking a sourdough roll from the basket. It was still warm, and the pats of butter had been pressed to look like tiny seashells.

"Nah, that's my brother Archer's thing."

"Besides cannibalism," I said, biting into my roll.

Cole laughed.

"You're funny," he said.

Boys never complimented me like this back home. There had been school Sasha, who was quiet, and home Sasha, who had plenty to say.

Now, it felt oddly switched. Because at home I didn't want to talk about anything, especially how I was doing (the correct answer always being "fine, thanks," whether it was true or not).

Sitting there in my cocktail dress, next to this smiling, attentive boy who had completely rolled with it when I'd told him about my mom and then gone right back to teasing me, I wondered. Maybe, in my months of grief, some of the weird, awkward parts of me had been polished away to reveal a bright newness underneath. Maybe the scars left by my middle school years had finally faded, and my grandparents were right that I could make friends here.

After our plates were cleared and the waiters came around with silver coffee pots, Cole asked if I wanted to get something to drink.

My grandmother nodded at me encouragingly, so I followed Cole over to the bar. He waved for me to go ahead, pulling out his phone and returning a text.

"Um, ginger ale?" I said.

"And a scotch old-fashioned," Cole added blandly, taking out his wallet and stuffing a dollar into the tip jar. The moment he ordered, I realized I'd made a mistake.

"So, you know what our grandmothers' book club *really* is, right?" he whispered as we waited for our drinks.

"Wine and gossip?"

Cole grinned, shaking his head.

"Nope. They read porn together," he announced dramatically.

"They do not!"

"Swear to god," he promised. "All that *Fifty Shades* stuff."

"That's not porn," I said.

"Then what is it?"

"Bathtub erotica?" I suggested.

To my surprise, he laughed.

"Ugh, that's worse," he said with a shudder. "Now I'm picturing my gran in the bathtub."

"Okay, fine, flannel pajamas erotica," I corrected.

"Much better!" He offered me a high five, and I took it, wincing at the force.

"Oww," I complained, shaking out my stinging palm.

"Don't be such a girl," he teased, smiling.

The bartender handed over our drinks, and I saw Cole

eyeing mine. God, I wished I'd ordered anything else.

I knew I should make a joke about it—something self-deprecating and clever. I was trying to think of one when a beautiful Persian girl hurried over, a silk dress swishing against the tops of her thigh-high suede boots. Her long brown hair was perfectly curled, and her makeup was expertly applied, and her eyelashes went on for miles. She couldn't have been more than five feet tall, but she was ridiculously intimidating.

"Cole!" she scolded. "Why was your family at my table, but not you?"

"I'm magic," he said, grinning.

"You're bullshit." The girl shook her head, pretending to be annoyed, but she was smiling. "Hi, I'm Friya."

"Sasha," I said.

"She's Eleanor and Joel Bloom's granddaughter," Cole said, slinging his arm around me.

"Really?" Friya smiled in my direction, as though that was all the information she needed. "That's so crazy. My dad works at Russ, Khan, and Bloom!"

"Hold up," Cole interrupted. "What happened with you and Nick?"

"We're over," Friya said. "That asshole. He wasn't helping that girl with her math homework. He was full on subtracting her clothes and dividing her legs. She literally failed summer school."

"Want me to beat him up?" Cole offered.

“God no,” Friya said. “But maybe give him really evil looks, so he worries you might?”

“Can do,” Cole promised.

Friya smiled. She was so confident, so effortless, the kind of girl who never worried about anyone’s approval. I wondered if she just rolled out of bed in perfectly layered gold jewelry.

I could barely handle Cole—adding this girl into the mix was too much. She didn’t even need to glance at my shoes for me to know they weren’t good enough. I got that just from existing near her. I was about to make an excuse and head back to the table when Friya’s phone buzzed with a text.

“Everyone’s down by the pool,” she said.

“Tell ’em we’ll be there in a sec,” said Cole.

“Well, it was nice meeting you,” I said, relieved it was over.

“Noooo, you have to come with us,” Friya insisted.

“Yeah, Freshman, you can’t bail on me now,” Cole teased, his eyes shining.

“Freshman?” Friya wrinkled her nose.

“He wishes. I’m a junior,” I said.

“Oh my god, Cole!” Friya scolded, giving him a shove. “I *hate* you.”

The pool was closed for the night, umbrellas folded and cushions removed from the chaise longues, but no one seemed to mind. In their cocktail attire, clutching drinks they'd brought down from the club, they looked impossibly cool, like a glossy magazine spread advertising a fragrance I could never afford. They were nothing like my classmates back home. Which, hopefully, was a good thing.

"There you are. *Finally.*" A tall black girl peeled herself off a lounge chair and pressed Friya into a hug. Her hair was twisted into two long braids, and with her gold hoops and gauzy, printed maxi dress, she looked like the kind of girl who got style snapped at Coachella. She introduced herself as Whitney. It was clear that she was in charge, and that Friya, for all her glamour and confidence, was eager to impress her.

Then there was Whitney's twin brother, Ryland, who was the prep to her boho in a pair of round glasses and ankle-length khakis. He barely glanced up from his phone, and I couldn't tell if he was permanently sour or if he just didn't find me all that interesting. And finally, there was Ethan, a surprisingly eloquent surf bro, who said it was, and I quote, "an absolute pleasure to make your acquaintance," with zero traces of irony.

"Same," I said, wondering how on earth anyone would ever think I belonged here.

I felt about seven years old, with my soda and my borrowed dress, staring at five of the most sophisticated teenagers I'd ever encountered.

They chatted about classmates I didn't know and

teachers I'd never heard of. I smiled, crunching the ice in my glass and watching without comment as Ethan slipped his arm around Whitney's back. She snuggled into him, her face lit up in the glow of her phone screen. She was tapping through stories from someone's house party, and she kept tilting her screen so he could see.

Cole pulled out a JUUL, passing it around. I took a pull, even though I never vape, just so I didn't look totally pathetic. Ryland wandered upstairs after a while and didn't come back. I sat down on his abandoned chair, barely saying a word, letting myself fade more and more into the background.

As I listened, I learned that over the summer, while I had moped around the house reading and feeling sorry for myself, Ethan had built houses in South America, and Cole had interned at a tech startup, and Whitney had done a pre-college program, and Friya had volunteered with an animal rescue. Somehow, they'd also found the time for family vacations to Europe and SAT courses and music lessons and off-season sports.

Their lives sounded stressful and overscheduled, and I got why they were hiding out here, drinking and smoking. And why they all seemed low-key pissed that their parents had dragged them out on the last weekend of summer, instead of giving them a night off.

Thankfully, I wasn't nearly as interesting as the drama that was unfolding on some girl's Insta stories. And so I was forgotten as they all leaned forward, watching the volleyball team play Never Have I Ever in someone's living room.

They were still engrossed in it when an elementary-school-age surf bro came down the path, cupped his hands around his mouth, and bellowed, "Ethan! Mom said to tell you we're leaving."

My shoulders sagged in relief.

"Thanks for the red alert, little man," Ethan called back, amused.

"Guess we should get back up there," Whitney said, stretching.

"Nice meeting you guys," I said politely.

"Same," they all said.

And just like that, they dissipated. I was the last one up the steps to the clubhouse, and when I glanced back down at the pool, I felt as though, if I closed my eyes and disappeared right then and there, no one would notice.

CHAPTER 7

MOST OF THE TIME, MY NIGHTMARES weren't so bad, but that night, they were relentless. I dreamed I showed up at my new school, except somehow it was twenty years ago. I chased my mother's ghost through the hallways, screaming at her to wait, to stop, to help me. And then I was lost, and suddenly my old middle school classmates surrounded me. Their laughter rang cruelly as Tara came forward, looming impossibly tall, with a dark horrible void where her mouth should have been.

"It's just a dare, Sasha," she crooned. "It's just a kiss."

I was dragged forward, powerless, and then my mother's body fell from the sky. Except it wasn't her, it was me, and the ground was shaking, crumbling, and then—

I pushed myself up in bed, horrified.

At least I hadn't screamed. That was my goal, to never, ever scream, because that would just make it worse: my startled grandparents rushing in to check on me, instead of my mom.

My phone, when I reached for it, said 4:53. Too early to get up, but I knew I wasn't going back to sleep. So I switched on my light and got an old fantasy novel down from the shelf, reading until the sun came up, and filling my head with magic instead of monsters.

Later that morning, I was squeegeeing the shower, my eyes scratchy from lack of sleep, when I saw Adam and his girlfriend in the backyard. They were sprawled across an enormous trampoline two houses down, reading thick paperback novels. They had sunglasses and headphones on, and a box of donuts sat between them.

It looked like a scene from one of those indie movies about sad white boys and the quirky girls who rescue them. Or maybe one of those aesthetic Tumblr photos I would have reblogged in middle school. Except this wasn't staged, and it wasn't fiction. It was two people, in real life.

I stood there for a minute, transfixed by the tiny, perfect universe of that backyard trampoline. By a girl who had said literally one word to me. A squeak from the squeegee against the shower door brought me back to reality.

Tomorrow was the first day of my junior year. The definitive end of my hiding out here and pretending none of this was really happening. Tomorrow, I'd become a student at the same high school my mom had attended when she was my age.

It was like I'd fallen into a story that wasn't mine, and was living the life of the missing main character, waiting for someone, anyone, to notice that I wasn't supposed to be here. Except I was here. This was my life now, and my mom wasn't coming back to claim it from me, and that was just how things were.

She'd never make me her special cheese omelet or proofread my essays or help choose an outfit for a first day. She'd never sit in the stands at my high school graduation. She'd never help me move into the dorms at college. I hated that my grandparents were the ones who would do those things now, stepping into every chapter of my life where my mom should have been.

Which is why, when my grandmother insisted on taking me back-to-school shopping at the last possible moment, I told her that she really didn't have to. But Eleanor seemed so excited about a "girls' outing" that I gave in and let her drive me to the mall.

I was expecting something indoors, with a Macy's and a food court. Instead, what I got was an upscale outdoor lifestyle center. It was all Spanish tiles and palm trees and elegant fountains and designer boutiques. A store selling two-thousand-dollar stationary bikes had a shirtless male model riding one in the window display. I stared at him in fascination, confused at how that was an actual job.

I couldn't imagine that my classmates actually shopped here. But then I saw girls my age ducking into Free People and Brandy Melville and Sephora, their arms loaded with bags, so apparently they did. I watched a group of blond girls cluster around a pink cupcake ATM, taking selfies.

One of them had on the exact Reformation dress I'd stalked on Instagram until I saw the price tag and quietly died. I tried not to stare, but I couldn't help it. I'd thought only influencers and models dressed like that. Not suburban teenagers hanging out at the mall.

Another girl walked past with her mom, both of them with matching Gucci bags. It was like I shouldn't even try. What was the point in getting some new sneakers or jeans? They weren't going to help me fit in here.

It was a losing battle. And one that I didn't want my grandmother to dedicate herself to.

"Grandma, you really don't have to buy me stuff," I said.

"There are rips in your jeans."

"That's the style," I promised.

"Not in Bayport," she retorted, marching into J.Crew.

I hung back, slightly terrified, as she prowled the racks, picking out "sensible basics" that I never would have chosen.

But then, I never shopped here. It was way too expensive. My mom and I shopped at the outlet mall, or at thrift stores, where you could buy like an entire wardrobe for the cost of one J.Crew sweater.

Although I doubted asking my grandmother to drop me off at the nearest Goodwill would go over well.

"These aren't really my style," I said meekly, after checking a price tag.

Not that I had a style. At my old school, I'd copied the status quo, wearing whatever my classmates wore to blend in. Secretly, though, I loved fashion. I followed influencers on YouTube and Instagram, studying their haul videos and their outfit posts, and wondering what would happen if anyone showed up at Randall High wearing over-the-knee boots with a beret and a plaid blazer.

"You're sixteen, your style will change," she said confidently. "Now what size do you wear in jeans?"

"Um, twenty-eight," I said.

"You should try the twenty-sevens, just in case," she said, leaving the twenty-eights on the table and hurrying me into the dressing room.

I barely had time to put on the first sweater before she'd peeled aside the curtain to get a look.

"Perfect," she said. "We'll get three."

I almost choked. They were sixty dollars each.

"I don't need three," I said. I didn't even need one. I had never in my life worn a merino wool cardigan.

"It's my treat," my grandmother insisted eagerly. "Now try the jeans."

They were too small. Of course they were. I couldn't even get them over my hips.

"I told you, I'm not a twenty-seven," I said, embarrassed.

"Well, that's a shame." Eleanor frowned. "Are you trying to lose weight?"

"No," I said, puzzled.

"Why not?" she asked, like it was a perfectly reasonable question.

"Um, well . . ." I blinked at her, unsure how to answer. I didn't have a problem with my weight. But apparently my grandmother did. This whole time I'd been panicking over price tags, but it turned out she'd been obsessing over the sizes.

Thankfully, the sales associate interrupted, asking if she could bring some new sizes, and as she made sympathetic eye contact, I realized that she'd overheard everything.

Even with bags of new clothing, courtesy of my grandmother's credit card and her philosophy on sensible basics, I still wasn't ready for school to start. But for some reason, my worry wasn't audible. If anything, my grandparents read my nervousness as excitement. Or maybe they just saw what they wanted to see, which would explain a lot.

"Big day tomorrow," my grandfather said at dinner that night. "You must be excited."

"Yep," I lied, smiling weakly.

"This is the year that colleges look at the most," my grandmother added, passing around a Pyrex dish of green beans.

"I know," I said.

They kept reminding me. Lately, my acceptance into a good college was one of their favorite conversation topics. They fixated on it with a laser focus, and I got that it was something exciting for them, so at first I'd encouraged it.

Maybe it was pathetic of me, but hearing my grandparents give advice about majors and SATs made me feel closer to my mom. I imagined her sitting in the same seat when she was my age, having the same conversation.

My mom was smarter than anyone I knew. Always reading—she was the one who had gotten me into the Lost Generation—and watching old movies, forever talking about long-dead artists and writers as though they were great friends of hers, as though Freddie Mercury or Dorothy Parker or Salvador Dali had sat in her salon chair just that afternoon, getting a trim. She'd gone to Claremont, a fancy private college halfway between Los Angeles and the San Bernardino Valley. She didn't finish, though. Thanks to my dad, and a course of antibiotics that made her birth control pills totally ineffective.

And now my grandparents had descended on me as though I were her do-over, their second chance to do everything right. As though, this time, they might actually get an invitation to a college graduation, instead of an insurance bill for an ultrasound scan.

So I smiled and listened as they talked about advanced placement classes and the best times to go on college tours, nodding along and saying yes, sure, that sounded great.

"And of course you already know Cole Edwards," my grandmother added. "Such a nice boy."

"A very good family, the Edwardses," my grandfather added.

"It's not like I'm marrying him," I said, resisting the urge to sigh.

"You never know," my grandfather said cheerfully.

Believe me, I did. I was already preparing to watch him from across the cafeteria, where he probably sat at a table full of intimidating jocks and their equally intimidating girlfriends. I pictured them easily: the type of girls who never got period pimples, and who wore lacy thongs during the mile run in gym, and who were always slathering their legs in seasonally scented lotion.

I zoned out, thinking about *those* girls, because there were always *those* girls. And they always seemed to know that I wasn't like them. I ate some green beans, relieved we weren't discussing my future anymore. Instead, my grandfather was talking about the new dental hygienist he'd been to see that morning.

"I asked what her husband did for a living," he said, swallowing a mouthful of veal, "and she said she had a wife."

My grandmother smiled tensely, sipping at her sugar-free organic iced tea.

"A *wife*," my grandfather repeated.

"We heard you, Joel," my grandmother said.

I slid down in my seat, inwardly cringing.

"I didn't know what to say, so I just said '*oh*,'" he continued.

"Well, you could have asked what her wife did," I said.

He stared at me. Blinked. Like the thought hadn't even occurred to him.

"It's just a suggestion," I mumbled.

"I didn't know she was *a lesbian,*" my grandfather said, shaking his head.

"So what?" my grandmother said, her expression scathing.

Go Eleanor, I thought. I assumed she was about to tell him not to be so closed-minded, but what she said instead was, "The woman's a dental hygienist, not our next-door neighbor."

I pushed some food around on my plate, my appetite gone. Like a lot of older people, my grandparents sometimes said things that were kind of racist. But I'd never heard them say anything outright homophobic before. And while discussing a total stranger, whose life didn't matter to them. It made me so uncomfortable.

Pearl whined at my feet. I slipped her a green bean, which she rejected, spitting it out on the Persian rug.

"Um, can I be excused?" I asked.

"Sure, sweetheart," my grandfather said.

I took my plate over to the sink and started rinsing it, out of habit.

"Just put it in the dishwasher," my grandmother called.

The dishwasher. Right.

I escaped up to not-my-room, trying not to freak out, but freaking out anyway.

I stared at the shopping bags in the corner, full of fresh notebooks and new jeans, everything waiting for tomorrow, when I would make my Baycrest High debut.

Please, I begged the universe, let it go okay.

And then: Please let me be the girl my grandparents think I am, for the next two years at least.

It had all been fine while I was playing Boo Radley in my mom's childhood bedroom all summer, reading by the pool and talking to no one except Dr. Lisa. But the truth was, I was terrified of what my classmates might see when they looked at me. Terrified that expensive sweaters and a blank slate wouldn't be enough to prevent a repeat of my catastrophic middle school years.

Back in seventh grade, when Tara was at the peak of her campaign to make my life miserable, she'd told the entire locker room that I'd made a move on her at a sleepover. What had actually happened was our friends dared me to kiss her during a game of Truth, Dare, Double Dare. But she'd left that part out. The part where everyone had giggled and insisted that we absolutely had to. She'd twisted it out of proportion, making me sound like I was so horny that I couldn't help myself. "And then Sasha *lunged* at me," she'd said with relish, as everyone listening gasped.

I hadn't lunged at her. I'd just crawled across our circle of sleeping bags and gone for it, rushing before I chickened out, or before my nerves overtook me. But it didn't matter. I wasn't on trial, I was automatically guilty.

"No wonder her boyfriend dumped her," Tara said with a smirk, as though daring me to say otherwise.

I didn't. I let Tara have the first and last word, and everyone took their cues from her.

For the rest of the semester, the other girls in my PE class had run shrieking into the next row of lockers, covering themselves theatrically while I tried not to cry. I'd squeezed my eyes shut and promised that I wasn't looking while they changed, that I would never, ever look.

Except I did look, sometimes. When our friends had dared me, I'd gotten a secret thrill at seeing what it was like to kiss a girl. Even though it was just a game. Because, honestly, I was curious. And then I'd let the kiss linger a second too long, and Tara had pulled away, and in that moment, I had inadvertently revealed a piece of myself. A piece that she'd seized with glee and used to torment me.

She'd told my boyfriend I didn't like him. That I was too scared to tell him myself. But I *did* like him. And that's what was so confusing.

Kissing Tara had felt no different than kissing a boy. So I'd pushed it down, and tried to forget, because it wasn't a big deal that I'd been excited to kiss a girl. I thought boys were cute, so I focused on them instead.

Still, the truth would spring up every so often, appearing in my peripheral vision in the form of long, tanned legs, or a laugh that sounded like music, or an actress on TV, or a pretty girl on Instagram. I pretended to be transfixed by their cute dress, or their amazing lip gloss, but just as frequently, I found myself staring at boys, with messy hair and skinny jeans, and it wasn't because I wanted to know where they shopped.

I never said any of my fears aloud. Because I didn't want to be that girl again, crying in a toilet stall in the middle school locker room, hearing the taunts and whispers from the other side of the thin metal door. So I put on blinders, and I shoved it down, into the secret parts of myself that I didn't share with anyone.

It never went away, though. Every time I thought a boy was cute, I was intensely relieved. Liking boys was easy. It was not liking girls that was hard. But I did it.

Still, carrying the truth around was exhausting. At least being invisible was safe. The alternative—being seen—was terrifying. And being seen as a girl who liked other girls? I'd gone through that hell once. I didn't think I could survive it again. Especially here, with my grandparents sticking their noses into everything. Especially now, with the way things were since last year's election.

My old town had been conservative, the kind of place that voted overwhelmingly Republican. It was stuffed full of churches we didn't attend, and while my high school had featured three different religious clubs, there hadn't been a Gay-Straight Alliance.

Bayport was the same shit, only wealthier. Half the town had voted for President Trump. Maybe they'd done it because he promised to save rich people lots of money. Or maybe they had deeper, moral reasons. But fifty-fifty weren't odds I wanted to chance. Especially in high school, which is already a uniquely hellish social experiment.

I wasn't sure how my grandparents would react, and I wasn't planning on finding out. Not after what I'd just heard at the table. Two years. I could be the granddaughter they wanted for that long.

CHAPTER 8

BAYCREST HIGH WAS JUST DOWN THE hill from my grandparents' house, and even though it was close enough to walk, my grandmother insisted on driving me.

We got there early, to meet the principal and make sure there weren't any issues with my schedule. And it felt so strange, walking this campus with my grandmother. I couldn't stop thinking about my mom, or how all of my firsts would be without her.

Like my first day as a high school junior. Baycrest was a collection of white mission-style buildings, all crushed against the back of the canyon. Palm trees sprouted along the pathways, and bright sprays of bougainvillea scaled the walls. The quad was full of circular café tables, topped with sky-blue umbrellas.

It looked like a resort. Or maybe a country club. Instead of fluorescent hallways, there were stone pathways and courtyards. The classrooms featured tinted windows, just like the luxury cars in the parking lot.

Eleanor dragged me toward a low administrative building with a bronze plate announcing that Baycrest High was a Blue Ribbon School, which made it sound like a prize-winning pie.

As she pulled open the glass doors, I caught my reflection. My flat-ironed hair, my minimal makeup—because I wasn't sure if the girls here thought it was trashy or try-hard to wear eyeliner. I'd spent an embarrassing amount of time choosing an outfit. I'd wanted something sufficiently neutral, which would neither stand out nor define me as any one particular thing. Finally, I'd gone with my new high-waisted jeans, my Vans, and a slouchy, cream-colored button-down I used to wear to work at the museum. It was boring and basic, but it did the job.

Still, I was convinced I was missing some small sign that would mark me instantly as an outsider. Some glaring error that would make girls scrutinize me in the hallway, cataloging all of the ways I was wrong.

The administrative office was overly air-conditioned, which was a bad omen for the rest of the day. I sat there shivering, wishing I'd brought a sweater while my grandmother filled in about a million forms.

"Mrs. Bloom? I'm Principal Mitchell."

"So nice to meet you," my grandmother said, shaking the principal's hand.

The principal beamed as she ushered us into her office, where a Stanford Alumni travel mug sat on her desk, along with photos of smiling girls in ballet leotards.

"Well, Sasha, we're so glad to have you," she said.

"Um, thanks," I replied.

All of this felt surreal and impossible, like I wasn't really here at all. And yet, when I pictured my old high school, surrounded by businesses that were still being rebuilt after the earthquake, I didn't feel like I was supposed to be there, either.

I was caught between implausibilities, and so I sat quietly as the principal reviewed my transcripts, doing that pleased nod to show that I was one of the Good Ones.

She assured us that Baycrest had a "very rigorous honors track," with teachers that assigned an average of one hour of homework per night, and then started reviewing my schedule.

Yearbook, of course. Honors Brit Lit. AP Euro. French 3. And, unfortunately, Phys Ed. Randall had only required two years, but here, I needed four.

At least it's block scheduling, I told myself. At least it's every other day.

"Since you earned an A in Algebra II last year, I'd recommend honors pre-calc," Principal Mitchell said.

I was pretty sure I'd been muddling my way toward a B-plus at best, except Mr. Hass had taken pity after my mom died. I didn't even remember completing my final packet, and yet my grade had come back an A, just like it had in every other class.

"Or I could stick with regular," I said.

"If you qualify for honors, you should push yourself," my grandmother said. "You don't want colleges to think you're looking for easy A's."

It was adorable she considered pre-calc an easy A. Because I definitely didn't.

"Honors it is," Principal Mitchell said, typing it into her computer. "And honors chemistry . . ." She frowned, looking at her screen. "Nothing left except a zero period."

I couldn't have a zero period. Already my grandmother had dragged herself out of bed at seven a.m. to putter around the kitchen while I ate breakfast and to drive me to school.

"How about regular chemistry?" I asked hopefully.

Math and science were my weakest subjects. But my transcript from last year was full of A's, and my standardized tests scores were high, and I could practically hear my grandmother analyzing how every breath I took would look to a college admissions board.

"If we switch your elective, we can make it work," the principal said.

My throat went dry.

"Do that," Eleanor instructed.

"But yearbook—" I started to protest. My grandmother shot me a look.

"You'll take something else," she said, as though it was already set in stone.

And then she raised an eyebrow at me, as if to say, *Sasha, don't be rude.*

"We have Computer Programming or Studio Art," the principal said.

"Studio Art," I said quickly, before Eleanor had me taking AP everything, with a nice, relaxing side of Computer Programming.

"There," my grandmother said. "Problem solved."

Just when I thought we were finished, Principal Mitchell handed me a slip of contact information for the school counselor.

I stared down at it, horribly embarrassed.

"I know you've gone through quite a traumatic time," Principal Mitchell said, making her voice Warm and Understanding. "So if you need someone to talk to, Dr. Okafor's door is always open."

Please, no, I thought. And then my grandmother plucked the paper from my fist and crumpled it into a ball.

"That won't be necessary," she said frostily. "Sasha's seeing one of the best adolescent psychologists in the area. So I'm sure you understand that we have this covered."

I swear to god, the temperature in the room dropped ten degrees.

I could almost see Principal Mitchell's breath cloud in front of her lips as she pasted on a fake smile and assured my grandmother that it had only been a suggestion, and one she could see was ill-advised.

"Very," my grandmother said, shouldering her bag to make it clear the meeting was over.

I stood up along with her.

Eleanor Bloom, ladies and gentlemen, I thought.

My locker was beige, and empty, and smelled like cleaning supplies. I stared into it, trying not to think about all of the people who had used it before me. Trying not to think of my mom, standing in this courtyard, unloading her textbooks on the first day of her junior year.

Had her locker even been on this side of the building, or was it in that bank near the senior lot? I guessed I'd never know.

All around me, students stopped to say hello to each other. To hug, or ask about each other's summers as though they hadn't already seen the pictures. Everyone was ridiculously well dressed, in this studied I'm-not-trying way. Even the boys in sweatpants wore the expensive kind that were all zips and slouch. Some of the girls had on fake eyelashes with their messy buns and festival shorts, or maybe they just had permanent lash extensions.

I was surrounded by the chatter and laughter of a school that I somehow went to, but in no way felt like mine. There was a horrible tightness in my chest, and I didn't know how to make it go away. I had too many AP classes, and a random elective I didn't want. My plan to quietly join the yearbook staff was ruined, and I had approximately three seconds to come up with a new one.

My grandparents were expecting me to flourish here, like a houseplant they'd coaxed back into bloom. But what if, despite their coaxing, I withered instead?

I didn't really have anything to drop off, but standing at my locker made me look busy and not alone, so I rifled through my backpack, pretending. I was testing my combination one final time when I saw Adam from next door, and the girl who had picked him up in her fancy car.

They were on the opposite end of the courtyard, both wearing sunglasses, and they were laughing hysterically at something. The girl's head tilted back, her hair loose and flowing. I couldn't stop staring. She was so effortless, so perfect, in a slouchy black sweater and army-green pants and lace-up boots, a tote bag draped over her shoulder. She swatted at Adam, and he twisted out of the way.

They seemed comfortable together, like they'd known each other their whole lives. When they crossed the courtyard, I could finally hear every word they were saying.

"Bullshit," Adam accused. "You're making that up."

"For real. He broke into the British Museum and stole like a million dollars' worth of dead birds," the girl insisted. "Out of everything you can steal from a museum, that's what he took. *Taxidermy.*"

Adam laughed, shaking his head in disbelief. "I hope they called him the *Birdglar*. Get it?"

"If I say no, can I pretend you never said it?"

They were so close that I might have called out to them then, saying *hello, remember me, with the dog?* but I didn't, because what if they stared at me blankly, or what if they weren't people you could just talk to unprompted?

And then the bell rang for homeroom, and the sea of students swallowed them up completely.

I made it through homeroom and first period pretending to be wallpaper. Honors pre-calc was dull but bearable, because at least math teachers didn't make you partner up or report on what you did over the summer.

And then I had English. There were already class copies of *Jane Eyre* on the desks. It had been the summer reading. Well, the first fifty pages at least. I sat down, watching everyone else choose seats together. Baycrest, with its nine hundred students, was tiny compared to my old school, but even at Randall, honors students were their own particular subset. I recognized a boy from my pre-calc, who was complaining to his friend how *Jane Eyre* was a "girl book."

I rolled my eyes. And then I spotted Friya, who was wearing a flowy sundress and arguing with a cute, dark-haired boy who had just taken the seat next to hers. I thought about waving hello, but didn't in case she didn't remember me.

"Seriously, Nick," she whined, her voice carrying. "Can't you sit somewhere else?"

"Who else am I going to cheat off of?" he said, and then promised, "I'm kidding."

A haughty girl wearing the tightest ponytail I'd ever seen slid into the seat next to mine. She unzipped her pencil case, unloading a ruler, three highlighters, and a mechanical pencil, and lined them up with intense precision.

"Come on, Friya, it was a joke," Nick pleaded.

I couldn't not look—they were practically a soap opera.

And then Friya glanced in my direction, and her eyes lit up.

"Sasha, oh my god!" she said, at earsplitting volume.

In a second, she had extracted herself from her desk. As she hurried over, the whole class stared at me like suddenly I was fascinating.

"Hey," I said, wondering what was going on.

"Michelle, would you switch seats with me?" Friya asked the girl next to me, turning on the charm. "Please? It would be, like, the most amazing favor."

"Whatever," the girl muttered, clearly unhappy about packing up her pencil case.

"You're the best," Friya told her, and then happily turned toward me, taking possession of her ill-gotten seat. "Seriously. I'm *dying*. How perfect is it that we're in the same class?"

"It's great," I said, cautiously returning her smile. I was so confused by what was happening.

Ms. Meade went over the syllabus and then assigned

a discussion topic. Friya immediately scooted her desk toward mine. On the other side of the room, the boy she'd ditched tried to get her attention.

"You have an admirer," I said, since she didn't seem to notice.

"Oh my god, ignore," she said, lowering her voice. "Ex-boyfriend," she explained, as soon as our teacher was out of earshot. They hadn't even been broken up for a week, and when he'd sat down next to her, she'd almost died.

"You're my literal savior," she announced.

"It was nothing," I said, embarrassed. After all, I wasn't the one who'd had to move seats.

"For real though," Friya insisted. "Girls helping other girls is, like, the most important thing. Right?"

And then she smiled at me, like we were already best friends.

When the bell rang, Friya grabbed my arm and pulled me past her ex-boyfriend.

"Can we talk?" he called.

"Later, Nick, okay?" she yelled over her shoulder, and then confided, "That's not happening ever."

We reached the entrance to the quad. I paused, waiting for Friya to make an excuse to go her own way, to say she'd see me around—and then I worried that she was expecting me to say it first.

"Cole's going to be so excited I found you," she said instead, smiling. "Just wait."

I followed her gratefully into the quad. And there they were, like an Instagram come to life: Cole, with his sunglasses on, an entire delivery pizza box on his lap. Whitney, scrolling through her phone, earbuds in. Ethan tapping out a rhythm on his Latin homework, using mechanical pencils as drumsticks. Ryland was nowhere to be found, but maybe he was just buying lunch or something.

"Eat me," Cole said, doing a high-pitched voice as he flapped the lid of the pizza box.

"You're a child," Friya told him, but she reached over and grabbed a slice anyway.

"Sasha!" Cole said. "How's life as a freshman?"

But he was grinning. Teasing.

"I'm older than you are, you snotwaffle," I retorted, sitting down next to him. It was the only empty seat. I took out my turkey on wheat, trying not to stare enviously at everyone else's slices of pepperoni mushroom.

"Where'd you get the pizza?" I asked, impressed.

"Ordered Postmates and pretended it was for a teacher," Cole said, looking smug.

"You ordered it to class?" Whitney asked skeptically, picking off her pepperoni and piling them onto Ethan's napkin.

"'Course not. I have free period before lunch," he said, leaning back in his seat.

"I thought you had Computer Programming," Ethan said with a frown.

"Nah, I'm the student aide. But Mr. Varma's so chill, it's basically free." Cole shrugged.

His hair was perfect, again. A golden swoop, defying gravity, with this little front piece that just brushed the edge of his eyebrow. The sleeves of his denim shirt were pushed above his elbows, and his pale khaki shorts revealed long, tanned legs dusted with blond hair. His leather sandals were practically falling apart, but his sunglasses were flashy gold Ray-Bans.

He was like one of those actors you see on television playing high school students, and you scoff, because teenage boys never look like that. Except Cole did. He was the kind of attractive that needed a warning label, because I wasn't mentally prepared for his bare leg to be inches from mine. I felt fluttery and strange, and I was hyper-aware of the way he reacted to everything and everyone. I didn't know how I was sitting here, but I had better get it right.

This was definitely a table of popular kids. Never mind that Friya was in my honors English or that Cole was a Computer Programming aide, which sounded unspeakably nerdy. I could tell from the way they carried themselves, from how relaxed they all were, sitting here as though they were holding court. Somehow, caring about academics wasn't a disqualifier at Baycrest, the way it had been at my old school. At Randall, the cool crowd had been the boys who bused in from Central and always had weed, and the girls who partied with them and were forever getting dress code violations.

"Hey, Sasha?" Cole said. "Can I ask you something?"

"What?" I said nervously.

He was going to ask me to leave. I was sure of it. Something about not enough seats at the table, and sorry, and then I'd have to slink away in front of the entire quad and would never be able to show my face again.

But he flapped the pizza box at me and inquired, in a growly monster voice, "Do you wanna eat me?"

"Yes, please," I said, reaching for a slice. The pizza was almost gone, and I felt bad, since Ryland wasn't there yet. I didn't want him to show up and think I'd taken his seat and his lunch. "So, um, where's your friend Ryland?" I asked.

Everyone stared at me, puzzled.

"He doesn't hang out with us," Whitney said disdainfully, as though it was obvious.

"Oh," I said. And then I stuffed my mouth with pizza, wishing I hadn't said anything.

"Can I put up a poster here?" someone asked.

It was Adam's girlfriend. She was carrying a stack of glossy posters advertising a club fair. There was something uncommonly magnetic about her, even here. She'd taken off her sweater, revealing a black bodysuit that scooped low in the back, exposing the sharp, tanned wings of her shoulder blades. Her bun was loose and casual, and her tote bag made her seem sophisticated and older. She looked amazing, and I couldn't figure out how she'd done the bun, no matter how much I stared.

"Go for it," Ethan said, scooting aside so she could reach the pillar behind our table.

"Hey, Lily, want some pizza?" Cole asked, using his monster voice as he flapped the box lid.

Lily. The name fit her perfectly.

"You should audition for *Avenue Q*," she told him, taking the last slice.

She made no move to sit down, and I realized with disappointment that this wasn't her lunch table.

She only stayed a moment, chatting with Ethan about their history essay.

I knew I was eavesdropping, but there was something about her. Something special. It was like she was drawn in pen while everyone else was in pencil. And I couldn't figure out how I was the only one who noticed.

Lily and Ryland were in my Studio Art class. They were sitting together, and Lily glanced up when I walked in. Our eyes met for just a second, and she actually looked disappointed to see me, as though whatever impression she'd gotten from afar was terrible.

I didn't think I'd had time to even make a first impression yet, but apparently I had. And it sucked. Awesome. I fought down a stab of frustration as I slid into an empty seat.

Lily bent her head and said something to Ryland, who snorted. Between his glasses and cardigan and oversized backpack, there was something much geekier about him now than there had been the night we'd met. When he reached into his backpack to dig for a pen, he had to unload a stack of graphic novels.

Mr. Saldana, our teacher, was every inch the city aesthete, from the unnecessary scarf wound around his neck to his graying stubble to his shoulder-length hair to the tweed vest buttoned over his T-shirt and jeans. He built furniture in his spare time, apparently, and explained how carpentry was an underappreciated art form as he handed out the syllabus.

"I see some familiar faces from Art Theory and Mixed Media. And some new ones," he said, staring at me, and then at a boy with blue hair who was gnawing on his sweatshirt strings.

He explained that we'd start with sketching, and then would move on to charcoals and eventually paints.

"We'll end the semester with a gallery show featuring your work," he said. "You can submit assignments you've completed in class or pieces you've been inspired to create on your own time. Sculptures, collages, photographs. Just no performance art—"

He raised an eyebrow at a boy who was all nervous energy and black hair dye, and a couple of people laughed.

"And the only requirement is that *everyone* must

contribute *something*," he finished. "Which leads me into our theme for the semester: put yourself out there, even in just the smallest way. In order to criticize art, which is another important component of what we're doing here, you must understand how brave it is to create anything at all.

"So," he said, clapping his hands. "What are we doing when we look at art? We're attempting to understand not just the piece in front of us, but the world itself, from a different point of view."

He handed out a sheet of paper. "And how do we do this? We must learn the grammar of art. In your English essays, you must discuss foreshadowing and metaphor, yes? In here, when we consider a piece of art, we'll use these criteria."

He motioned toward the sheet of paper.

"Let's try it out, no pressure. I'm going to put some art on the projector. Stuff you've seen. Really famous pieces. What is it about them that speaks to you?"

I stared down at my vocab sheet, skimming the words and their definitions: *line, tone, texture, shape, movement, scale.*

The art he'd chosen was all basic stuff. Rembrandt. Picasso. Dali. But using the language on our sheets was hard.

My classmates struggled on, commenting on the symmetry and the subtlety and the colors. It was painful listening to them. And even though I knew I could have done better than most, I still wasn't going to raise my hand and go for it. I didn't quite have the lay of the land yet. Besides, being quiet was safer than showing off.

And then Mr. Saldana flashed a riotous polka dot room onto the projector.

"Anyone know this?" he asked.

Yayoi Kusama, I thought, in the silence.

"It's Kusama," Lily called.

"Go ahead," the teacher said, and Lily made a face, like, *I wasn't volunteering, I was just stating the obvious.*

"Okay," she said. "Well, what I love about her is that she invites us into her fever dream. She makes mental illness seem beautiful. She overwhelms us. There's no negative space. No harmony. Our eyes don't know where to focus, and through the lack of focus, we become unglued from our own reality. It's thrilling and terrifying, seeing the world like that."

I'd never heard anyone my age talk like that before. Like she wasn't afraid of being laughed at, or being different. By talking about what she saw in the art, she'd inadvertently revealed a piece of herself. There was no way I could ever do that.

"Yeah, what she said," a floppy-haired boy called, and a couple of kids laughed self-consciously.

Lily just shrugged, like she was used to being the smartest one in the room. Like it was all an amusement, and she had nothing to prove, and so what if people laughed? I was slightly in awe.

We kept going. I didn't raise my hand once. Not for Diane Arbus or Jackson Pollack or Andy Warhol. I just sat there, bending the cap on my pen back and forth and sinking lower in my seat, too self-conscious to say anything at all.

CHAPTER 9

MY GRANDMOTHER SERVED LAMB CHOPS for dinner that night. It was in honor of my first day, she claimed, as though I had, at any point in my life, loudly announced a craving for grilled sheep. I stared down at the quivering, lime-green blob of mint jelly on my plate, and the watery moat of meat juice that had formed around it, not feeling particularly hungry.

It was beginning to make sense why my mom had never pressed me about school. Why she'd combed back my hair with her fingers and asked, "Good day?" I'd nodded, and that was it. Because I'd barely had time to buckle my seat belt that afternoon before my grandmother's questions had started: How were my classes and did I like my teachers and with whom had I eaten lunch?

And now I was pretty sure we were going to rehash it again, with my grandfather.

"So," he said. "How was your big first day?"

I resisted the urge to sigh.

"Great," I said, trying to sound upbeat. "So great."

"Tell him where you sat at lunch," my grandmother prompted, looking smug.

"Um, with Cole Edwards," I said through a mouthful of potatoes. "And with Friya, whose last name I don't remember."

"Michael Nassiri's daughter," my grandmother supplied, beaming triumphantly.

"That's wonderful, sweet pea," my grandfather said. "Making nice friends already."

"Yep," I said, trying to be happy about it, even though, for the entire lunch period, I'd been terrified of doing or saying even the slightest thing wrong.

But clearly I'd done something right, because my grandparents looked *so* pleased. My grandmother went on about what a wonderful young man Cole was, and how Friya was always doing so much charity work, and her father was so handsome, and I nodded, wondering how anyone could think that I fit in with them.

It felt like an elaborate joke. Especially the part where, here, in this glittering oceanfront town, they thought I was worth noticing, too. Back home, in the dreariness of the inland empire, I had been just as unappealing as the endless beige strip malls.

Across the table, my grandfather fed the dog scraps, and then shot me a wink, thinking he was being covert.

"Tell him which honors classes you're taking," my grandmother prompted, as though we were in a play and I'd forgotten my lines.

Didn't we have something else to talk about? Apparently not. So I dutifully recited my class schedule.

"Good, good." My grandfather nodded. "I hope you know there's going to be a lot of homework."

"I know," I said. "I've already started."

I regretted the words as soon as they were out of my mouth.

"How much do you have left?" my grandmother asked.

"Um, a history worksheet and some math," I said. "I already did the English. But it's block schedule, so nothing's due until Wednesday."

"You better not leave it for tomorrow," my grandmother warned.

"I won't," I said, even though I'd been thinking about it.

As if she could read my thoughts, she launched into this whole speech about how you should always do homework on the day it's assigned so you have the opportunity to ask questions.

"I will," I said. "I promise."

"Come on, Elle, give the kid a break," my grandfather said.

"Because that worked out so well with Alice," she retorted.

Instantly, the room went quiet. Too quiet.

She shouldn't have said that, and we all knew it.

"Um, I'm going to get back to my homework," I said, standing up and bringing my plate over to the sink.

"This is her most important year, Joel," my grandmother whispered as I rinsed my dishes. "I have to stay on top of her or she won't get into a good college."

"Give the girl some credit," my grandfather whispered back, and I realized they thought I couldn't hear them.

"Tuition's the same whether she gets into UC Riverside or UC Berkeley," my grandmother retorted. "Which one would *you* rather pay for?"

I dropped my cup into the sink with a loud clatter. I couldn't help it.

"Just put it in the dishwasher," my grandfather called.

I did, and then I escaped upstairs, my heart pounding.

They couldn't actually intend to pay for my college. That was insane. But it did explain the sudden intense interest in my schoolwork. I'd always known that I had to be on top of things, because there was no money for college, so merit scholarships dictated my future.

One of my mom's rules had been to never, ever ask my grandparents for money. Not the time the car got towed, or the summer all my friends went to this expensive sleep-away camp, or when our laptop straight-up died in the middle of finals week.

"There are strings attached to everything your grand-parents give," my mom would warn whenever it looked dire. And then she'd work late at the salon, or pick up a Sunday shift at the blow dry bar in Cabazon, and the crisis would be averted.

But college wasn't a busted laptop. It was the first time I'd get to choose for myself how and where I wanted to live my life. And if my grandparents were willing to help with that, then I guessed I didn't mind giving up yearbook, or taking too many AP classes, or indulging their fantasies about Cole asking me to homecoming. A few nights ago, when I'd put on my mom's old dress and looked in the mirror, I'd been unsure who I was, and who I was supposed to be. But maybe that was a good thing. I knew what my grandparents wanted from me. So maybe that's who I was supposed to become.

CHAPTER 10

MY SECOND DAY AT BAYCREST WAS no less disorienting than my first. I still felt like I'd been dropped into a life that wasn't mine, but at least I knew where the bathrooms were and that I should bring a sweater. I hated that my grandmother had been right about my needing those.

I was switching books at my locker between classes, lost completely in my own thoughts, when someone yelled, "Dog thief!"

It was such an improbable accusation that I had to turn around and see what was happening. When I did, I nearly crashed right into Adam.

Instead of his Academic Decathlon jacket, he wore an eighties acid-wash bomber and a knitted vest. His hair had been mussed into a kind of faux-hawk, which looked ridiculous.

That's when I realized—*I* was dog thief.

"I thought it was you," he said, grinning.

"Loving the outfit," I said, since I couldn't not.

"Oh. Yeah." He laughed. "Student government. We're filming a segment for the morning announcements. Join a club! Have some school spirit!"

He wiggled his fingers in an ironic rendition of jazz hands.

"So you're in . . . Time Travel Club?" I asked.

"Hey, no spoilers," he warned.

"Exactly what a time traveler would say," I pointed out, and he grinned.

"Wait, are we permanent neighbors now?" he asked.

"Afraid so," I said.

"And we're locker neighbors, too," he said, spinning his combination.

His locker was only three down from mine.

"We've got to stop meeting like this," he joked. "Otherwise people will talk."

"Let them," I said, playing along. "I have nothing to hide except this ill-gotten bag of jewels and the seventeen bodies in my basement."

"Seventeen? Jeez, that's dark," Adam said.

Oof, he was right. I watched as he dumped the contents of his backpack into his locker. "You didn't bring a change of clothes?" I asked, trying to switch subjects.

"What for?" He shrugged.

I shook my head. It was so strange to think that he was dating Lily. He didn't seem like her type. Not that I knew what her type was.

The bell rang, and Adam flipped up the collar on his ridiculous jacket.

"Stay cool, daddio!" he called, flashing a peace sign and strutting off.

The rest of my week unfolded without incident. It was like I'd fallen headlong into an alternative universe, one where I lived in a weirdly spotless house and ate home-cooked dinners and sat at a lunch table full of pretty, popular people.

The whole experience was bizarre. And the absolute strangest part was how Cole kept smiling at me, and finding excuses to tease me."

I spent our lunch period soaking up the strange sensation of having a coveted seat in the quad, and of people assuming that I deserved to sit there. I wasn't dead mom girl or earthquake girl. Although I did come close on Wednesday.

We had an earthquake drill in third. I wasn't expecting for it to feel any different than it had every other year. Emergency drills were standard, like bringing no. 2 pencils for Scantron tests or playing Heads-Up 7-Up whenever we had a sub. At least during earthquake drills, you didn't have to sit there with your head down and your thumb up, knowing that you would never, ever be picked.

But that morning, as Ms. Meade made us crouch under our desks, protecting our necks, my heart sped up. I couldn't breathe. I was back at the museum, scrambling under the cash register.

I saw the displays fall and heard the distant screams of everyone in the museum scrambling for shelter. And then

I pictured my mom, in the back room of the salon, with nothing to duck under.

Spots of darkness colored the corners of my vision, and I felt nauseated and clammy.

I tried to breathe normally, because I wasn't going to go to pieces here, in my English class, in the middle of a stupid drill. I just needed to hold on another ten, maybe fifteen seconds, and—

"Sasha!" Friya whispered, trying not to giggle. "Sasha! Look!"

I opened my eyes, realizing I was pressing too hard into the back of my neck.

"Huh?" I asked, confused.

"Julia's underwear," she whispered, motioning toward a girl whose jeans had slipped down and whose yellow Pikachu print panties had ridden up.

Friya was waiting for my reaction. Her mouth was twisted into a smirk, and her eyes glittered with amusement. And suddenly I was back here, in this place where I was on the giving end of the joke, instead of the receiving end. I knew I was supposed to laugh or roll my eyes or whatever. Because Julia's outfit wasn't crouch-under-the-desk proof.

So I forced myself to smile, because Friya had no clue I was a hundred miles away, reliving the worst day of my life. And I wasn't about to tell her.

Julia finally figured it out about her underwear, tugging

her shirt down. Our teacher called an end to the drill, and I climbed back into my seat, realizing that, in a weird way, Friya distracting me had actually helped. I wasn't in my own head anymore, replaying my personal nightmare. I was just here, in the present.

When Friya told the story at lunch, she embellished it so that we were both "in hysterics." I knew she was only doing it to impress Whitney, who was too busy taking selfies to care. She'd learned about some new posing trick where you made triangle shapes with your legs and arms, and she looked ridiculous doing it. The boys weren't paying attention at all. Some guys from their soccer team had dropped by, carrying bags of fast food from an outing off campus and making us all jealous that we weren't seniors yet and didn't have the privilege.

At least I'd finally figured out how everyone was connected: Ethan and Whitney were dating, and Cole was Ethan's best friend, and Friya was Whitney's. But of course that was just the current state of things. They'd all known each other forever. Their parents were friends, and so they'd become friends, in this simple TV sitcom kind of way that I'd never thought happened in real life. At least, in a way that had never happened to me. My mom never got along with the other parents. She was too young, and then too young and single.

It was sheer luck that my grandparents knew Cole's

grandparents, and that Friya's dad worked at my grandfather's firm. I had been stitched into their quilt somehow, a last-minute addition.

Without them, I don't know what I would have done. Eaten lunch alone in the library, I guessed.

I saw Adam occasionally by the lockers, and he was always friendly. But then, he was our junior class representative, and friendliness was pretty much his personal brand. His girlfriend completely ignored me. Lily and I had Phys Ed together as well, and she paired off with a friend, their heads bent together as they walked field laps, an unbroachable unit.

As much as I hated Phys Ed at my old school, at least here it was a break from notes and slides and quizzes. I'd never worked so hard in my life. When I wasn't in school, I studied, and when I wasn't studying, I slept so deeply that I didn't even dream.

The nightmares of endless earthquakes, of bodies being pulled from rubble—sometimes my own, sometimes my mother's, sometimes people I barely knew—were gone. It was a welcome reprieve. Although I worried that they were still there, lurking in the corners of my school planner, waiting for an opening to come back.

In Studio Art, we'd started sketching our first still life. It was a simple tableau of fruit and a pitcher of water, set on a tablecloth. Mine was awful. Whatever talent I had with a camera lens didn't translate to charcoals. My hands felt clumsy, the whole piece precarious, as though at any moment I could set down a bad line that would ruin the whole thing. Plus, I hated the way Mr. Saldana prowled around the room, watching us.

"Ahh, no," Mr. Saldana said, pausing over my shoulder on Friday. "Sasha, is it? You're not drawing what's there. You're drawing what you assume is in front of you."

I stared up at him, confused.

"What's the difference?" I asked.

"That banana is overripe," he said, nodding toward the tableau. "And yet yours is perfect. The dots are too symmetrical. And see that flaw near the top? You have drawn what you know to be a banana. But you haven't drawn *that* banana."

"Oh," I said, realizing he was right.

"You must do more than look quickly and assume," he went on. "You must *see*."

If any other teacher had said that, I would have rolled my eyes. But something about Mr. Saldana, with just the faintest traces of an Argentinian accent making his sentences roll off his tongue like poems, made his pronouncement sound serious.

"I'll try," I promised, and then I stared up at him, unsure how exactly I was supposed to do that.

"Start over," he instructed.

CHAPTER 11

THAT WEEKEND, I TRIED TO MAKE my mom's old bedroom feel more like it was mine. I sorted through my clothes and put everything school appropriate into my top drawers. For months, I'd kept stuffing everything back into my duffel bags, but I didn't have time in the morning to dig through the mess. And even though I knew the best solution was to just use the closet, I didn't think I could bear it. Already my life was so mixed up with my mom's. My wardrobe didn't need to be mixed up with hers too.

When I opened the bottom drawer of the dresser, my camera stared back at me. I'd forgotten I'd stashed it there, in a mess of T-shirts I wore as pajamas and socks that had shrunk unevenly at the laundromat. I took it out, feeling the familiar heft of it in my hands. And then I turned it on, hearing that soft click as the lens engaged, telling me it was ready to capture photos.

But I wasn't.

My mom had bought me this camera, spending more than she should have on my fifteenth birthday. "I can't wait to see your photos," her note had said. Except she was gone, and she'd never see any of the pictures I took again, and the next time I snapped a photo, it would be of a world that didn't have her in it.

Better to leave my camera in the drawer. So I put it back, and then got started on my never-ending homework.

There was a sheet of paper waiting for me on the kitchen table on Monday morning, next to a cup of Icelandic yogurt. I approached it cautiously, nervous that it was something awful. My heart sped up as I tried to think what was so bad that it had to be written out formally.

But it was just a list of clubs my school offered, printed out from the internet. Someone had highlighted Mock Trial and put three yellow stars next to it.

I stared down at the paper, confused. First of all, I hadn't realized we had a home printer, and second of all—what?

"Oh, good," Eleanor said, padding into the kitchen. "You found it. I thought you might want to familiarize yourself with Baycrest's extracurriculars."

"Um, thanks," I said. "But why is Mock Trial highlighted?"

"Because the first meeting's after school today. I wrote the classroom down on the back."

I flipped the list over, and sure enough. I'd noticed tons of club flyers papering the hallways, but I hadn't stopped to investigate. It wasn't like yearbook was an after-school activity.

"It's so helpful that your school has a Facebook page," my grandmother went on. "You can find out everything. Have you been on there?"

"Grandma, no one uses Facebook," I said, opening my yogurt. "Besides, I'm not sure Mock Trial's really my style."

The moment I said it, I knew it was a mistake. Pearl, who'd been dancing around my ankles, begging for, of all things, lemon yogurt, went silent.

My grandmother sighed.

"Sasha," she said, as though she hated having to spell it out. "This isn't about you. It's about college." Of course it was. "You don't have any extracurriculars."

"I have yearbook, and my job at the museum."

"Those are from last year," she reminded me. "Joining Mock Trial will really demonstrate an interest in pre-law. It's a smart choice."

I didn't know why she thought I was interested in pre-law. And then, suddenly, I did. I half-remembered a conversation over the summer, in those grief-fogged days, when my grandparents had asked me what I planned to study in college.

I'd said art history, and when I saw the horrified look on my grandmother's face, I'd backpedaled that I was also thinking of English. And she'd said law schools loved English majors, and I'd said, "Oh, really? That's great," and now we were here.

To my grandparents, a career in the arts wasn't an option. A career in the arts was my dad, working as a home inspector and monopolizing our only car on the weekends to drive to LA and play open mics while my mom and I walked to the laundromat.

According to my grandparents, there were pretty much three choices: doctor, lawyer, or business executive. Professor was okay. So was dentist or engineer or clinical psychologist. But anything that wasn't a guarantee was a gamble.

My mom had been pre-law, even though she'd taken more literature and art classes than anything else. I wondered what she would have been if she'd finished.

Alive, whispered a small voice in the back of my head, which I tried to push away.

"So it's decided," my grandmother said. "You'll stay for the Mock Trial meeting today."

"Um, actually—" I said.

I had to tell her that I didn't want to. That I wasn't interested in Mock Trial, or being a lawyer, at all. But then I thought about my grandmother printing out the list of extracurriculars and leaving it there for me, like a present. Which made me think of the new clothes she'd bought me, and how she was driving me to school in the mornings, and how much of an interruption my presence was in their lives.

And when I opened my mouth to say I wasn't doing it,

what came out instead was, "I'm not sure what time Mock Trial ends, so maybe I should just walk home?"

That afternoon in Studio Art, Mr. Saldana made us stop sketching a couple of minutes early. Which was fine by me, since we were copying postcards, and my landscape was lopsided.

"We still have ten minutes until the bell," he said mildly, raising an eyebrow at this girl Justine, who had started to pack up. "And I wanted to take that time to talk about Art Club. The first meeting of the year is today after school. Actually—Lily? Would you mind coming up here?"

Lily shrugged and said it was fine.

"Great," Mr. Saldana continued. "I'll let our club president tell you about it."

Lily moved to the front of the room. She was wearing tight black overalls today, with a striped shirt underneath, and these tough, pointed-toe boots with metal heels. Her lipstick was bright red, and her hair was in two little teddy-bear buns. I loved it so, so much. It was quirky and bold, the kind of look it took confidence to pull off.

And Lily had confidence in spades. The way she gazed at us, calmly, not at all perturbed to be singled out.

"Okay, hi," she said. "You probably already know about Art Club. We're the ones who put on the student art auction at the end of every semester, and we did the beards on the trees last year, and we were also responsible for the buckets of sidewalk chalk at Spring Fling. So basically, if you're into urban exploration, art installations, or just really idolize the Algonquin Round Table for some reason, check us out. We could use some new blood. Which we use to paint with. Kidding. Sorry. Zero blood sacrifices are necessary."

This was the kind of club I wanted to join. As Lily talked, I imagined it for a moment. The two of us becoming friends. Going to art galleries together. Flipping through fancy magazines in the café of some bookstore, sipping cappuccinos and poring over the fashion and the photography.

"When are the meetings again?" Justine called without raising her hand.

"Mondays and Wednesdays," Lily said. "After school."

The same time as Mock Trial.

Friya had warned me at lunch that Mock Trial was a bad idea. That it was a smug boys' club full of khaki-wearing douchebags. I'd thought she was exaggerating, but it turned out she was *underselling* its awfulness.

Todd, the club president, had the kind of snide demeanor that make you fantasize about punching him in the face. It was easy to come up with his yearbook superlative: *Most Likely to Be Your Boss*.

I sat there amid a group of eager freshmen boys while, at the front of the room, the team sat facing us with matching pins in their lapels.

"As newbies," Todd said, smirking at the four of us, "you'll be timekeepers. And if you impress us, then next year you might get promoted up. This is serious business, freshpeople. Last year, our team placed in the top three in the county and went on to compete at state." He paused, letting that part sink in.

"Being part of a winning team," Michelle from my English class piped up, "is being a winner, no matter your role."

Next to me, a boy with braces rubber-banded together so tightly it made my mouth hurt just looking at him nodded seriously, taking notes.

I hated it so much. I mean, sure, I could see how it looked good on a résumé. But not coming in as a junior. My presence disrupted the flow of the entire system.

Sure enough, Todd pulled me aside after.

"So I understand you're a junior," he said. "Were you in Mock Trial at your old school?"

"Um, no," I told him.

Todd nodded, as though he'd been expecting my answer.

"Well, you're going to have to start at the bottom," he let me know in his pompous way. "So I really hope you weren't thinking that just because you're a junior you could skip the grunt work."

I stared at him, confused. I hadn't been trying to angle my way into some fancy role. I didn't even know anything about Mock Trial except that my grandmother had told me to join.

"What are you talking about?" I asked.

"Don't play dumb," Todd said. "You're obviously here to pad your résumé for college. Junior year. Not enough extracurriculars. But you know what? You should have started thinking about that earlier. We're all fighting for the same few spots at Stanford, and since neither of us are minorities, well." He let out a short bark of a laugh. "It's every man for himself. Or woman—sorry—didn't mean to offend."

My jaw almost hit the floor, and I tried to disguise it as a cough.

"Um, I'm not trying to get into Stanford," I mumbled. "I just thought—new school. I should join an activity we didn't have at my old one."

"And how many AP classes are you in?" Todd asked.

"Um, four," I admitted.

He raised an eyebrow, as though saying "yeah, right."

"Well, I'll tell you right now," he said, "even though we're not posting the list until tomorrow: You're a timekeeper. Your job is to stare at the clock while the rest of us run the show. If you're lucky, you might get to make photocopies. But that's it."

"Great," I said. "That's fine."

"So we'll see you Wednesday, Stanford?" he said, with just a hint of malice.

No, I wanted to say. This was a huge mistake, and now it's turned into an even bigger misunderstanding, and I never, ever want to come back. I want to run screaming from your horrible racist, sexist face and pretend none of this ever happened.

But I couldn't. I had to do this. I'd promised my grandparents.

So I took a deep breath and pasted on a fake smile and promised, "Yep, see you Wednesday."

On my way to my locker, I paused outside Mr. Saldana's classroom, catching a glimpse through the thin rectangle of glass at what was going on in there. Music was playing, some kind of bossa nova, and tubes of frosting were strewn everywhere, and a Van Gogh was on the projector. The Art Club was decorating cakes to look like *Starry Night*.

Mabel, from my PE class, was holding up her hideous rendition, her fingers coated in frosting, and everyone was laughing uproariously.

"It's SO bad," she gasped.

"Shitty Night!" Ryland dubbed it.

"Starry Blight?" someone else called.

I realized I'd been standing in the hallway watching for too long, so I forced myself to keep walking. To unload the heavy textbooks from my locker, and then to walk all the way home, up the hill that looked innocent enough in the mornings, but turned out to be a hell of a hike in the afternoon.

"I heard someone joined Mock Trial," my grandfather said at dinner.

We were eating *bœuf bourguignon*—the Julia Child recipe, my grandmother was quick to point out, as though there was some other less appetizing recipe for the exact same thing that I was worried she'd used instead.

"Yep," I said, my mouth full.

All afternoon, I'd had this awful pit in my stomach at the thought of going back to Mock Trial. I honestly wasn't sure I could bear it. But if I was going to bail, I had to tell them.

I was pretty sure they wouldn't make me keep going back if they knew how awful it had been. I didn't know what I was supposed to get out of it other than a line on a résumé.

"Actually," I said, but before I could say anything else, my grandfather was already off, telling me how great it was that I was showing an early interest in the law, talking about how all these millennials expected to go into the arts and be their own bosses, and then wound up moving back home and never getting anywhere.

It sounded very Fox News. I heard him watching it almost every night, after dinner. The light from the television flickered across the stairs the few times I'd come down for a glass of water. But the thought of walking past the den, of having to see my grandfather glued to the screen, soaking all of that in, made me decide it was better to just drink from the bathroom tap.

"I'm not a millennial, Grandpa," I reminded him.

"Well, whatever you are," my grandfather said, "I'm glad you're keeping a good head on your shoulders. Studying hard and dating that Edwards boy—"

"She already said they're not dating," my grandmother cut in, glaring at my grandfather. "You never pay attention."

"I pay attention just fine," he said, his tone a warning.

I slid down in my seat, fiddling with my napkin. It was so uncomfortable, watching them fight. Hated that I was stuck here to witness it. Hated that by going to that terrible Mock Trial club, I still wasn't doing enough to make them happy with me.

Think about college, I told myself as my grandparents continued to bicker. Think about how you've already been here four months. Think about something besides how much you wish you could go to Art Club. And become friends with Lily.

Getting that out of my head was harder than it should have been.

No, I told myself. That's not the plan. Stick to the plan.

CHAPTER 12

"SAW YOU WALKING TO SCHOOL THIS morning," Adam said, pulling open his locker on Tuesday. He had on his Academic Decathlon jacket again. Oh god, I hoped I wasn't going to get one that said Mock Trial. Whitney would never let me live it down.

"Yep," I said. I'd finally convinced my grandmother she didn't have to drive me. A small but amazing victory.

I'd spotted Lily's sleek Mercedes while I was walking down the hill. They'd sped past, windows down, music blasting, missing me entirely, or so I'd thought.

"The uphill sucks, just so you know," he said, as if I wasn't painfully aware. I'd stubbornly worn my ankle boots yesterday, and I had the blisters to prove it.

"I'm planning on levitating," I said.

Adam snorted.

"We can give you a lift home if you'd like," he said. "I'm sure Lil won't mind."

The offer was tempting. But it felt weird that Adam was offering, especially since Lily didn't seem to like me. If Ethan did that, inviting some random girl to ride with him and Whitney, I was pretty sure she'd pitch a fit.

"That's okay," I said. "I don't want to impose on your girlfriend."

At this, Adam burst out laughing. He laughed so hard that he had to lean back against his locker, and so long that more than a few heads turned curiously in our direction.

"Lily isn't my *girlfriend,*" he finally got out. "She's my *sister.*"

"Your sister?" I spluttered, because I was not expecting that at all.

"Her mom married my dad like eight years ago," Adam explained. "So we're stepsiblings, technically. Except Gracie, our half-sister, is six, and you try explaining fractional genetics to a little kid."

Stepsiblings. Wow. I'd gotten it all so wrong.

"Hold on," I said, my brain racing to process this unexpected development. Because if they were siblings, that meant— "Lily lives two houses down?"

"Yeah. Try to keep up," Adam joked. "So you want a ride or not?"

"No thanks," I said, because Adam's offer and this new information still didn't change the fact that Lily disliked me, and that I couldn't quite figure out why.

•••

Over the next few weeks, life fell into a routine. On Mondays and Wednesdays I had Mock Trial, and on Thursdays, at Cole's urging, I stuck around after school, hanging with the girls on the bleachers while the boys had soccer practice. Whitney came to cheer for Ethan, and Friya gleefully posted stories because she knew it would irritate her ex.

"He doesn't 'do' school-sponsored activities," she told me one afternoon, rolling her eyes.

"Neither do I," Whitney said. "That shit is lame. No offense, Sasha."

"None taken," I said. "Mock Trial is lame."

It was worse than lame. Still, I didn't know how to tell my grandparents that I hated it.

Every night at dinner, I'd try and fail to work up the courage. Either they were in a good mood, which I didn't want to ruin, or else they were bickering, which I didn't want to interrupt. I'd experienced enough of my own parents' fights as a kid to know the best action was to just stay out of it. So I let my grandparents do their thing, and I answered their questions about my day, and I watched them exchange little glances showing how pleased they were that I was everything they'd hoped for. That I was exactly the girl they'd wanted.

I could be that girl, I told myself, as I went dutifully to my horrible Mock Trial meetings and sat with Cole's crowd at lunch. I just had to keep doing the things I was already doing. It was that simple and that hard.

Part of me had expected it to get easier being around Friya and Whitney. That underneath their intimidating exteriors, I'd find some interest we had in common, or at least something interesting to talk about. Except they remained at a distance. They'd invited me in, and that was precisely the problem: I'd needed the invitation, when no one else at the table did.

But then there was Cole. Whenever I caught myself editing some joke or some reference, or sitting silently for too long, wishing Friya would just shut up about her ex, he'd look over at me and say something charming. Or else he'd roll his eyes and nudge my leg under the table, letting me know that he was annoyed, too.

He was smart in school—taking all honors, even though he downplayed it. He ran late to lunch sometimes, staying behind to help the students in Computer Programming. I saw him in the classroom on the way to my locker, watching as he joked around with the younger students. He even made a point to say hey to them around campus. It was sweet, the way he was concerned about everyone else.

The way he was concerned about me. Whenever he turned his attention toward me at lunch, I'd flutter inside just a little bit, because his eyes were bright as sea glass, and his hair defied gravity, and he always had some excuse to touch my arm, or my back.

And I'd think, See? You do like it here. You're just miserable because your mom is dead. Because you miss pancakes and Thai food and walking around the house with no pants on. The only reason your life doesn't feel right is because nothing in this town feels right, because it was never supposed to be yours in the first place.

Still, I'd pause outside Mr. Saldana's classroom after Mock Trial, catching a glimpse of the Art Club and wishing I could try it on and see if it fit. There were maybe seven or eight of them, and they always seemed to be having the best time.

Once, they were watching a slam poetry competition. I watched through the doorway, entranced by the rhythmic beat of someone's voice, by the pulsing, pounding way they were using their words. By how everyone was eating pizza and sitting on their desks, staring at the video on the projector, totally into it, and not at all embarrassed to admit that.

There was this tug in my gut like I was supposed to be there with them. Like they weren't strangers or random classmates, but people I was supposed to know.

Except I didn't know them. I didn't know Lily, who wasn't dating Adam and who lived two doors down and dressed amazing and always had something interesting to say—but never had anything to say to me.

Instead, I knew Friya, who was always begging Ethan to airdrop her his Spanish homework, and Whitney, who put mustard on her french fries because ketchup has too many carbs.

Every night, I'd go home and fall face-first into my

enormous pile of homework and endure my grandmother's endless questions. The one thing I'd look forward to was getting the texts Cole sent before bed. *Evening soundtrack,* he'd say, sending me a retro music video. I'd curl up in bed with my phone, watching, knowing that he was waiting on the other end. He figured out that I was into weird news articles, and he'd send those too.

What's the verdict, Fresh? he'd write. And I knew that was my opportunity to steer us into having a real conversation, instead of just the joking opener to one. But I always held back, sending a clever comment instead of an honest answer.

I wished he wasn't putting all the pressure on me to take the conversation from friendship to something more. That for once he'd be the one to confess something meaningful. To assure me that he was someone I could really talk to. But he never did, no matter how much I imagined it.

But once I pictured one thing different, I started picturing others. What it would be like, for example, to belong to a different school club. To have different friends.

Lily was right there. I saw her every day, across the locker room in Phys Ed, in black lace bras and striped boyshort underwear, scraping her hair into a bun as she laughed over something with Mabel. Or else she was across the room in Studio Art, deep in concentration as she sat next to Ryland, her modicum of artistic talent eclipsed by his. Rarely, I saw her in the quad, or her car, or in the backyard on that enormous trampoline. And I'd wish I could wave and go over. I'd wish and I'd wish and I'd wish.

I'd wish my mom was still alive, because the thoughts I kept trying to shove down about Lily were thoughts that my mom would have been cool with. And I wasn't sure I could say the same thing about my grandparents.

Most nights, I'd hear them watching TV downstairs, and I'd know they were nodding in agreement when the president said he didn't need to release his tax returns, and I'd wonder what else they were nodding in agreement with. And the despair would creep in, and I'd remind myself that I was fine not having things I wanted.

CHAPTER 13

THE WEEK OF THE HOMECOMING GAME kicked off with a pep rally, which in and of itself wasn't terrible. The terrible part was that the pep rally took place at eight a.m. on Monday. Which meant that Whitney, Friya, and I slouched in the stands, yawning, with zero pep to rally.

From the way everyone around us looked half asleep, I gathered they felt the same. At my old school, we'd had pep rallies right before lunch. The same boys would always heckle, and the cheerleaders would do a dance routine full of strategic high kicks, and I'd stand off to the side with the yearbook camera, secretly relieved that I didn't have to participate.

It felt different to sit in the stands with my friends instead of taking pictures. I looked around at the sea of students, who were only just now starting to coalesce into something recognizable. People looked familiar in the halls now, not strangers anymore but classmates: the quiet boy who ate nothing but hot dogs, the loudmouth girl who loved horses, the impossibly tall drama kid who wore three-piece suits, and the emo girls who hung on his every word.

Enormous butcher-paper banners hung above the bleachers, decorated in class colors. Ours was green and featured an enormous painting of a box of Junior Mints, which was either clever or terrible, I couldn't decide. It was spirit week, apparently. The run-up to the homecoming game, wherein we were supposed to get really amped about our football team, and being juniors, I think simultaneously.

"Get ready to have some spirit," Whitney whispered, rolling her eyes.

"I'm *literally* still asleep," Friya complained.

The boys joined us, Cole stepping over everyone so he could sit next to me, instead of just taking the end. His hair was still wet from the shower, which killed me, and he was wearing his soccer warmups, gray with sky-blue stripes, which brought out the green in his eyes.

"Too early," Ethan complained, yawning.

"Nah, ya gotta rally," Cole said, grinning. "Get it? Rally?"

"Terrible," I told him, and he gave me a soft punch in the shoulder. My sleeve felt warm even after he moved his hand away.

And then Adam bounded onto the floor of the gym dressed in head-to-toe green, like a deranged leprechaun. There was even green in his hair. He was in his element, I had to give him that. Unfortunately, we were expected to be in it along with him.

"Come on, freshmen!" the cheer started. "Wake up those sophomores!"

And then it was upon us, a wall of pep, an entire bleacher section of screaming, flailing freshmen. By the time it got to the sophomores ("Wake up those juniors!"), Cole was drumming his palms on his knees, going, "We gotta win this, guys," and when it came to us, his scream was deafening.

After the requisite "You can do better than that," Cole turned toward us, pleading for us to step it up.

So I screamed, feeling ridiculous. But then I caught Cole's eye, his mouth wide open, screaming even louder than me, and we locked eyes, shouting together, and I was surprised that it was actually kind of fun. My heart was pounding, and I felt alive.

"See?" he whispered after it was over, his lips thrillingly close to my ear. "You just had to rally."

"No one actually goes to the homecoming dance, right?" I asked at lunch on Tuesday.

I'd spent the past day quietly freaking out and wondering if my friends were planning to go without me, and I was the last person in the world to realize.

"God no," Friya assured me.

"Total waste of a Saturday night," Ethan promised.

At my old school, homecoming had been a thing. I'd covered it for yearbook, getting shots of the seniors who'd been voted king and queen, watching all of the friend groups pose in front of the canvas backdrop, finding out from Instagram who had been at the wild afterparties.

"We're going to the game, though," Whitney said. "Our football team's terrible since Archer graduated, so it's like . . ." She trailed off, frowning.

"*Schadenfreude*?" I supplied, at the same moment Whitney said, "Acceptable."

Cole laughed, throwing his head back, and I felt my cheeks heat up.

"God, Freshman, what would we do without you?" he teased, patting me on the shoulder.

There was some commotion on the opposite side of the quad, where a few members of the football team had decided to have an impromptu hot dog eating contest.

We all glanced over, weirdly fascinated by the spectacle.

Schadenfreude, I thought again. Pleasure at the misfortune of others. A removed sort of amusement, exactly like what we were experiencing now.

My grandparents seemed surprised that I wasn't going to the homecoming dance. They'd seen it on the school's Facebook page apparently, and my grandmother was all excited about helping me choose a dress and going to the salon together for manicures.

I actually felt bad explaining to her that we were just going to the game and then getting together at someone's house. She couldn't quite understand the concept, and I was worried that if I kept trying, suddenly she'd understand too well that Cole was having a legit house party, where there weren't going to be teacher chaperones. So I told her that he was taking me to the game.

"Sounds like things are getting serious," she said, immediately brightening. "And he's considering asking you to go steady."

I don't know how I kept a straight face.

"Wow, that would be so great," I said.

My mom would have given me a look, detecting the thick layer of sarcasm. But my grandmother just smiled even wider, and I could practically hear her thinking about how much easier it was to get what she wanted the second time around.

On Thursday, Mr. Miller made us run laps in gym. Someone had stolen the Frisbee apparently, which meant our unit on Ultimate Frisbee had to hit pause. In honor of spirit week, there had been one-dollar cupcakes on sale in the quad, and after eating those, the last thing any of us felt like doing was laps.

"This is how they exercise inmates," I overheard Mabel complain.

"High school is *such* a panopticon," Lily agreed, tying

her hair up into a knot.

I watched the two of them link arms and set off toward the field.

Mabel was part of the drama crowd, even though she also did Art Club. She was a sort of minimalist, high-fashion goth, with a pageboy haircut and an Instagram full of exquisite flat lays. She was almost as intimidating as Lily.

Except Lily wasn't intimidating. She was more than that. She was a force.

I jogged the first lap, because Mr. Miller was blowing his whistle and calling out anyone who wasn't hustling. A few of my classmates gave him the finger when his back was turned.

Ahead of me, two senior boys were laughing. One of them stopped to tie his shoe, and the other waited for him, jogging comically in place. The boy who was in no way tying his shoe reached down beneath a bush and unearthed a soggy, bloated tennis ball. He grimaced and tossed it to his friend.

"Gross," his friend complained, laughing, as he caught it.

"Pick up the pace, Natasha!" Mr. Miller yelled.

For a moment, I thought he'd said Sasha. I glanced over at him, confused, since I was jogging. And that was when I felt my ankle roll over something small and hard and spherical.

The tennis ball.

I went down, landing on my side in the ochre sand. I

was so surprised by it that I couldn't breathe. My ankle throbbed. I felt nauseated from the pain.

"Shit, you all right?" one of the boys called.

"Hey, toss back the ball," the other one urged, cupping his hands.

"Grow up," Mabel called, kicking the ball back into the bushes.

And then she stood over me, holding out her hand.

"Here," she said, helping me up. "Go slow in case it's broken."

"It's probably fine," I said, which was more wishful thinking than empirical observation.

A flash of pain shot up my ankle when I put weight on it.

"That's definitely a sprain," said Lily, who had joined us. "You have to ice it, or else it'll puff up."

"Like a frittata," I said stupidly.

No one knew what to do with that, and honestly, neither did I.

"We'll take you to the nurse," Lily said. "Here, put your weight on me."

I stared at her in surprise. But it made sense. Mabel was so much taller, while Lily and I were almost the same height.

"Um, thanks," I mumbled, my cheeks turning red as I slung my arm around her shoulder.

I'd barely even spoken to Lily before, and now I could

feel the warm, soft fabric of her T-shirt under my bare arm. I was close enough to smell her shampoo, or deodorant, or whatever it was that hinted of sandalwood. I felt dizzy, and my heart was racing.

Oh god, I hoped I didn't smell like my lunch. Or my gym clothes, since I hadn't washed them this week. Because "Sasha Bloom smells like BO" was the last thing I wanted Lily to think of me.

Thankfully, the nurse's office wasn't too far. I got set up with some ice packs on the world's most uncomfortable cot, and Mabel and Lily hung around for a while, in no hurry to get back. I didn't blame them.

"Who steals a gym Frisbee?" I wondered aloud.

"Who tosses around a soggy tennis ball?" Lily returned.

"Yeah, someone might get hurt," I said, deadpan. Lily snorted.

"Can you drive home on that?" Mabel asked, nodding at my right ankle.

"I actually walk," I said.

"I'll give you a ride," Lily offered.

"Um, you don't have to," I said, hoping it hadn't sounded like I was angling for her to offer.

"You live two houses down," she said, like I was being ridiculous.

And maybe I was. So I smiled and said thanks, and after the bell rang, Lily followed me to my locker, watching as I unloaded books into my bag.

"Which class is that for?" she asked, nodding at a Diane Arbus art book I'd gotten from our school library.

"It's not," I said. "I mean, um, it's just for me."

"You're into photography?" Lily asked, sounding surprised. "Do you take photos as well?"

I nodded, even though it had been a while. I used to take my camera everywhere, but that was back in a different life.

"Well, I mostly take portraits," I said. "I read somewhere that a good portrait is like a quiet epiphany. So that's what I try to photograph. Epiphanies people don't even realize they're having."

I'd said too much about myself, I realized. I broke off, horribly embarrassed.

"Epiphanies people don't even realize they're having," Lily repeated. "That's one of the better descriptions I've heard of art."

"Um, thanks," I said, surprised. I'd been afraid that I'd gone too cerebral, talking about photography. The girls at my lunch table would have laughed. But Lily was totally here for it.

"You'll have to show me your portraits sometime," Lily said.

"I could show you now," I offered. I wasn't sure she'd talk to me again, and anyway, what did I have to lose?

I took out my phone, opening an album of my favorites.

"Wow," she said softly, enlarging a photo of an elderly

woman staring up at an enormous taxidermy buffalo. It was black and white, shot from below, her face rippling in shadow. "Grandparent?"

"Just a docent," I said. "I took that in the museum where I used to work."

"You worked in a museum." She didn't say it as a question.

"Before I moved here," I said, not wanting to get into it.

Lily kept scrolling, looking at the portrait I'd taken of a cheerleader during a football game. I'd used a long exposure, which had created trails of light and color whenever she moved. Her pom-poms were a soft blur, her smile in sharp focus. It had been too experimental for the yearbook.

"Friend of yours?" she asked.

"Not really. I just thought—you see how her smile's the only thing that isn't moving?" I said.

Lily snorted and shook her head.

"You should join Art Club," she said.

"Yeah, well." I shifted my backpack onto one shoulder. "It's at the same time as Mock Trial."

Lily frowned.

"You're doing Mock Trial?" she asked, surprised. "What for?"

"Pre-law," I said, shrugging.

"Weird." Lily made a face. "Wouldn't have pegged you as the future-lawyer type."

"I'm not," I said. "I'm just doing it because, well, it's complicated."

"I'll take your word for it," Lily said, digging out her keys.

Adam was waiting for us in the lot, and when he saw me, he started waving vigorously, with zero embarrassment.

A couple of people were staring, and Adam gave them a head-nod. "What's up?" he said pleasantly. "Don't forget to buy tickets to the homecoming dance!"

And then he frowned in my direction.

"What's with the limp?" Adam asked.

"Some dicks in our gym class," Lily said. "We're giving her a ride."

"But it's so out of the way," he said, deadpan.

Her car was ridiculous inside, with buttery leather seats and one of those fancy backup cameras that helps you park.

"Nice car," I said, since I couldn't not say it.

"It used to be my mom's," Lily explained. "She had to get an SUV for the soccer carpool."

"She calls it her suburban hell vehicle," said Adam. "Even though she secretly loves it."

"She really does," Lily agreed.

Adam reached for the console to plug in his phone, but Lily swatted his hand away.

"We're not listening to your dumb podcasts," she told him, plugging in her own phone. "We have time for one good song."

"Then how come you never play any?" Adam retorted over the opening bars of Dua Lipa's newest single.

Lily turned it up savagely, until it was more noise than music.

I watched them from the back seat, fascinated. They were every inch bickering siblings, and I couldn't figure out how I'd missed it at first. How I'd seen them sprawled on their backyard trampoline, sunglasses and headphones on, ignoring each other, and had mistaken it for some grand romantic moment.

"Hey, Sasha, are you going to the homecoming dance?" Adam asked.

"Um," I said, trying to figure out how honest to be without hurting his feelings. "Well, my friends aren't, so . . ."

"I knew it! No one's going," Adam said, slouching down dramatically. "Freaking Felicia Sawyer never should have been elected homecoming chair."

"That dance is a lost cause," Lily said. "Who wants to pay fifty bucks to hang around an overly chaperoned gym full of freshmen?"

"When you put it that way," Adam said, glaring.

"Is there another way to put it?" Lily asked. "Besides, Sasha's probably going to Cole's party."

I was surprised she even knew about that. It didn't seem like her scene.

"I was planning to," I said. "You?"

"Maybe," Lily said.

"I have to help out at the dance," Adam said. "Although I'll be devastated if I miss the return of Grilled Cheezus."

"Grilled Cheezus?" I asked.

Apparently, at Cole's last party, Ethan had gotten so

drunk that he'd hatched an elaborate plan to cook everyone grilled cheese sandwiches and parachute them off the third-floor balcony.

"Oh no," I said.

"Oh yes," Lily said. "He set up a whole station in the kitchen. *Mise en place,* like an actual restaurant. He was not messing around. And then he climbed onto this little faux balcony, bellowed 'GRILLED CHEESE,' and tossed them into the crowd."

"It was amazing," said Adam. "People called him the Grilled Cheezus for months. He even grew out his hair."

"That's commitment," I said.

"That's Ethan," Lily said, shaking her head.

"It's too bad he hangs around with such doucheholes," said Adam, giving Lily a significant look.

"Adam!" Lily scolded. "Those are Sasha's friends you're talking about. Right, Sasha?"

She was staring at me in the rearview, a slight smirk playing over her lips, daring me to say it out loud. And I wished I didn't have to. Because they'd been nothing but nice to me, and okay, maybe I sometimes got the impression that they weren't that way to everyone, but it wasn't like they were actively making anyone's life miserable. At least, not that I saw.

"Right," I said. "They're my friends."

CHAPTER 14

AN UNEXPECTED SIDE EFFECT OF TWISTING my ankle in Phys Ed was that Cole seemed genuinely concerned the next day. He even offered to give me a ride to the homecoming game.

When he pulled up, dressed in his varsity jacket with shoeblack across his cheeks in warrior streaks, I was surprised it was just the two of us. I'd thought it was more of a carpool, not a one-on-one situation.

"Where's everyone?" I asked.

"Just us," Cole said. "For a change."

"So Whitney made Ethan take her to dinner?" I guessed.

"Yep," Cole admitted. "We could have joined, but I kind of wanted a break from hanging with them. Hope it's okay."

"Are you apologizing for not taking me to dinner?" I asked, charmed.

"Only if you would have said yes. To dinner." He glanced over at me, as though gauging my reaction. It was like one of his text messages. All suggestion but no substance.

"Well, I don't know," I said. "Because in order to answer a question, someone has to ask one."

Cole shook his head, grinning.

"Touché," he told me.

Was he flirting? Was I? I couldn't figure it out. Any of it. Why we were alone, why Cole was staring at me like that, or what I should do if he was finally trying to make something happen between us.

Go for it, I supposed. It would cement my place at their lunch table, and maybe then I wouldn't have to panic so much about whether Friya and Whitney wanted me around. And it would certainly delight my grandparents.

"Also, you're welcome," Cole said.

"What for?" I asked, buckling my seat belt. His car smelled like boy—like expensive cologne and fast food and sports equipment and air freshener.

"Brought you a school sweatshirt," he said, gesturing toward a sky-blue hoodie balled up in his back seat. It was actually a nice gesture.

"Is it clean?" I asked, only half-teasing.

"It's definitely been washed in the past six months," he said, grinning.

I gave the sweatshirt a tentative sniff, but thankfully he was just messing with me, and its cleanliness was acceptable.

Everyone was already at the game when we got there.

The stands were filled, like the game was actually a big deal. And it wasn't just students, either. There were so many adults, and almost all of them were wearing school sweatshirts or varsity jackets. Some had even brought little kids.

"Wow," I said, looking around.

Cole's hoodie was hilariously massive on me, but he insisted it looked cute.

"Hey, Ariana Grande!" Friya called, waving us over. "Nice sweatshirt."

We huddled onto the bleachers, sitting on a blanket Ethan had brought. He produced a flask, too, from the pocket of his varsity jacket, passing it down the row. I didn't want them to make fun of me for skipping it, so I tilted the flask to my lips, tasting something strong and harsh that might have been whisky.

"God," I said, coughing, pretending I'd taken a larger swig.

Cole, meanwhile, passed around a vape, and I was slow on the uptake that it was weed this time, and not just dessert-flavored tobacco.

"Um, I'm fine," I said when he offered it to me.

He'd pushed up the sleeves on his own sweatshirt, and I could see a bruise on his arm.

"What happened?" I asked, frowning at it.

"Soccer practice," he said, shrugging. But he tugged down his sleeves anyway, acting self-conscious.

The game was more exciting than the girls had made it

out to be. There was a new player this year, a freshman, six-two and built like a brick wall, who was killing it on the defensive line.

People were losing their shit for him. I thought they were screaming MOOSE, which couldn't have been right. And then I saw the back of his jersey and realized they were shouting RUSSE.

Cole and Ethan were getting hammered. They had some elaborate drinking game set up that they couldn't begin to explain. After the flask was emptied, Ethan mostly slouched down in his seat, watching the game with laser focus and making the occasional comment like, "Sports is such a metaphor, you know?" while Cole got more and more worked up.

"Come on, come on, come on!" he yelled, surging to his feet.

"I didn't realize you were so into football," I said after the ball went out of play.

"I'm not. But a couple of these guys played with my brother. He only graduated two years ago."

Cole twisted around, flicking his chin a couple rows back in the stands. Archer was here, wearing an old letter jacket that he was practically bursting out of. It had barely been a month since I'd last seen him, and it looked like he'd been doing nothing but guzzling down protein shakes and hitting the gym. Even next to his muscled friends he was intimidating.

"I think he ate another Hemsworth," I said.

"Better them than me," Cole said cynically, and before I could really process it, he'd draped his arm around my shoulders.

I stiffened in surprise. God, he was warm. Like a furnace. The boy smell was back, and was practically intoxicating. Before I could think about what I was doing, I leaned toward him.

He felt so nice and soft. And then our team completed a pass, and Cole shouted at an earsplitting volume, surging to his feet.

"Get it! Get it!" he yelled.

We were about to score a touchdown. Everyone around me screamed, jumping up. People were losing it. Whitney was even filming it on her phone.

The other team intercepted at the last possible moment, and our stands let out a collective groan. Except for Archer, who was screaming obscenities at the top of his lungs, even after everyone else quieted down.

Next to me, Cole winced. He reached for the vape again, and I stood up, needing a break.

"Um, I'm going to get a Coke," I said. "Anyone want anything?"

"I'll have a *Diet* Coke," Whitney said sweetly.

"Same," Friya said.

"You know what I could take down right now?" Ethan said, his pupils enormous. "Truffle mac 'n' cheese."

I waited to see if he was joking, but he stared back at me, completely serious.

"Um, I don't think they have any," I told him, "but I'll see what I can do."

As I made my way down to the concession stand, I really hoped, for the sake of my wallet, that they weren't serving truffle mac 'n' cheese. I'd had a shock the first time I went through our school's lunch line and saw the menu included sushi.

"Alice?" It was a woman's voice, soft and tentative. "Alice Bloom?"

I found myself face-to-face with a plump blond lady around my mom's age, whose energetic five-year-old son was covered in blue cotton candy.

"No," I said, my throat dry. I felt a little sick at the accusation. "Um, that's my mom."

"You look just like her," the woman said, staring at me. "Is she here? I'd love to say hello. It's been, god, eighteen years?"

The woman swiveled her head, searching for my mom in the crowd.

I swallowed, trying to keep from falling apart. It was almost unbearable to talk about her like this, here, with some complete stranger.

"She's, um, she's not here," I said.

"What a shame," the lady said. "Does she have Facebook? I didn't realize she lived in town."

"No, she doesn't," I said.

I needed to get away from this eager, friendly woman whose questions felt like knives going in and twisting.

"Well, what's her email then?" the woman pushed. "I just moved back—had to get this little one into a good school district, you can't imagine how hard that is. Anyhow, I'd love to reconnect."

"She passed away," I blurted.

"Oh my god," the woman said, her mouth hanging open, frozen in this little round tunnel.

She blinked at me, as though it was my fault that she wasn't having a joyous reunion with her old classmate. I stared back, wanting to be anywhere else. The woman's eyes darted into the crowd, searching for a way out. "I'm so sorry to hear that. I—well, we should be going. Come on, Atticus. Let's find Daddy."

The woman bustled away with her sticky kindergartner, and I stood there, my chest heaving, trying not to cry. I wasn't going to cry at a football game. That was even worse than crying at school. But it was too much all of a sudden. Too many parts of my mom, and her life, and the ways they were never supposed to intersect with mine. These adults who were at the homecoming game—they were my mom's classmates. People who had known her when she was my age, who had sat in her third period and stood in front of her in the lunch line and signed her yearbook.

I hadn't realized before, but I certainly realized now. Here, among her old classmates, I was just asking for more confrontations like the one I'd just had. I looked like her. Everyone always said so, calling me "mini-Alice" or "her twin," even perfect strangers.

And probably someone else, who wasn't lonely and new in town, with a sticky kindergartner plastered to her leg, might have reacted better, but I didn't want to find out, because places like homecoming games were supposed to be safe. They weren't supposed to be filled with reminders of my dead mom.

I darted into the concession line. It took me a moment to recognize the familiar peacoat and high ponytail in front of me. Lily.

I froze. She was so close, her back only inches away, her hair swinging with each shuffle forward so it was practically in my face. I could smell her shampoo, herbal and tangy. She had a mini Kanken backpack on, sky blue, with a Hermione Granger keychain hanging off it, and enamel pins that represented everything from political slogans ("nasty woman" "black lives matter") to a cute cartoon dumpling colored like a rainbow. It looked almost like a pride flag, but was probably just some weird joke from *Adventure Time*. She also had a NASA pin, and an anthropomorphized avocado, and a tiny gray Totoro.

She twisted around, noticing me.

"Hey," she said. "How's the limp?"

"Cured," I said. "Experimental procedure. My DNA is now half hedgehog."

She laughed, her whole face lighting up. If Cole was stained glass, she was a lighthouse.

"You know, hedgehogs are illegal in California," she said. "They might kick you out."

"One can only hope," I said drily.

It never ceased to surprise me how I could do this. How I could be falling apart one moment and full of witty remarks the next. How my brain and mouth could function just fine through utter despair.

"So, you enjoying the game?" I asked.

"Ryland is," Lily said with a shrug. "He's very into—what's it called?—when you're pleased by someone else's misfortune? *Schadenfreude*."

"Damage-joy," I said, and Lily stared at me. "That's the literal translation."

"Weird," she said. And then she glanced down at her phone, which was lit up with a text conversation.

I watched her type, her ponytail sliding over one shoulder, her lashes fanning against her cheeks.

"I love Harry Potter," I blurted, like an idiot. Lily looked up, confused. "Your keychain," I explained. I wanted so badly to impress her.

"It was like my entire childhood," Lily confessed. "I had the biggest crush on Emma Watson."

For a second, I thought she actually meant a real crush,

because I'd definitely had a thing for Hermione. But her mouth was twisted into this ironic smirk, and I got that she was making fun of herself.

"Didn't everyone?" I retorted. "I mean, her eyebrows are iconic."

I wondered if I should have admitted that, but Lily just smiled.

"'It's Levi*o*sa, not Levio*sa*,'" she quoted, doing a surprisingly good impression.

My mom had gotten me the first book on tape when I was seven. We'd done a chapter each night, like a bedtime story, except better, because she'd crawled into bed with me, and we'd closed our eyes and listened together, under my glow-in-the-dark stars.

"You okay?" Lily asked, shaking me back to the present. "You seem kind of sad."

I was surprised she'd noticed. My friends never did.

"I was thinking about my mom," I confessed, and somehow, with her, it wasn't painful as I explained about the bedtime audiobook.

"What happened to her?" Lily asked, point-blank.

"She died last spring," I said.

"I'm really sorry," Lily said. But she said it like it was okay, and not weird or uncomfortable to be talking about. "It gets easier to live with, if you're wondering."

I stared at her, wondering how on earth she knew that.

"My dad died when I was four," she confessed.

I had about a million questions, but before I could ask any of them, Whitney and Friya showed up.

"What's taking so long?" Whitney complained.

"For real, you totally disappeared," said Friya. And then they spotted Lily.

"Oh," Friya said. "Hi."

"Hi," Lily said, her smile strained.

We lapsed into awkward silence. Somehow, the four of us didn't work at all. It wasn't like Lily and I could pick back up our conversation, and Whitney was complaining about how completely wrong her horoscope had been for today, and trying to show it to Friya.

I'd never been so relieved to reach a concessions window.

CHAPTER 15

I WAS TREMENDOUSLY NERVOUS ABOUT Cole's party. I didn't know how these things worked, or if it was okay to show up alone, but Whitney and Friya hadn't texted me about going together, and I didn't want to be needy, so I didn't ask.

Instead, I panicked over the one thing I could control: my outfit. And then I spent far too long trying and failing to pile my hair into a messy topknot before looking it up on YouTube and realizing I needed more than just bobby pins and hope. They never tell you that part, how the simplest-looking makeup and hair is actually insanely complicated and full of hidden parts. The moment I realized the girls with perfect ballerina buns were going around with socks balled up on their heads broke me.

"Sasha?" my grandfather said, poking his head out of his home office when I came downstairs. I could hear the television blaring in the background. The president was vowing to build a border wall between the US and Mexico. "That's quite an outfit."

"You don't like it?" I asked, frowning. It was just an army jacket over a floral sundress and some boots.

"You look like your mother." He smiled wistfully, and my stomach twisted. "Where are you headed in that getup?"

"Cole's having some friends over," I said. "Grandma already knows about it."

My grandfather nodded, and then took out his money clip, peeling off a twenty.

"Grandpa, no," I protested. They already gave me an allowance.

"You should always have cab fare to get home," he insisted, and then tapped the side of his nose. "I expect I'll forget I gave this to you in the morning."

Before I could even say thank you, he disappeared back into his office.

Cole lived in the same subdivision, a couple of streets up. His house was enormous: white and modern, with this weirdly sculptural aesthetic where you couldn't tell if something was a piece of art or an expensive chair. The street was piled with cars, and as I stood there, double-checking my makeup in my phone camera, a group of girls staggered out of an Uber, giggling.

"It's like we're back in high school," one of them shrieked in delight.

I waited for them to go in first. I knew this was actually

Archer's party, a get-together consisting of whoever was in town for the homecoming game. That Cole had only gotten to invite people because he'd threatened to tell their parents.

But I had a secret: I'd never been to a house party before. And now I was at one full of college students wearing USC hoodies and reeking of pot.

The party sprawled through the huge, echoing house, each room revealing another cluster of people I'd never seen before and was pretty sure didn't go to our school.

In the kitchen, I finally found a familiar face: Ethan. He was with a group of drunk senior boys from the soccer team, who were sitting on the floor in a pile of broken, uncooked spaghetti.

"It's wild," Ethan kept saying, shaking his head.

"It's spaghetti," I told him.

"Watch this." He held up a stick between his hands, and then bent it until it snapped. "Three pieces," he informed me, picking them up. "Spaghetti never breaks into two pieces. Always three or four. Can you believe it?"

One of the guys, who was actually wearing a hemp poncho, broke another strand of spaghetti to demonstrate. Four pieces this time. The boy next to him, who was filming it with his phone, howled.

"Spaghettiiiiii," he hooted.

"Cool, well, I'll leave you to your work," I said, backing away slowly.

I poured myself a drink, mixing Coke with rum, because

I knew at least that was a thing. I didn't know the ratio, though, and when I cautiously took a sip, I suspected I was way off.

"Hey," Ethan called, holding out a piece of spaghetti. "You need a stirrer?"

"Sure," I said, grabbing it. "Thanks."

"It's eco-friendly," he said. "Save the environment, right?"

"Where is everyone?" I asked.

"Cole's probably in the screening room," Ethan guessed.

I didn't think I'd heard him right. But sure enough, after some wandering, I found an actual screening room, with a projector screen and reclining leather seats. In the back was a Ping-Pong table, which some boys were using for beer pong, and the screen door was open, spilling out onto a backyard deck.

Thankfully, I spotted Cole immediately. He was wearing his Supreme hoodie and skinny jeans, barefoot, dashing around playing host.

"You need anything?" he asked. "A drink? A napkin? A potted fern?"

"The fern, definitely," I told him.

"I'm going to need to see some ID for that." He grinned, taking a few steps closer, and staring down at me through his criminally long eyelashes. I could smell pot on him, and his eyes were dark tunnels instead of stained glass.

"What happened last night?" he pouted. "You left early."

"Oh, um." Friya had begged me to bail with her. She'd gotten ketchup on her top on the way back from the concession stand and declared she was so over the game anyway. I'd taken the ride, since I'd figured Cole was too wrecked to drive me home. "Football's not really my thing," I finished lamely.

Even standing so close to me, Cole was still playing party host. He made a face, momentarily distracted.

"Jared! Use a coaster, you heathen!" Cole roared.

"Suck my nutsack, Colon," some boy from the soccer team yelled back, joking.

"Sorry. Some people have zero manners," Cole said.

"Who are all these people?" I asked, twisting around. I recognized a lot of them from our school, but there were dudes with full-on beards walking around.

"Archer's friends." Cole rolled his eyes. "I hate it when he comes home and does this. Our parents treat him like a god."

"Thor, son of Odin," I joked.

"Nah, he's the other one," Cole said. "The asshole god."

And then he leapt across the room for a moment, being like, "Jared, I was serious about that coaster, dude."

He slapped one down on the table and then slunk back.

"I like your house," I said. "You never told me you have a screening room."

"It's my mom's." Cole shrugged. "She's a producer."

"Of movies?" I said, impressed.

"Yeah. Well, she used to be. Now she just complains about digital."

"Gah! Netflix!" I said, shaking my fist.

"Exactly," Cole said. "Hey, come upstairs with me. I have something to show you."

"Okay?" I said, wondering what it was. Part of me was hoping puppy.

Cole reached for my hand. He'd done that once before, and it was both electric and thrilling, the way mine felt dwarfed in his.

I didn't know where we were going, or what we'd do when we got there. I just knew that I was at a house party with a boy who liked me, and I was pretty sure, at some point very soon, he was going to kiss me. And I was going to kiss him back, and hopefully not be terrible at it. And then I wouldn't have to stress over Whitney's passive-aggressive comments, or worry about my place at their lunch table. Then I'd belong.

We tangled down a hallway and through the living room, where I caught sight of Friya on the sofa. She was sitting on Nick's lap, the two of them making out hungrily, as though their breakup had only made them more starved for each other.

"Wow," I said. "Really?"

"Yep. They've been like that all night," Cole said, shaking his head. "I give up."

"I thought they were over," I said.

"Nah. Friya got a thrill out of saying that because it meant Whitney had to listen to her talk, for once," Cole said, being strangely insightful. I shot him a weirded-out look, and he shrugged. "What? Nick and I go way back. Plus Whitney and Ethan have been a thing since freshman year. Who do you think gets stuck hearing about all their shit?"

"You contain multitudes, Cole Edwards," I told him.

"Twelve vitamins and minerals in every bite," he assured me.

And then he squeezed my hand and led me up the stairs, through another hallway and past some sort of lofted gaming area where a bunch of jacked-looking dudes were sprawled in beanbag chairs, screaming as they played Fortnite.

We passed a laundry room, where a couple was going at it, door ajar, and then Cole stopped, told me to wait until I heard a secret knock, and disappeared into a dark room.

He was definitely going to kiss me. Except, the longer I stood there, my heart pounding, the more I started to wonder if it wasn't an elaborate prank. I could picture the joke easily: Cole leaving me standing outside that door for the rest of the party. Cole and Whitney and whomever else was inside, hands over their mouths so I wouldn't hear their laughter, spying on me to see what I would do.

Or no one in the room at all, Cole slipping out a second

door, through a bathroom, leaving me alone, waiting, hoping, forgotten.

And then a knock sounded from inside the room, and Cole's muffled voice called, "You may enter."

I pushed open the door.

The room was awash in candlelight.

Candles flickered on his bedside table, his dresser with clothes trailing from half-open drawers, his bookshelf full of sports trophies, the stack of AP textbooks on his desk.

It smelled like vanilla. And tuberose. And ocean breeze. And jasmine.

And Cole was standing in the middle of it, his shirt off, the top button of his jeans undone, the *Calvin Klein* of his boxer briefs on full display.

"Surprise," he said, grinning.

He looked like a model. Like he'd walked straight off Instagram and was standing shirtless in the center of the room. A kiss seemed too tame for him to have gone to so much trouble. My stomach twisted at the question of just how much more than a kiss he was expecting, but I tried to push past it, because I was almost seventeen, and clearly I'd missed a couple of things hiding behind my camera for the past few years.

"Wow, you didn't warn me we were performing a ritual sacrifice," I joked, gesturing toward the candles.

No one laughed.

Instead, Cole stepped forward, putting his hands on my

hips. His touch burned. I could feel my heartbeat everywhere. And he said, "I borrowed them from my mom. For you."

He beamed like he'd figured out the secret to the universe. And maybe he had. He tilted my face up toward his, using just one finger under my chin. His chest was all muscle, and his arms were powerful, and suddenly, he was kissing me. It was wet and smoky and minty, and I couldn't believe it.

I couldn't believe he'd done this for me.

He steered us over to the bed, and when I pulled away for a moment, he lounged backward on his green duvet, staring up at me.

"You know what?" he breathed.

"What?"

"I've been wondering what color your panties are all night."

"Oh," I said, surprised he'd been thinking about them. About me. It wasn't like I'd been wondering the same thing about him.

"I'll show you mine," Cole purred, taking my hand and gliding it down the zipper on his jeans, releasing the dark bulge of his black underwear. "Now you."

I had to do it, I realized. We were already here, in his bedroom, surrounded by a dozen flickering candles, fortified by rum and Coke, kissing. And it wasn't that I didn't want to. I was curious what it was like, and if I'd enjoy it.

But I was also afraid that I wouldn't enjoy it, and that he'd notice.

He was so handsome. With his shirt off, his jeans gaping open around his waist, he was marble, a statue of a hero they erect in the town square. Oh god, *erect* was really the wrong word. Now I couldn't stop thinking about it.

Erect erect erect.

I slid off my jacket. I had on a dress underneath, floral and short, with spaghetti straps. Against dress code. I saw Cole clock it, licking his lips. He watched as I pulled it off, as I sat there across his legs in just my navy-blue bikini briefs. I didn't have a bra on. The straps had shown, and I'd worried one of the girls would say it looked tacky, but now, without one, I felt far too exposed.

"Nice," Cole said appreciatively, leaning back in bed and pillowing his arms behind his head and staring up me with dark, hungry eyes. The bruise on his forearm had turned purple, and there were small scars on his rib cage, marring his perfection. They made him seem less marble and more real. A living, breathing teenage boy, alone in his bedroom, with me.

"What are we doing?" I asked.

"Whatever you want," he said, waiting for me to make the next move.

I'd never been undressed with a boy before. But the internet is a wonderful crash course, because I knew exactly what to do. At least, I knew what other girls did in this situation. I reached for his jeans, pulling them off entirely, sliding them down his legs and then running my lips over his ankles, kissing his calves, his knees, his thighs. Working my mouth, and my courage, up.

I glanced at Cole to see how I was doing. He was staring down at me, grinning, his cell phone propped upright on his chest.

"What are you doing?" I asked suddenly.

"Relax," he said. "Keep going."

"You're filming me," I said, aghast.

"I am not," Cole protested.

I grabbed the blanket at the end of his bed and pulled it over me, covering myself.

"Show me your phone," I demanded, holding out my hand.

He wouldn't give it to me.

"Chill, Sasha. I just took some photos to look at later."

For a moment, I didn't think I'd heard him right.

"Photos?" I said, horrified. "You have to delete them! Right now!"

"I'm not going to share them with anyone," he promised. "Come on, you look hot."

I stared at him in total disbelief. How could he possibly think this was okay?

"Cole, I'm serious," I said, grabbing for his phone.

He twisted out of the way, laughing, holding the phone over his head.

He's such a nice boy, my grandmother had said, from such a good family. He's the right sort of person to know.

I didn't even know how bad they were. I just knew it was me, in a boy's bedroom, topless, kissing him below the waist. The kind of pictures my mom had always cautioned me never to send to anyone, not even a boyfriend. The kind of photos that had undone girls at my old school.

Cole was still holding the phone over his head, grinning, like this was all a big joke.

"What's the matter?" he asked.

"You," I snapped, tremendously angry.

I tugged on my dress, grabbed my jacket, and got out of there. There was no reason to panic. I could fix this. Friya and Whitney would help me.

I ran downstairs, spotting Whitney immediately. I was hoping for Friya, but Whitney would work.

"Whitney!" I said. "I need your help!"

"What's up?" she asked, sounding bored.

I explained what Cole had done, expecting sympathy, or anger. What I didn't expect was for her to laugh so hard that she had to hold on to a weird sculptural chair for balance.

"He paparazzied you?" she gasped. "Oh my god, that's hilarious!"

"Hilarious?" I didn't think I'd heard her correctly. "He took pictures when I had my clothes off. Without my permission. And then he refused to delete them."

"Honestly?" Whitney said. "You should be flattered. I mean, Cole? He totally has his pick."

It was like we were speaking different languages, and something vital was getting lost in translation. So I tried again.

"Whitney, this is serious," I said, completely freaking out. "You have to help me get rid of the photos before he does something with them."

"It might already be too late," Whitney said, grinning. She was enjoying this.

"Too late for what?" Friya asked, poking her head in.

"Cole took nudie pics of Sasha," Whitney crowed, giggling.

"I hope you mowed the front lawn," Friya said. "Because I know this girl Chloe who posted soooo many bikini photos last summer, and you could completely see her muff puff in every one."

Whitney cracked up.

"Oh my god, that was hysterical!" she said. "Remember how I made all those people comment about her hairy potter? She was *so* confused."

Whitney cackled.

I stared at them, blinking, wondering why we were discussing someone else's crotch hair.

"Also, big news. We don't hate Nick anymore," Friya went on, oblivious.

"Really?" Whitney screeched. "Tell me everything."

And Friya was off, talking a mile a minute about how he'd finally apologized over DM, sending like a whole novel.

I was going to be sick. This couldn't be happening. These couldn't be my friends. I mumbled that I was going to get a drink, and then I staggered out into the yard. My heart was hammering, and suddenly I hated this party so, so much.

It was grotesque and terrible, and I wished I'd never come. Ethan was wandering around, dropping pieces of uncooked spaghetti into everyone's drinks and telling them to save the environment. Some girl was vaping into her friend's phone. A cluster of college-age jocks was loudly playing flip cup on the patio.

I was angry at Cole, but I was angrier at Friya and Whitney. The first day of school, in English, when I'd helped Friya avoid her ex, she'd said girls sticking up for other girls was the most important thing. But now, when I really needed her, it turned out she didn't believe that at all.

"Hey," someone said. It was Lily. A few strands of spaghetti poked through her topknot, no doubt Ethan's work. She peered down at me, concerned. "You okay?"

I must have looked really rough if Lily Chen was stepping in. Like, sprained-ankle, face-plant rough.

"Not really," I said. "Actually, no. I'm not okay."

Lily sat down next to me. Her perfume smelled deep and woodsy, and I wanted to breathe it in until the party dissolved entirely. Until it was just the two of us somewhere quiet and far, far away from all of this.

"What's going on?" she asked.

I explained about Cole.

She didn't laugh. Instead, her eyes burned with rage.

"That asshole!" she fumed. "Come on, let's get his phone and fix this."

"Really?" I said, surprised.

"Of course," she said, frowning. "I'm really freaking sorry he did that to you."

"You sure I shouldn't just lighten up and be flattered he even wanted to hook up with me?" I said. It came out more bitterly than I'd intended, and Lily frowned.

"Who said that?" she demanded, and then, before I could tell her, she guessed. "Whitney."

"And Friya."

"Those bitches," Lily swore. She stared out at the backyard for a moment, all keyed up, her knees bouncing, her mind whirling.

"I don't even want to tell you the rest of it," I said darkly.

"Well, now you have to," Lily insisted, so I did.

"I never should have hung out with them in the first place," I finished, shaking my head. "And I definitely shouldn't have come to this party."

"Don't say that," Lily said sternly. "It's their fault if they want to be garbage people, not yours."

She'd known all along they were awful, I realized. And

she'd thought I was one of them. I'd told her I was one of them. No wonder she'd been so cold and so dismissive.

She certainly wasn't being dismissive now.

Lily's rage was beautiful and terrifying. She was like a vengeful spirit, glittering with anger, and it made something inside my chest flutter, just a little bit.

"Well, come on," she said, pulling me to my feet. "We've got to see a douchehole about a phone."

CHAPTER 16

LILY DRAGGED ME UPSTAIRS, THROUGH THE living room full of strangers, and then stopped at the top of the stairs, lost.

"Which one's his room?" she asked.

I showed her, and she didn't even knock. She just burst in.

The room smelled sickly sweet, the aftermath of so many candles. They were all blown out, though. And Cole wasn't there.

"Shit," I despaired.

"Oh, we'll find him," Lily promised, stepping closer. "Let's go."

I looked down, realizing that we were holding hands. Hers was the same size as mine, soft and a little cold, as though she'd been holding a drink for a while.

She pulled me back into the downstairs throng, pushing her way through the party. Word had apparently gotten out, because it was even more crowded now. And I fought down a stab of disappointment as we squeezed through a packed hallway, because obviously the handholding was necessary.

Cole was in the screening room, playing a game of beer pong, not a care in the world. He'd tossed on a hat, which sat back on his head at a rakish angle. He was laughing as he aimed the Ping-Pong ball toward his opponent's cups.

"*Cole!*" Lily thundered.

He held up his index finger without even looking over, like, "one minute." Like, "this Ping-Pong ball is more important than you." And then he made his toss.

The ball sank into the cup, and he pumped his fist.

"Whoooo!" he crowed. And then he turned to Lily, glowing from his win.

"What's up, Lil?"

"Phone," Lily said, holding out her hand. "Right now."

"Jeez, better do what the lady says," some dude hooted.

Cole looked confused as he dug out his phone.

"Unlocked," Lily instructed with a withering glare.

She went into the photos, and I was so embarrassed at the thought of Lily seeing them. Even though they were dark and grainy, you could still see it was me, topless. He'd gotten his torso in the bottom of the frame, his underwear bulging upward like Mount Olympus, which made it all look so much worse.

Wordlessly, Lily deleted them, and then she opened the

settings, deleting the trash, wiping the data, making sure they weren't uploaded to the cloud. Making sure he hadn't texted them to anyone.

I held my breath the entire time.

And then Lily solemnly raised Cole's phone, holding up her middle finger and snapping a pissed-off selfie.

"All yours," she said, tossing it back to him.

"Sasha," Cole said. "Wait—"

"She's not talking to you right now," Lily said, pulling me away. "Come on."

It was the nicest thing anyone had ever done for me.

I told her so, and she shrugged, embarrassed.

"Anyone would have done the same," she said.

"Except for my friends," I mumbled.

I twisted around, looking for them, half dreading that I'd find them watching the whole thing and giggling.

"Hey," Lily said. "You want to get out of here?"

"Yes, please," I said without hesitation.

We climbed into her car, which felt oddly intimate, just the two of us.

"Hold on. Gotta tell Ryland I bailed," she said, sending a quick text. "So he doesn't worry."

"It's nice that he would?" I said. It came out as a question.

"They may be twins, but they're nothing alike," Lily said.

She drove down the block, which was so quiet that you could sense the ocean looming there, in the distance. She paused at a stop sign, turning toward me. Her hair was coming undone and her necklaces were tangled together and her lipstick was gone, but she still looked amazing. I wondered how she did it. How she was so effortless all the time, and so bravely herself.

"Pick an adventure," she said with a little half smile.

"I don't even know what there is to do in this town," I said. "But my grandpa gave me twenty bucks tonight, so how about you choose and I finance?"

"Deal," she said. And then she tapped the steering wheel for a moment, thinking.

Someone pulled up behind us, flashing their brights and honking.

"Oh my GOD, go AROUND!" Lily yelled.

A huge truck full of dude bros from the party raced past us, and then braked hard. As if in slow motion, one of the boys shimmied out the sunroof, dropped his pants, and bent over, mooning us.

The boys howled as they drove away.

"Well, that was unexpected," Lily said drily.

"I've seen far too many boys with their pants off tonight," I replied. "This better not be a bad-things-come-in-threes situation."

"An unholy trinity of butts," Lily said, somehow keeping a straight face.

"My only request is that wherever we're going is naked-boy-free."

"Guess the nude beach is out," Lily said, deadpan. And

then her eyes lit up, and she smiled a private smile and refused to tell me anything else.

We went through the In-N-Out drive-through, getting shakes and burgers. Lily insisted I needed mine with chopped chiles, which I didn't even know was a thing. Apparently there wasn't just a secret menu, but also a secret-secret menu, known only to those who scoured the internet for foodie videos.

I loved that. I loved picturing Lily alone in her bedroom, watching people sample street food and try off-menu burgers. She had a running list of restaurants and foods she wanted to try all over the world, and she knew the best places to find approximate versions in Orange County. While we inched toward the pickup window, she told me about purple-yam-flavored soft-serve and soup dumplings and cheese tea. I had no idea those were even foods, much less ones you could get twenty minutes away.

"Don't worry, this is just part one," Lily assured me as the pimply teen boy working the drive-through handed us our Neapolitan shakes and Animal Style Double-Doubles with chopped chiles.

"What's part two?" I asked.

"Not telling. You relinquished your ability to choose this adventure," Lily reminded me.

She drove back down PCH and stopped at the light outside our subdivision. I had a stab of disappointment at the thought that it was over, that we were just getting fast food and going back home.

But Lily turned down a street neither of us lived on, an expression of mischief lighting up her face. She stopped the car outside an enormous Cape Cod–style house, with the flicker of a television in their living room window.

"Who lives here?" I asked as we got out of the car.

"No idea," she said, pressing the flashlight button on her phone and motioning for me to follow.

There was a narrow set of weathered wooden stairs to the side of the house, and as Lily shone her light into the darkness, I realized where we were going: a secret beach.

Bayport was full of them, tiny strips of sand that weren't strictly private, but could only be accessed either on foot or from the surrounding mansions.

I followed her down the staircase, stopping to take off my boots. I could hear the ocean before I could see it, cold and swift and churning.

There was a little yellow lifeguard stand on the beach, and Lily went right for it. We sat on the edge of the platform, our feet dangling, as we sipped our milkshakes and ate our cheeseburgers, which really were amazing with the chopped chiles.

It felt dangerous and thrilling, being at the edge of everything, just the two of us, with no one else in sight. Behind us, on the cliff, the glass-faced houses glowed like lanterns, and I wondered if we were glowing too.

"Better?" Lily asked, and I nodded.

Perfect, actually.

"The ocean's supposed to be calming, right?" I said. "Because our bodies are like seventy percent water."

"Actually, they're seventy percent dinosaur pee," said Lily.

"What?"

"I read this article about how the amount of water molecules on Earth stays the same, which means most of them were already drunk back in the Jurassic period," Lily explained. "So there's a very high probability that most water is just recycled dinosaur pee."

"What about those Tumblr posts that are like, we're all made of stardust?" I asked.

Lily shrugged and took a sip of her milkshake.

"Stardust and dinosaur pee," she said. "Tell your friends."

"I kind of don't have any."

"You don't need friends like them," Lily said. "Trust me. You really don't."

"I believe you," I said.

She chewed her straw for a minute, and then admitted, "Freshman year, Cole tried to hook up with me."

I stared at her in surprise.

"Our school does this winter ski trip," she went on. "He asked me to stop by his hotel room, said it was about our *Romeo and Juliet* essay. And when I got there, he was sitting on the bed wearing nothing but a ski hat. On his crotch."

"What happened?"

"He took the ski hat off." Lily shook her head. "It was super awkward. Like, fourteen-year-old me was not expecting to see a dick. I don't know which of us was more embarrassed. I shrieked and ran away, and I couldn't even look at him afterward. But I told Whitney, and she made it a thing. She kept giggling and calling me a prude and putting her ski hat over the saltshaker. When I begged her to stop, she got mad at me for being upset."

"Sounds like Whitney," I said.

"She doesn't know how to be a real friend. And Friya's so sick of being a sidekick, except when it comes down to it, that's her choice. I can't believe I ever used to hang out with them."

Lily used to be friends with this crowd. Of course. It made so much sense now that Cole had offered her the slice of pizza, her friendliness with Ethan, and how Friya and Whitney had reacted when they'd seen who I was standing with in the concessions line.

"Wow," I said. "I had no idea."

"When we met, I thought you were one of them," Lily said.

I snorted, remembering.

"What?" Lily said.

"When we met, I thought you were dating Adam."

Lily laughed.

"Zero chance," she said. "Even if we weren't stepsiblings."

I took a sip of my milkshake, and the silence stretched on for a moment too long.

Lily glanced down at her lap, as if embarrassed.

There were still a few strands of spaghetti in her hair, and I plucked them out without thinking.

"Spaghetti," I said, showing her.

"It was almost as good as the grilled cheese," she said, with just the faintest trace of a smile.

"You don't know," I said. "Maybe after we left he gathered all the pieces and made a big plate of Bolognese."

"And then he parachuted it off a balcony," Lily added.

I smiled, and Lily smiled back, full force, like we were sharing a secret. She had one of those rare smiles that turn a spotlight on you, that make you feel, at least for a moment, as though you've executed the most triumphant performance of your life and have just received a standing ovation.

I could feel my heart beating way too fast, from the million grams of sugar in the milkshake, and the craziness of the night, but also from something else, from this sense of freedom. Here, on this beach, it felt as though Lily and I were free to do anything we wanted. Except I didn't know what I wanted.

Or, I did know, and it terrified me.

And then the alarm went off on my phone.

"What time is it?" Lily asked suddenly.

"Oh crap," I said, showing her. "It's late."

I had ten minutes to get home before, well, I wasn't sure. But I didn't particularly want to find out.

"We've got this," Lily promised, jumping off the lifeguard stand.

I followed after her, and the two of us ran, barefoot, across the beach and up the narrow staircase, laughing and cursing. We made it back just as the clock hit eleven.

CHAPTER 17

MY GRANDPARENTS INSISTED ON HAVING BRUNCH that Sunday at the club. I really didn't want to see anyone again after Cole's party, so I tried to get out of it, claiming I had a migraine, but my grandmother just shot me a look until I said okay, I'd get ready.

"Wear something with a V-neck, it's more flattering," she called.

This time, as my grandfather pulled through the gates, I had a nervous pit in my stomach. I was dreading seeing anyone, especially here, in front of my grandparents. It felt like there had been this enormous shift, and suddenly the cracks I'd suspected were there all along had become visible.

Fault lines, they were called. Places where it was only a matter of time until an earthquake occurred. It didn't matter how quiet or safe things seemed—the cracks were still there, hidden beneath the perfect surface, waiting.

I felt faintly ill at the thought of running into Cole, and it was only when we were already inside that I remembered his parents were out of town.

The brunch buffet was in the same place as before. In the bright October sunshine, the room was transformed. It was loud, bustling, cheerful. Kids ran around in church clothes, and men in dry-fit golf polos waited in line at the omelet station.

I loaded up my plate with bacon and hash browns and sliced fruit, and some bougie-looking pastries called kouign-amann.

"All those carbs, Sasha?" my grandmother said, making a face.

I'd been so distracted I hadn't even thought about it. I'd just grabbed whatever had looked good, since I figured we might as well get our money's worth.

"Oh. Um," I stared down at my food, embarrassed. It was mostly grease and sugar, but then, I'd had enough alcohol the night before that the thought of eggs or yogurt made me queasy.

My grandfather, whom I hoped would come to my rescue, continued scrolling through his phone, squinting at the screen even with the enlarged type. He was on Facebook, reading the comments on someone's post.

"Unbelievable," he mumbled. "There's so much fake news."

"A lot of women in our family have thick thighs," Eleanor

went on. "It's just a fact. We'll never be thin. But we can always be better."

She kept going, explaining her gym routine, which sounded exhausting, and like you'd always be stressed about running out of clean underwear, doing Zumba and yoga that many times a week.

I picked at my fruit, wishing she'd give up. So I was having an unhealthy breakfast. It wasn't a crime.

"Really, Eleanor, leave the poor girl alone," my grandfather said.

"I'm just giving her advice," my grandmother huffed. "Everyone could stand to lose five pounds. It makes a big difference in the face."

"Well, I think you look beautiful, sweet pea," my grandfather told me, winking. "I'm going to get some of those pastries. They look scrumptious."

But before he could get up, a tall, elegant man approached our table carrying an egg-white omelet.

"Good morning, Blooms," he said, beaming. He had a perfect slick of black hair that was going gray at the temples, and his sleeves were rolled just so.

"Michael, hello," said my grandfather.

"Hey there, Joel. Sorry to interrupt. Just a quick work-related question; I won't take up too much of your time," Michael promised.

And then—oh god.

Hovering just behind him was Friya. She carried an

identical breakfast and had an upbeat smile pasted on. She and I regarded each other for a moment, and then Persian George Clooney turned his attention toward my grandfather, the two of them discussing some problem with a new secretary.

"So did you have fun last night?" Friya asked me.

Wow. Of course I didn't have fun last night. Which I thought Friya definitely knew.

"Yeah, *Lily* and I did," I said.

"Wait, was she even there?" Friya laughed. "I guess I was super distracted." Her eyes lit up as she leaned in, suddenly excited. "Did I tell you Nick and I got back together?"

"Congratulations," I said hollowly.

"I know, right?" Friya bubbled. "This whole hating him thing was getting *exhausting*."

"I'll bet," I said, since my grandmother was listening, and it wasn't like I could say anything. She really wasn't bringing it up. The thing with Cole. It was like my crisis had been such a small blip on her evening that it hadn't even registered. "Thanks for the advice about Harry Potter," I added.

Friya frowned, like she had no idea what I was talking about.

And then my grandmother cut in with, "I'm so glad you girls are friends."

"Sasha's the best," Friya said, smiling. "And it's, like, so cute with her and Cole."

I almost choked on a piece of cantaloupe. Why on earth would she say that? It was such bullshit. *She* was such bullshit.

My grandmother beamed, like Friya was the answer to all of the questions I'd been evading.

"Now tell me," my grandmother began, asking about Friya's extracurriculars. I picked up a kouign-amann, taking an enormous bite as Friya and my grandmother chatted about some dog charity. It was hard to believe this was the same girl who had given zero shits about my crisis, and then had babbled about herself, because when it came to Friya, she was her own favorite subject.

There was no way I could sit down at their lunch table on Monday and pretend nothing was the matter. No way I could act like it was completely fine that Cole had taken topless photos of me, and the girls had laughed and made fun of some girl's pubes when I asked for their help.

I was done.

"Daddddy," Friya whined. "I'm going to be late for my massage."

He glanced at his watch, one of those flashy silver things, and agreed that they really did have to get going, but it was a pleasure running into us.

After that, brunch dragged on forever. My grandparents seemed to know an overwhelming number of people. By the third old lady Eleanor just had to say hello to, I kind of zoned out.

As I stood there, miserable, waiting for it to be time to go home, I had a terrifying realization: *This* was what my grandparents wanted for me. This life. This world. These people.

And if I wasn't careful, one day I might look around and discover that I was a lawyer at my grandfather's firm, that I was at this brunch of my own volition, eating an egg-white omelet, married to some boy from a good family because everyone thought it was a good idea, not because we actually loved each other.

I'd said yes too often, agreeing with everything my grandparents wanted because I didn't want to rock the boat. Except I'd never stopped to really think where that boat was headed. And now I knew: it wasn't to a lighthouse, but to a yacht club.

I'd screwed up, letting them think I wanted this. Letting them think they could steer me in whatever direction they wanted. Because we'd gone too far, and there was no coastline in sight, and I didn't know how to tell them that I wanted to turn back.

On the drive home, my phone buzzed with a text from Cole:

hey you around

Oh, god. What if Lily hadn't erased all of the pictures? Was that why Friya had been so fake nice to me—because she knew?

In a bit, I wrote back.

ok can I call you in like 10 min? Cole texted.

Um I guess. What's up? I asked. Calling me didn't sound good. At all.

need to talk

I stared down at my phone screen, feeling ill.

"Sasha, what's going on?" my grandmother asked. "You're buried in your phone."

"Sorry," I said. "I was replying to a text."

"From whom?"

"Um, Cole?" I said.

"Oh." My grandmother sounded pleased. "That's all right then. It was very nice of him to take you to the football game."

I mumbled that I guessed so, not really wanting to get into it.

"And did you have fun at his party?" my grandfather asked.

"Yep," I said tightly.

"It's such a relief, you dating such a nice boy," my grandmother said.

The sentence hung there awkwardly as my grandfather pulled into the driveway.

I needed to correct them. I had to correct them.

"Actually, we're not—" I began.

"We should have him over for dinner," my grandfather said, cutting me off.

"That would be wonderful," my grandmother said. "I

can make my chicken pesto. Or maybe the porcini risotto. Sasha, find out if there's anything he doesn't eat."

"I don't know if he—" I began, trying to think up an excuse. But my mind was blank. All I could think was, *He needs to talk. On the phone.* "Eats mushrooms," I finished lamely.

"Then it's a good thing you're texting him right now," my grandmother said.

Ugh.

"Okay, I'll ask," I promised, desperate to escape the conversation.

And then I went up to my room and scrolled through Instagram as I waited, mindlessly liking photos without really looking at them. My stomach was churning. I hated not knowing what Cole wanted to talk about. Hated feeling tethered to my phone, waiting for it to ring.

When he finally called, he sounded sheepish, and embarrassed, and hungover, his voice crawling over gravel as he asked point-blank if I was going to tell anyone about what he'd done.

"You mean the topless pictures you took without my permission and refused to delete?" I said, not bothering to sugarcoat it.

"I messed up," Cole admitted. "But I really wasn't going to show them to anyone. I just, you know, thought it would be hot. To have some."

"Well, you could have asked," I said.

"I could?" he asked hopefully.

"I would have said no."

"Bummer." I could hear the smile in his voice. The way he didn't quite understand that all wasn't forgiven. "Not even if I sent you some first?"

"*Cole*," I scolded. "I need you to take this seriously."

"I am," he insisted. "That's why I called. Because I seriously need a favor."

"Which is?"

"Can you maybe not tell your grandparents about this?" Cole asked. "Because I'd hate if it got back to my gran. She's pretty Catholic."

So that's what this was about. Damage control. I was unspeakably disappointed all of a sudden. I'd expected—I don't know. A real apology. A sense of awareness. Except of course not. Cole expected to get away with things—ordering drinks underage, having food delivered to campus, and now how he'd behaved toward me.

It wasn't like I was so desperate to tell my grandparents that I'd taken my clothes off in a boy's room. I could just picture Eleanor's panic, her horror that I was my mom all over again when it came to boys and bad decisions. Her fear that she'd become a great-grandmother at sixty-five. Still. It would have been nice if Cole let me make that decision for myself.

"Um," I said. "I guess I don't have to say anything."

"Perfect," he said. "Okay, great. Glad that's settled."

There was this long pause, and I wondered why we were still on the phone, and then he asked, "Hey, since you're here, you have Tanaka for AP Euro, right?"

"Right," I said warily.

"Do you think he's going to ask us about trade routes on the test?"

I closed my eyes. Took a deep breath. Waited until I was reasonably certain I wasn't going to sound pissed before I answered, "Um, well, he was really cagey when this girl in my class asked, so we should probably go over them."

"Hundred percent," Cole said.

And then, before I could fully process the fact that we were talking about the AP Euro test, he hung up.

CHAPTER 18

I WAS WALKING TO SCHOOL ON Monday morning when I heard a horn blast behind me. I turned around, afraid that it was Cole.

It was Lily.

"Hey," she said, rolling down her window. "Climb in."

Adam waved merrily from the passenger seat, apologizing for his backpack as I climbed in. Everything felt different as I buckled my seat belt, like we were actually friends, instead of people who sat at the same lunch table, just pretending.

Lily barely even knew me, and still, she hadn't hesitated before rolling up her sleeves and trying to fix what was wrong. That was more than I could say about anyone else.

I'd thoroughly stalked her on Instagram, going back far enough that I could see the break when she'd stopped hanging around with Cole's crowd. When the pictures changed from group selfies with Whitney and Friya to beautifully photographed food and art museums and a *Stranger Things* Halloween costume with Adam and Ryland that was absurdly spot on.

But none of that prepared me for climbing into the safe, small world of her car without warning. She'd seemed impossibly distant for so long, someone I could only admire from afar, but now, she was within reach.

She had on her cat's-eye sunglasses again, and a soft teddy bear jacket, the same kind I kept seeing on influencers.

"Cute jacket," I said.

"I just got it," Lily said.

"It's horrible," Adam said. "You look like my grandma's toilet rug."

"Your face looks like my grandma's toilet rug," Lily shot back.

"Subject-noun agreement," Adam said gravely.

I shook my head, amused. They had grammatical rules about insults. It was too much.

Adam took a huge bite of a sugary pastry he was holding, and my stomach gurgled appreciatively. The car smelled amazing.

"Wow," I said, taking a deep breath. "What is that?"

"Pineapple bun," Lily said. "Want one?"

"Yes, please," I said.

Adam passed me a little oval-shaped pastry in a cellophane bag. It was fluffy and sweet and buttery, with a sugary crumble on top.

I took a bite and almost moaned.

"So good," I said. "Except I'm confused about the pineapple part."

"They only look like pineapples," Adam explained. "They taste like plain Danish."

"Plainish," Lily and I both said at the exact same time.

"Wow, you guys portmantied!" Adam grinned, delighted.

I ate another bite of the pastry. I'd never had anything like it.

"Where did you get these?" I asked.

"85 Degrees," Lily and Adam said.

"It's a Taiwanese bakery," Lily explained. "They have sea salt iced coffee too. It's amazing. We should go sometime."

"Sure," I said, trying to downplay how excited I was at the idea of Lily taking me to a Taiwanese bakery that put sea salt in their iced coffee.

Lily's locker and homeroom were on the other side of campus, which explained why I never saw her. Adam and I started to walk toward our lockers, and Lily went the other way.

"Wait," I called, and she turned around. "Can I have lunch with you today?"

Lily's grin was a beautiful thing.

I glanced over at Friya's empty seat in English, confused. Her Spanish class was next door, so she was always early.

And then she walked in holding hands with Nick. He

was beaming, a beanie tugged low over his hair, the sleeves of his denim jacket pushed up. Friya was giggling and playing with her hair, and looking like she was fully aware everyone was watching them.

She slipped into her seat, flashing me a grin. Nick, who had followed her over, stared down at me.

"Sasha, right?" he said, like I hadn't been in his English class for the past six weeks. Like I was a stranger whose identity he needed to verbally confirm to be sure.

"Yep," I said.

"Listen, could you do me a solid and switch seats with me?" he asked.

"You don't mind, do you?" Friya added, her expression pleading.

"No," I said, my mouth dry. "I don't mind."

I packed up my things, trying to remember where Nick sat. And then I did: he was next to Michelle. They were doing to me exactly what they'd done to her on the first day of class. I'd been so flattered when I was on the receiving end. But now I could see how horrible and selfish it was, the way they rearranged people as though we were objects on a shelf. As though this school, and everything in it, belonged to them.

I found Lily in the courtyard behind Humanities. There was literally no good reason I could think of to stick a fountain there, and yet someone had. It was disused, though, a giant empty bowl.

Lily was balancing on the edge, a container of snack bar sushi on her lap.

"It used to be filled with the blood of my enemies," she joked, nodding at the fountain, "but for some reason, people found that off-putting."

"Can't imagine why," I said, sitting down and taking out my turkey on wheat. "Can I vent for like one second about what just happened in English?"

"Go for it," Lily said, picking apart a piece of ginger and dropping it into her puddle of soy.

I ranted about the seat change, and Lily rolled her eyes, agreeing that they'd been rude, and that she was sorry I had to sit next to Michelle Warner, who was a level-four bitch.

"I know," I said miserably. "We're in Mock Trial together."

"That's right," Lily said. "I keep forgetting you do that. I don't know how you can stand them."

"Me neither," I said.

"It's weird, because two years ago the Mock Trial crowd was awesome," Lily mused. "And then a bunch of people graduated, and Todd's army of assholes took over, and everyone with a soul fled to debate."

I'd seen the debate team around, mistaking them at first for the drama crowd, because they were so loud and quirky. They seemed nice.

I sighed, feeling sorry for myself.

"Okay, I have something that'll cheer you up," Lily said. "So we're doing this unit on monuments in Paris. Les

Invalides, Hotel De Ville, all that stuff?"

I nodded, impressed by her accent.

"And Mlle Dupont mentions how under the Arc de Triomphe is the Tomb of the Unknown Soldier. And this girl Chloe raises her hand and says, 'Okay, but wouldn't they know who the soldier is?'"

Lily snorted with laughter before continuing, "We're all staring at her, like 'What are you talking about?' And she explains, 'Well, if all the *other* soldiers came home from war, or died or whatever, and there was *one* soldier missing, why wouldn't they know who he is?'"

I burst out laughing.

"No!" I said, delighted.

"Yes!" Lily crowed. "And poor Mlle Dupont had to explain that 'Unknown Soldier' was actually a metaphor for the thousands of war dead."

"What's a metaphor for what now?" Ryland asked. He and Adam had come from the lunch line, and they both had wrap sandwiches and lemonade. "I heard, like, the last sentence of that story, so you're gonna need to tell it again."

Lily did, and it was even funnier the second time.

"I keep picturing Chloe—it was Chloe Machado, right?" Adam said, and Lily nodded. "I keep picturing her sitting there, staring at this picture of the Arc de Triomphe like, 'OMG, how has no one figured out the name of the *single* soldier who was missing in action during World War I?'"

Ryland cackled.

"Dumb questions give me life," he said. "I'm like a dumb questions vampire."

"That metaphor doesn't work," Lily told him.

"Why not?" Ryland demanded, laughing.

"You're literally going to make me explain it?" Lily tossed her crumpled chopstick wrapper at him.

It was so different sitting with them, watching them goof around and delight in being ridiculous. It felt relaxed. Comfortable. I bit into my sandwich, realizing that, for the first time, where I was sitting seemed to fit.

"Borderline acceptable use of literally," Adam warned.

"Oh my god, don't you have some academics to decathlon?" Lily asked, not very nicely.

"Don't you have some art to club?" Adam shot back.

That was when I realized.

"Crap, I have Mock Trial after school today," I said with a grimace.

"Ditch it," Lily said. "Come to Art Club instead."

"There's going to be pizza," Ryland said. "And no offense, but your lunch is making me sad."

My perennial turkey on wheat sandwich was making me sad, too.

I could skip one Mock Trial meeting. It wasn't like my grandparents would find out.

"Maybe," I said.

"If you don't, you'll regret it," Ryland said.

"Six out of ten dentists agree," said Adam.

"It's four out of five dentists," Lily retorted.

"Fine, fourteen out of fifteen dentists agree," said Adam.

Everyone glared at him.

"Stop breaking humor," Lily complained.

Which is how I found myself staying after class for the Art Club meeting instead of walking down the hallway to Mock Trial, where I was supposed to be. Where for ninety hideous minutes I was supposed to stare at the clock to see how much longer I was going to have to stare at the clock.

I chatted with Ryland as everyone trickled in. Surprisingly, he was a closet YA novel enthusiast. Mostly, he was obsessed with graphic novels, but his particular arena of nerd also extended to books. We talked about our favorites, and I could see why he and Lily and Adam were friends. I hadn't gotten it before, but I did now.

Mr. Saldana came into the room after the pizza arrived to see how we were doing.

"Sasha," he said, spotting me. "What a nice surprise. What brings you to Art Club?"

"Lily convinced me," I said.

"She's a photographer," Lily called from the other side of the room. "You should see her work!"

"I'd love to," Mr. Saldana said.

"Um, maybe next time?" I felt terrible. Mr. Saldana thought I'd joined Art Club for real instead of just stopping by for the afternoon. And now he was expecting to see my photos, which would inevitably lead to the confession of how none of them were more recent than last April.

"It's a deal," Mr. Saldana said, grabbing a slice of pizza.

"Great," I said weakly.

"'Photographs alter and enlarge our notions of what is worth looking at and what we have a right to observe,'" he continued. "Susan Sontag. She wrote a wonderful little essay on photography. I think I have a copy, actually. . . ."

He turned around, rummaging one-handed through his bookshelf, before pulling out a slim volume. He gave it to me, insisting I take it home and read it.

"I have a hunch you'll really get something from this," he said.

"Thank you." I stared down at the little book.

"It's not a how-to manual," he warned. "It's more about the ethics of seeing the world through a camera lens. What we have a responsibility to capture, and how we use our power to capture those things."

"With great power comes great responsibility," I joked.

"Yeahhhh Spiderman!" Ryland called.

Mr. Saldana laughed.

"Exactly," he said. "And the added responsibility of returning that book. I don't charge library fees, but I take overdue fines out of your class grade."

With that warning, he took a bite of his pizza and headed off.

After he left, Lily put on a documentary about this painter Chuck Close, who was face blind, but had become a famous portrait artist anyway. He broke faces down into little squares, using painting to see what was obvious to everyone else.

It was a smaller group than I'd thought, just six of us. Mabel wasn't around, even though I'd seen her in the hallway between classes, and when I asked Ryland about it after the documentary, he shrugged and was like, "It's callbacks for the fall play."

He sounded sad over it, and when I asked, he said, "If she gets a decent role, she won't be around as much."

"You have to stop moping about that and say something," Lily told him, joining us.

"Did you want to audition?" I asked Ryland, confused.

They both laughed.

"God no," Ryland said.

"He has a crush," Lily put in. "On Maaaaaabel Choiiiii." Ryland swatted at her, and she grinned in his face. "But he's just waiting for the universe to deliver happiness instead of going after it himself."

"I'm waiting for the right moment," Ryland returned.

"If you do that, you'll miss your shot," Lily warned. "Because there's no such thing as the right moment."

Lily's eyes met mine for just a moment, as though she wasn't just saying it for Ryland's benefit. I frowned, confused at what she meant, but she had already looked away, and I wondered if I'd imagined the entire thing.

CHAPTER 19

FROM THAT DAY ON, I SAT with Lily at lunch. It was so natural, so seamless a transition, that it seemed things had always been that way. Of course we were friends, of course we had lunch together, laughing at Adam and Ryland's quips and rolling our eyes over their puns. Of course we teased Ryland when Mabel stopped by and he lost his cool, especially after she announced that she had a callback for Rizzo in *Grease*.

It seemed impossible that I had spent so many weeks smiling and nodding as Whitney laughingly made little digs at everyone, and as Friya internet-stalked her ex. That I had cared about keeping Cole's attention, which turned out to be the *opposite* of what I wanted.

Nick was back at their lunch table now. I saw him sitting there on Tuesday. Cole was slouched down, stuck between the two couples, playing with his phone and looking completely miserable. I remembered what he'd said, about how much it sucked to be stuck between two couples and their drama. I felt a little bad for him, but not bad enough to walk over and say hello when he waved at me.

I wasn't desperate for their acceptance anymore. It didn't get me anything except an unwanted seat at a lunch table where I'd never truly belong.

"You're not staying for Art Club?" Lily asked after eighth period on Wednesday, when I started to pack up my things.

I wanted to. God, I wanted to. Missing one Mock Trial meeting was acceptable. Missing two felt like a decision, one I was terrified to make without telling my grandparents. Especially after what had happened the last time I'd mentioned wanting to quit.

"I can't," I said, making a face. "I have Mock Trial."

After all, a promise was a promise.

"Wow, look who decided to grace us with her presence," Todd said when I walked in.

"Sorry about Monday." I cast around for an excuse. "I wasn't feeling well."

"Then you should have notified your team captain," he said, referring to himself in the third person.

"Sorry." I mean, it wasn't a big deal. I didn't do anything essential.

"You may only have a small part," Todd went on, "but your real job is to prove yourself. To impress me. And you can't do that if you don't show up."

He was actually enjoying this. He threw a pleased smirk in Michelle's direction, and she grinned back. It was an absolute delight sitting next to her in English, let me tell you.

"Got it," I said.

"Well, are you going to make it up to the team?"

I hope not, I thought.

"Um, I guess?" I said.

"Right answer," smirked Todd. And then he picked up a heavy law book with yellow sticky tabs and said, "We need photocopies of the tabbed articles for everyone. Stapled."

I wanted to scream. Instead, I pasted on a smile and promised, "Eleven copies coming right up."

That night at dinner, I took a deep breath and jumped.

"So," I said. "I think I'm going to quit Mock Trial."

The sentence floated there, clunky and awkward. My grandmother frowned.

"You can't quit," she said. "Where's this coming from?"

She sounded upset. My heart sped up, and all of the lines I'd carefully rehearsed in my head disappeared.

"Well, the other kids on the team aren't very nice," I said lamely.

"Who cares?" my grandmother said. "This isn't about making friends. This is for college."

"But that's the thing," I said. "I'm like one of five time-keepers, and the others are freshmen, and—"

"So tell them to put you to work," she said, making it sound like the whole thing was my fault. "You're very capable."

She didn't understand. And she wasn't going to. I couldn't ask Todd or Michelle to put me to work. They'd laugh and make snide comments and send me off to the netherworld of the photocopy room. There wasn't a way to fix this. I just wanted to bail.

"Grandma, I've tried," I said. "But I don't want to do it anymore."

"You made a commitment," my grandfather said, as though I had exchanged sacred vows and married Mock Trial, instead of showing up to a couple after-school meetings.

"I agree," my grandmother put in. "You can't have *nothing* down on your résumé for junior year."

"Actually," I said, "I was thinking of joining Art Club."

As soon as the words were out of my mouth, my grandmother winced.

"Art Club?" she said, making it sound awful. "Sasha, be serious."

I was being serious.

"How's that going to look?" my grandmother went on. "Quitting Mock Trial in the middle of the semester. What's to say you won't quit this Art Club?"

Before I could get a word in, my grandfather added, "Quitting isn't smart, and I'll tell you why. Because you'd be walking off a winning team. And you know what that makes you look like? A loser."

It was scary how I knew exactly where he'd gotten that language from.

"Joel," my grandmother scolded. "You can't talk to her like that."

"How's what I said any different from what you said?" he argued.

"Sasha, you're not quitting," my grandmother said, "and that's final."

I went upstairs and sprawled across my bed, hating everything. Just once I wanted my grandparents to let me make my own decisions. To see me as an actual person, instead of some person-shaped doll they could move around to their liking. It was no better than Cole and his crowd: Friya arranging my seat to suit, Whitney asking me to move my lunch so it wasn't in her Instagrams, Cole literally placing me into his fantasies.

They were being so unreasonable. At least by quitting I'd gain something I wanted and lose something I didn't.

Except I didn't know how to make that happen. Because Mock Trial was my grandparents' idea, and telling them it had been a bad one was basically telling them that having me around wouldn't go the way they wanted.

That *I* wasn't the granddaughter they wanted.

I'd been the daughter my mom had wanted. At least, I'd

pretended. She'd assumed I was out with friends whenever she worked weekends. Instead, I was sitting alone in my room watching girls I didn't know try on their new spring wardrobes on YouTube.

But at least that was my choice. My grandparents had effectively prevented me from choosing anything. And I hated that so much. Living here, I'd found out who my grandparents wanted me to be, but I'd never tried to figure out who I was.

I sprawled on my bed, staring at the room that was starting to look like mine. At the stack of textbooks on the desk, and the pile of clothing spilling out of the hamper. At the disappointing still lifes and landscapes I'd made in art class.

And then I stared at the drawer where I'd stashed my camera. The drawer for lost socks and dingy bras. And I thought about Mr. Saldana's book, tucked into my bag. He'd never done anything but correct my work before, and suddenly he was showing an interest in me and my photography. And now I was going to disappoint him by going back to being just another mediocre student in his class.

It was ironic how I could capture people perfectly on camera, but when it came to real life, everything was underexposed and off-balance.

The only person I ever felt in focus around was Lily. And I had no idea what that meant. Just that, if there was anyone who might understand how frustrated I was, it was her.

I reached for my phone, sending her a text.

Told my grandparents I wanted to quit Mock Trial and they lost their shit.

Her response came back almost immediately.

Ugh. Sorry. And then, after a moment, **Want to hear a radical idea?**

I said that was my favorite kind, and then I waited as the three dots blinked across the screen. I pictured Lily in her bedroom, even though I'd never seen it, sprawled across her bed, barefoot and wearing sweatpants, her hair up in a messy bun. I pictured the case on her phone, covered with sunflowers. That case, cupped in her hands, right now.

Finally, my phone vibrated with her response: **Quit and don't tell them. I mean, how are they going to find out?**

I stared down at what she'd written. Lily was right. It wasn't like they'd get some note from the attendance office saying I was skipping. It was an extracurricular activity. The first district competition wasn't even until January. That would give me plenty of time to break it to them gently.

Interesting, I wrote. **But what about my résumé? Pre-law, remember?**

You can still put Mock Trial on your résumé! Lily wrote. **I mean it's not a lie, you were a member of the team.**

She was right. Oh my god. It had never even occurred to me.

Mind blown, I wrote back.

And after you quit, you can hang with me in Art Club, Lily wrote, followed by a string of heart and smile emojis.

I like this plan.

Me too, Lily said. **So much.**

Cole was waiting by my locker the next morning. He was sipping a green juice, and his hood was flipped up, and he looked pensive.

"Um, your locker brings all the boys to the yard?" Adam said, spotting him.

"Evidently," I said, frowning.

"Do you need a minute?" Adam asked. "Because I don't really need my chem book until third period, so . . ."

"Thanks," I told him.

And then I went to go see what Cole wanted.

"Whattup," he said, holding out his smoothie. "Want a sip? It's a Green Monster."

I shook my head.

"Um, Cole?" I said. "Why are you waiting at my locker and offering me your smoothie?"

"Because you're ignoring me," he said, sounding hurt. "You stopped sitting at our lunch table, and when I asked Friya, she said something about Harry Potter that didn't make any sense?"

I groaned. I *really* didn't want to have this conversation here.

"Don't worry about it," I said bitterly. "I found some people who actually want me around."

"Come on, Sash, we miss you."

"Yeah, I'm so sure," I scoffed. Off Cole's confused look, I explained, "Friya asked me to move seats in English so she could sit next to Nick."

By his expression, Cole clearly hadn't known about this.

"Damn it, Friya," he groaned.

"And Whitney doesn't seem to care I exist, so." I shrugged. "Guess it's just you."

"What, I don't count?" Cole asked, joking.

"*You* took topless pictures of me without my consent, so your opinion doesn't matter," I told him.

Cole sighed. Closed his eyes a moment. And then opened them, being completely serious.

"Sash, please. I need you," he said.

"No, you don't," I told him. "You just need to not be eating lunch with two couples. It's a completely different thing."

And then the bell rang for homeroom and I left him there, looking upset. But Cole wasn't my problem. And his problems weren't my problem. And I wished he'd just forget about me, like the rest of his friends already had.

That afternoon, I marched up to Todd Burnham's locker and handed him my handwritten letter of resignation. The letter had been Adam's idea. He and Lily and Ryland had stood over my notebook at lunch, helping dictate as I wrote it out.

"What's this?" Todd asked, staring down at it.

"I'm quitting," I said. "And just so you can't accuse me of not taking it seriously, I put my resignation in writing."

"Well, not everyone is cut out for Mock Trial," he said. "Good luck with Berkeley. Or—sorry—was it Stanford?"

I rolled my eyes.

"See you around, Todd," I said, and then I walked out to the student lot and got a ride home with Adam and Lily.

When we pulled onto our block, Lily asked if I wanted to hang at their house for a while. I glanced at my grandmother's car in the driveway, really not wanting to deal with her. She was used to me staying late on Thursdays anyway.

"Sure," I said, trying to sound less excited. "I could do that."

Their house was the opposite of my grandparents'. Warm and colorful and chaotic, with mid-century furniture and brightly patterned rugs and a shelf of cut-glass awards that it turned out Lily's mom had won as a software developer.

Where my grandparents' place felt cold and unlived in, this felt like a home. Everywhere I saw small personal touches.

"We should bake something," Lily said. "It's almost Halloween, and I feel like I haven't done anything celebration-y."

"Same," I said. Part of it had to do with the holiday falling on a Wednesday this year, which flat-out sucked.

"I volunteer to eat whatever you're making," Adam said, which earned him an eye roll from Lily.

"Wow. Big sacrifice," she told him.

"Um," I said, staring down at my yellow silk top. "Got an apron?"

"Better. Come on."

Lily grabbed my hand and pulled me upstairs to her bedroom.

It was black and white and minimalist, except for an entire wall of bookshelves that were arranged by color, creating a floor-to-ceiling rainbow.

"Wow," I said, going over to have a better look. I'd never seen someone with so many books. She had everything from John Green to Eudora Welty. And none of it was alphabetized. "How do you find anything?"

"That's the downside," Lily said. "But I figure it's the coolest pride flag ever, so it's worth a little disorder."

"Pride flag?" I said.

Lily shrugged and said, "Yeah. I'm gay."

She said it like it was the most normal thing in the world to admit aloud, without even a hint of self-consciousness. I stared at her, totally caught off guard.

"Oh, wow," I said, surprised, "I had no idea. It's, um, great. That you told me."

I trailed off, embarrassed. There was this incredibly long moment of silence, and then I started laughing.

"Did I make it awkward?" I asked, wrinkling my nose.

"Little bit." But Lily was smiling. "But not in a bad way? Sorry. It's super weird, having to constantly tell people, or not tell people. I'm still figuring it out. Note to self: showing off my giant bookshelf rainbow is maybe not the best reveal."

"Even though it's awesome," I said.

"Even though it's awesome." Lily's smile stretched wider.

She disappeared into her closet for a moment, rattling around. And I had a few seconds to process what Lily had just said.

I couldn't imagine ever admitting something so huge that casually, and it blew me away that she was able to. But then, that's how Lily was. Bold and matter of fact. She'd said she had a crush on Emma Watson when she was younger, and there was that little rainbow dumpling pin on her backpack, which I'd figured was from a cartoon or an anime. Of course it wasn't. The hints were all there, and still I hadn't put them together.

But then, no one had been out at my old high school. Not even Brandon Wasserman, who did both ballet and gymnastics, yet never had a hair out of place.

"You can borrow this," Lily said, emerging from her

closet. She tossed me a sweatshirt. It was soft and gray and said *Shakespeare on the Hill Summer 2017* across the back.

"For baking," she explained. "So you don't get anything on your shirt."

"Right," I said. I'd forgotten why we'd come up here in the first place. "Thanks."

I tugged it on. It smelled like Lily, like her woodsy perfume, which reminded me of the party that weekend.

"Did Cole know?" I asked. "When he pulled the naked stunt on you?"

Lily shook her head.

"I only figured it out the summer after freshman year," she said with a self-conscious shrug. "I kept obsessing over this one girl at theater camp, and Ryland was like, 'You have a crush on her, and I have never seen you have a crush on anyone ever.' And he was right. And then she broke my heart and stole my favorite jeans."

"That's a lot to take in," I said. "But I'm very sorry about, not in chronological order: your jeans, your broken heart, and Cole's penis."

Lily smiled.

"All apologies should be so disorderly."

She tugged on a sweatshirt of her own, which read *Gryffindor Quidditch* across the front, and then flipped her hair upside down, gathering it up into a knot. God. It killed me how she could just do that, how she didn't even need to look in a mirror or watch a tutorial or use a million pins and dry shampoo.

"Are you dead?" Adam called, thundering up the stairs. "And if yes, what am I supposed to do with the bodies?"

"We are extremely dead," Lily told him seriously.

"Somehow, I feel like you two would be terrible at a murder mystery party," I said.

We all trooped to the kitchen, where Adam sat down at the table, making it very clear that he was only there for the eating part, not the baking.

"Shortbread cookies?" Lily asked, reaching for a cookbook that had Mary Berry on the cover.

I stared at it in surprise.

"I'm obsessed with the *Great British Bake Off*," I said.

"'I expect nothing less than sheer perfection,'" Lily quoted.

"Why is *everyone* into that show?" Adam complained.

"Because it's full of drunk grandmas and dirty baking puns and is hosted by queer comedians? Except it's somehow weirdly wholesome?" Lily returned.

"What she said," I told him.

"Whatever," Adam said. "It looks dumb."

"So does your face," Lily shot back, grinning.

Adam slunk off and put on some music while Lily and I followed Mary Berry's recipe.

We left the dough to chill in the freezer and joined Adam in the living room to start on our homework.

I was wrestling with my chemistry, and Adam was like,

"You're calculating molar mass wrong."

Lily craned over to see what I was doing. "Yeah, you need to divide, not multiply."

I swore and began erasing.

"Stupid H Chem," I muttered.

"Yeah, it's brutal," said Adam. "I wish I'd taken regular."

"My grandmother insisted on honors," I said miserably.

"That sucks," Adam said. And then, without even looking up from his Spanish worksheet, he asked, "Why'd you move in with them, anyhow?"

Lily must have kicked him under the table, because he mumbled "ow," and glared at her.

I should tell them, I realized. Lily had told me about losing her dad, and being gay, and the girl who'd broken her heart. I'd almost told Cole.

So I took a deep breath and admitted, "It all happened really fast after the earthquake."

"Wait." Lily turned toward me, her eyes huge. "That giant earthquake up in San Bernardino?"

I nodded.

"Were you there?" Lily asked.

They were both staring at me, and I felt horribly uncomfortable.

"Yeah," I admitted, my voice small. "I was there. I was—I was working at this museum, after school, and all of the displays started falling."

I stopped. I'd never told this part of the story before. At least, not to anyone who wasn't Dr. Lisa.

"And my mom was at work, too. And she got hurt. And that's how she died," I finished awkwardly. "My dad's not an option, so my grandparents took me in."

Lily and Adam were staring at me with all of the sympathy I'd been so eager to avoid. Except, somehow, coming from them, it was okay.

"Oh my god, Sasha," Lily breathed. "Why didn't you say anything?"

I shrugged, considering. "Haven't you ever just had something awful happen and been desperate to walk away without people forcing you to wear it across your chest like a scarlet letter?"

"Points for the Nathaniel Hawthorne reference," said Lily. "And yeah. Totally. I wasn't even in kindergarten when my dad died, but I still remember the looks."

"My awful thing was getting you as a stepsister," Adam teased, grinning.

"Whatever," said Lily. "You were a total disaster before I made you cool."

"This is cool?" I asked skeptically.

"This is my maximum level of cool, yes," said Adam. "What's the line? 'Look on my Works, ye Mighty, and despair!'"

"Wow, Percy Shelley," I said. "That was an honors English deep cut."

"Academic Decathlon, baby," Adam preened.

"His maximum level of cool," Lily repeated sadly.

CHAPTER 20

OVER THE NEXT FEW WEEKS, I stayed after school for Art Club, and when my grandparents asked me about Mock Trial, I smiled and said it was the same as always. Because I was pretty sure Mock Trial was the same as always, just without me.

And whenever they asked about Cole, and when he was coming to dinner, I said probably after the soccer season wound down. And my grandparents said great, and to let them know, my lies gliding past them undetected.

It was worth it, though, lying to them. I actually wished I'd done it sooner. For the first time in a long time, I felt like could breathe again. Like I wasn't under constant pressure, all while dragging so much baggage with me. Like I'd traded up for an emotional suitcase with wheels.

I felt myself sliding further and further down a path that I'd only meant to explore for a moment. A path that was so unexpectedly wonderful that even if I could turn back, I wouldn't have wanted to. Not when I got to spend lunch sitting on the edge of the fountain, laughing at whatever ridiculous thing Lily or Ryland or Adam had just said. Not when I got to ride to school with people who never made me feel embarrassed or left out, or even the tiniest bit weird for loving books and photography and having no idea what the Kardashians were posting on Instagram.

I was edging closer than I'd ever been to the person I was supposed to be.

Part of that was my Studio Art class. I'd written it off at first—paints and charcoals weren't my thing. But just because I wasn't great at them didn't mean they weren't worth learning. It was like Mr. Saldana said: there was value in considering a different perspective.

I read the book he'd given me, which was surprisingly wonderful, all about the philosophy of taking pictures. The language was gorgeous, and the ideas in there blew my mind. When I gave it back to him, he smiled and asked me about it, and then made me show him my photos.

"They're from last year," I hedged, but he bent over my iPhone anyway, zooming in and studying them for a while before pronouncing them "Just lovely." I captured a sense of yearning from a distance, he said. And then he handed me Berger's *Ways of Seeing* with a wink.

It turned out photography was about working with light, but sketching was about working with shadows. When I figured that out, suddenly drawing made so much more sense to me. It was like creating a negative instead of a photograph. It was the opposite of what I was used to doing. I didn't turn into a great artist overnight, but even I could see the improvement.

Another part of everything feeling so much better—the main part—was Lily. Maybe it was because she'd lost a parent, too. Or because the family she had wasn't the family she'd started with. But she got how it felt not to fit in.

And she liked girls. Which didn't mean she liked me. I had to keep reminding myself over and over. We were friends, and that didn't have to lead to anything more. No matter how much I dreamed of what it would be like if it did.

We'd started texting at night, conversations that were only supposed to last a couple of minutes, but which stretched on into the early hours. Curled up in bed with my phone glowing in my cupped hands and Lily on the other side, I felt less alone than I had since moving here.

Just read about Kintsugi, and it made me think of you, Lily texted once. **It's the Japanese art of repairing broken ceramics with gold.**

She sent me pictures, delicate plates and bowls with unexpected threads of gold winding through them.

They're beautiful, I wrote back.

I think so too, Lily said. **The idea is that neither damage**

nor repair are shameful. That actually they're what makes these pieces unique, because without the broken places, they'd just be ordinary.

I stared down at what Lily had written, wondering if we were still talking about art.

But the broken thing isn't beautiful, I pointed out. **It has to be repaired first.**

That's easy, Lily promised. **All you need is someone else to hold the broken pieces together until they've set.**

In November, the Art Club went on a field trip to Los Angeles. There was this museum that had an exhibit Lily wanted us to see. Six of us drove up: Lily and Ryland and me in her car, and Mabel with two seniors who I didn't know all that well, Adrian and Danica.

It was strange leaving Bayport, which I hadn't done since my grandparents had driven me there. But it was stranger still to be so much closer to where I used to live.

I didn't say much on the drive up. Just stared out at the miles between myself and the town I'd grown up in, watching them disappear.

My mom and I had gone into LA together when I was little. We'd even driven past this museum before, which featured an enormous art installation of art deco lamp-posts outside, creating a forest of light. It felt disorienting to be going there now, to visit something I'd seen before, in a different life.

The art installation was better up close. The hundreds of

antique lampposts, arranged in columns, gave the impression of an ancient Greek temple.

"Wow," I said, staring up at it.

I couldn't figure out how it was so much more than the sum of its parts. Because it wasn't anything special. Just lampposts. But somehow, having been moved here, with nothing else changed, they were art. And I loved that.

My mom used to say there was one question she asked as a hairdresser: What else can it be besides what it is? And I felt certain the artist had asked himself the same question when he created this.

But you could ask that question of a person, too. What else could I be besides what I am? Answering it was the hard part. Although, ever since I'd started hanging around with Lily, I felt like I was getting closer.

As we were waiting to buy tickets for the museum, the streetlamps turned on, the whole installation flooding with light.

"Look," Lily said, her hand on my arm.

It was like my whole body filled with light and warmth when she touched me, even if it was just the sleeve of my jacket. It was the sort of thing friends did all the time. Like how she linked arms with Mabel during Phys Ed.

"I wish I'd brought my camera," I said, staring at the soft, warm glow beneath the lampposts.

"I brought mine," Adrian said, digging an enormous DSLR out of his messenger bag.

I stared at him in surprise. He wasn't someone I'd ever

talked to. A tall, thin senior in eighties-style glasses and white jeans and gold chain jewelry, who'd always seemed more interested in music than anything else. But it turned out he was also into photography.

"You shoot with a fixed lens?" I asked, curious.

"Better depth of field. Actually, would you two mind jumping in there? I have an idea."

"Sure," Lily said, pulling me toward the lampposts before I could protest.

I'd always been ridiculously self-conscious in front of a camera, half afraid that a secret part of myself would surface in the picture for everyone to see. Or that I'd have food in my teeth, or underwear lines, or I'd look fat, or deeply unhappy, or . . . or anything.

"Be natural," Adrian called. "I don't want anything too posed."

"So," Lily said, grinning. "Life on the other side of the lens."

"I know." I looked around at where we were. It was so different from the inside, where we were standing. "It's like Narnia. They always came in at the lamppost, remember?"

"That's right! I'd forgotten about those books."

"Lil, can you lean back a little?" Adrian called.

"He's very editorial, isn't he?" Lily rolled her eyes and did as he said. "But he's good. You should see the stuff he exhibited in the gallery show last year."

"Gallery show?"

"The one Mr. Saldana makes all of his students submit work for," Lily reminded me.

"Right. That."

I figured I'd wait until the last minute and hand in whichever piece I produced in class that sucked the least. I had five more weeks before the deadline.

I smiled weakly, trying not to stress about it. Or about the fact that my grandparents thought I was on an extra-credit trip for class. Or that I was being photographed by a boy with a lip ring and patent leather Docs.

"Could you guys stand closer together?" he yelled. "Maybe hold hands?"

My heart sped up at the suggestion. I looked over at Lily, who shrugged.

All of a sudden her warm hand was in mine, and she was holding on tightly, like I was someone worth holding on to. I could barely breathe. It was so lovely, and so thrilling, being here with her.

"Perfect," he called, and I realized he was right. It was perfect.

The instant we walked inside LACMA, I started to quietly panic. I hadn't been in a museum since the day of the earthquake, and something about being back in one made me feel queasy, and a little off.

But Lily was smiling at me, waiting for me to love it, so I tried to stop imagining the floor shaking and the displays falling and the light fixtures crashing to the ground. Instead, I thought about how it had felt when Lily took my hand in hers for Adrian's photos.

I took a deep breath, and then another.

"You okay?" she asked.

"I'm okay," I confirmed. And after another few moments, I was.

Part of it was that the museum was amazing. There were real Magrittes—including that famous one with the pipe.

"Wow," I said, staring at it.

Danica was already posting everything to her Insta story, including the Magritte, and barely even looked up from her phone.

"Don't get too excited," Mabel warned. "He painted a ton of those. Lots of museums have one. It's not like it's the *Mona Lisa*."

"That's depressing," Ryland told her. "Stop ruining art."

"I'm just saying." Mabel shrugged. "It's the traveling production cast of paintings."

"There's nothing wrong with a traveling cast production," said Adrian. "Bring culture to the masses. Let art chill and be accessible."

"Are you calling me an art snob?" Mabel demanded.

"I'm just saying," Adrian teased, borrowing Mabel's earlier words. She glowered, and he gloated, and their argument was so obviously a flirtation that I couldn't blame Ryland for seeming so defeated.

Lily and I exchanged a look. He was such a good guy. A little too obsessed with manga and anime, but he was kind and creative and adorable, and it was easy to see the two of them together.

"That's the exhibit we came for," Lily said, pointing to a sign that advertised Chagall: Fantasies for the Stage.

"Theater and art," she explained over her shoulder. "Something for everyone."

The exhibit was amazing, full of hundred-year-old opera and ballet costumes, yellowed and covered with beadwork so delicate it seemed that if you breathed too intensely they might crumble to dust right there. They'd been painted too, made to look like fantastical beasts and woodland creatures. I only knew Chagall from his paintings; I hadn't known he'd also designed costumes.

"I would have loved to live back then," Lily said wistfully, staring at a leotard painted with leaves and vines that had gossamer wings trailing down the back.

"Me too," I said. "I always wanted to live in Paris in the twenties."

"Drink absinthe in cute cafés," Lily added.

"Fall in love with a penniless writer."

"Cause a scandal by wearing trousers."

"Die charmingly of tuberculosis," I teased.

"Inevitable," she said. "It was the only fashionable way to go."

We laughed. And I stared at the costumes, thinking,

these were there. These pieces were created for a different world, one that existed before any of us were alive. One that was gone now. And it wasn't because of a natural disaster, but because time buried things the way earthquakes did.

"What are you so quiet about?" Lily asked.

I told her.

"Well, you can't idealize the past too much," she said thoughtfully. "Being a woman was dangerous. Being gay was illegal."

"So I guess it's better to be alive now."

"Is it, though?" Lily smiled sadly. "I mean, compared to a hundred years ago, sure. But I have this awful suspicion that, ever since the election, we've started going backward."

"I don't get how so many people can be filled with so much hatred," I said. "What happened?"

"It's horrible," Lily said, her dark eyes serious. "My mom's glued to the news cycle. She's in online groups now where she calls Congress and writes letters and does action items, and she's never cared about politics in her life."

"I think my grandparents voted for Trump," I confessed. "They say stuff sometimes."

Lily made a sympathetic face.

"Last fall, when I came out," she said. "The world felt safe. Like we were on the cusp of this amazing revolution. But all of that's gone now. I leapt, and while I was still falling, strangers took away my soft place to land."

That was exactly how losing my mom felt. Like she was my safe space, and I had nothing to worry about so long as she was around, because of course she loved and accepted me. And now that she was gone, I didn't know what to do.

"I'm sorry," I said.

"So am I," Lily said. "But not sorry enough to take that rainbow pin off my bag. I'm not ashamed of myself, I'm ashamed that the world isn't good enough yet. Because it should be."

"It really should," I said.

We were both quiet a moment, but it was a good silence, a contemplative kind. I felt so awful, hearing Lily talk like this. Having her think that I wasn't feeling any of these things too, and not knowing how to tell her that I was.

So I stared at the costumes, these gorgeous relics from a world that had been harder to live in than the one we lived in now. From a time that I knew was objectively worse, but had painted in my head as something so much better.

"Can you imagine living in a world full of such beautiful things?" I asked, staring at the costumes.

"We still do," Lily said, turning toward me, her eyes bright and wonderful and still a little sad. "You just have to look for them."

And I thought, I want to. God, I want to. I thought, My favorite thing in this museum is you.

I wished I could save this moment forever. This small nothing of a moment: Lily and me gazing at turn-of-the-century costumes on a cloudy fall afternoon. The soft, tender expression she had when she saw something beautiful. The way she brushed my arm or my hand with hers, as though it was the most natural thing in the world, and not an impossible source of electricity.

Every time she did it, I died slightly. Because I didn't just want her to like me as a friend. The way I felt about her was bigger. More. The way I felt was everything, and it left me spinning just to think about it.

So I tried not to. I tried to think about the art, and to drift over, away, to be less obvious. To chat with Ryland or Lily or even Adrian, who seemed delighted to meet another photography enthusiast. After we started talking equipment, Ryland shot me a thumbs-up, because we'd bored Mabel so much that she'd gone to hang with him and Danica instead.

On the drive home, as we sped down the 405, we passed the line where Los Angeles turned into Orange County.

"Orange Curtain!" Lily yelled. She was driving, her hair whipping wildly in the wind.

"Booooo!" everyone yelled back.

I was stuck in the back with Mabel while Ryland rode shotgun.

"Orange Curtain?" I asked.

And so Ryland explained.

"It's like the Iron Curtain," he said. "With Capitalist Europe on one side, Communist Europe on the other."

"Except it's urban liberals on one side, and suburban conservatives on the other," Mabel said with a sigh.

After that, the mood was pretty much dead. Lily turned up the music, and we passed the next few freeway exits listening to Troye Sivan and not saying anything.

And I thought about what Lily had said in the museum, about losing her soft place to land. About how she didn't regret coming out, despite the world changing around her into a less accepting place. I wasn't like that. Even with a soft place to land, I'd still been hiding. And now, keeping parts of myself hidden was so second nature that I couldn't even be real with the one person who would understand. Lily looked at me and saw this illusion, this outline. But really, it was all just smoke and mirrors.

When I got up to my room, I had an email from Adrian on my student account.

These came out so dope, he wrote.

Attached were the photos he'd taken of us.

The ones of Lily and me together. He'd done something with his settings. Made everything brighter and dreamier, until the whole world went out of focus except for the two of us. We were standing between the lampposts, her in the light and me in the shadows. Her head was tilted back, and she was laughing. And I was reaching toward her, in awe.

It was like a flipbook, going through the photos, watching as Lily reached for me, too, as we stood there, our hands clasped, looking silly.

And I realized it wasn't the holding hands that he'd had wanted to capture. It was the reaching for each other just before.

CHAPTER 21

LATER THAT WEEKEND, I TOOK MY camera out of the drawer. I was hoping it would feel good in my hands again, but it still felt wrong. It still made memories come flooding back, aching, painful memories of my mom. Instead of turning it on to shooting mode, I only made it to playback. And then I scrolled through the memory card, reliving all of the moments I'd captured.

There were my classmates at the Valentine's Day dance, the girls with red heart stickers on their cheeks, their arms around each other, grinning. There was the freshman couple dancing with their foreheads pressed together, her eyes shut and his open. There was the old man who ran the antiques store, and our neighbor's toddler in a yellow rain slicker, and a mechanic climbing one of the enormous wind turbines, and Barista Todd in silhouette pouring a foam heart into a cup of coffee.

I scrolled back too far, and all of a sudden my mom's face

was glowing up at me from the LCD screen. Her smile, the small space between her front teeth that had come back even after orthodontia. They weren't good photos of her. That was the worst part. They were photos you take when it doesn't matter. When you're testing out the light or the framing. When you've taken so many that they're meaningless.

I couldn't do this. She'd bought me this camera and told me she couldn't wait to see what pictures I took with it. So how could I use it now? This thing I loved was too tangled up in her. And I didn't know if I'd ever be able to untangle it.

I hadn't realized that Ethan and Whitney and Nick were in a band together, so it surprised me when Lily brought up going to see them play in a student showcase.

Their show was the weekend after our museum trip, at some place called the Den. Lily gave me a ride. It turned out to be a cross between a coffee shop and a community theater. A velvet curtain separated the space where people hunched over their laptops from the back room with the stage.

It was dark inside, the floor and walls painted completely black. The room was narrow, and the stage was small, and it was absolutely packed.

Some other band was onstage when we got there, rocking out in their matching snapbacks and tie-dye tanks.

They were all on guitar and bass, and they mostly just seemed to be making a lot of noise come out of some very tiny speakers.

Some freshman girls right by the stage were losing their minds, screaming and holding up their phones to send their friends snaps.

"One can never account for taste," Lily said sadly.

"They'll look back in a few years with utter embarrassment," Ryland said, joining us.

"The band or the fans?" I asked, and he snorted.

After another few torturous minutes, one of the guitarists mumbled into the mic, "Yeah, so we're Poop Emoji, thanks so much for listening."

"Hey," someone said, clapping me on the shoulder as Whitney and Ethan's band was setting up.

It was Cole, in sweats and a baseball cap, looking slightly disoriented. Friya was with him, in a backless cream mini dress and precarious silver ankle boots, looking like she was headed to a nightclub instead of an all-ages show.

"Wow," Lily said appreciatively. "You look hot."

"Good, because I feel ridiculous," Friya complained, tugging on her hemline. "Nick and I had a fight. So I only came to cheer for my friends. And to show off how amazing I look to make him feel guilty."

And then I glanced toward the stage, where sure enough, Friya's ex-boyfriend was plugging in a guitar. He looked even cuter than he did in our English class, in his tight T-shirt and black ripped skinnies and Vans, his hair all a mess. He spotted Friya and waved, but she just huffed, turning away like she wasn't interested.

"I should have worn leggings, to show him how much I don't care," Friya complained.

"No way, you look totally smokin', Free." This from Cole, who was scrolling on his phone, not even paying attention.

Ryland rolled his eyes. He clearly didn't want to be here, cheering on his sister's band and hanging out with her friends. But his parents were on call and couldn't make it, so they'd insisted he turn up. Lily and I had come as moral support.

It had been a while since I'd hung out with Cole, and I was surprised at how he kept smiling at me, how he offered to buy me a soda and asked how I'd been.

"Well, I quit Mock Trial," I said.

He did a slow clap.

"About time," he said. "I never liked you hanging around with all those assholes."

"Now I hang around with all these assholes," I joked, motioning toward Lily and Ryland. Adam was at an overnight for Academic Decathlon, which was apparently amazing. I'd take his word for it.

"Psh. These two? They're good people," Cole said, grinning. "Quirky, like you."

"Killing it with the compliments tonight," I teased.

"Aah, you just forgot how charming I am," Cole insisted.

Oddly, it was true. I *had* forgotten how easy he was to talk to. How goofy and boyish. How, even dressed in sloppy bro clothes, he was still devastatingly attractive.

"What happened?" I asked, staring at his hand. His knuckles were scraped and bloody.

"Soccer." Cole shrugged.

"Isn't soccer a no-hands kind of sport?" I said.

"I messed up at the gym," he said. "Had a bad spotter." And then he bumped his hip gently into mine. "Nice to know you care, Freshman."

"I don't," I told him, moving away.

"Well, I'm going to keep on believing it anyway," he said.

He stared down at me with his sea-glass eyes, and I realized that whatever was between us was still there, no matter how frustrated I was with what he'd done at the homecoming party, or how badly he'd botched the apology. But just because I was attracted to him didn't mean I was obligated to do anything about it. Half the girls in our school were probably attracted to him. It didn't make him boyfriend material.

He dug out his vape and offered it to me before taking a pull. I watched how much he inhaled, and he wasn't just getting a buzz. Something told me he hadn't hurt his hand at the gym, either. I wasn't sure what was going on with him, but I also knew that I didn't have the bandwidth to care.

"You better not be driving," I warned.

"Nahhh, Ethan gave me a lift."

The band started, and Lily, who'd been talking to some people from school I didn't know, came back and asked where I'd been.

"Here," I said, confused.

"I've been taking really good care of her," Cole said seriously.

Lily rolled her eyes.

"Hi, Cole. Bye, Cole," she said, taking my hand and leading me toward the crowd. We pushed our way to the front, joining Friya and Ryland.

On the stage, Ethan was on drums, a bandanna tied around his forehead, looking totally in his element. Whitney, in some sort of lace coat and feather earrings, crooned into the microphone, her voice soft and oozy like liquid velvet. Nick was scowling and strumming his guitar. And one of the Aidans from my math class was on keyboard.

The crowd was thick around us, writhing and excited and a mass of energy. Cole, who had followed us, squeezed my arm and grinned. Lily was on my other side, in a skin-tight black bodysuit and mom jeans, her ponytail swinging.

The moment they played the opening chords, the crowd went crazy.

"I'm getting a Coke," Ryland said, disappearing instantly.

"Dance with me in case Nick looks over," Friya begged Cole.

"No way," he said. "Dude will kill me."

"He will not, you're like my brother," she shot back.

And then the music got too loud for us to do anything except scream and dance. I'd listened to a couple of their songs online, and thought they were just okay. Somehow, here in this narrow room, with the sound echoing off every surface, they were great. Lily and I danced together, screaming because they were our friends, kind of, sort of. Next to us, some fangirls were freaking out, and Lily caught my eye and laughed.

Friya was glaring at the fangirls, who were shouting, "WE LOVE YOU, NICK!"

A fast-paced song came on, and I felt Lily's soft, warm hands grab my hips. We were so close, dancing with each other, grinding on each other, Lily's smile luminous in the dark. My heart hammered, and the room spun, and I felt like I could lean in and kiss her, and she'd kiss me back, hard.

I was certain we were supposed to kiss, right then, as the song built to its crescendo and Whitney's sultry baritone crooned this amazing refrain about waves crashing the party.

And it terrified me. Because I liked boys, and I knew that about myself, but I also knew that the way I felt about Lily meant it didn't matter if I also liked boys.

The crushes I'd had on girls before had been small. Hypothetical. Contained. This crush felt bigger, as though, no matter how I tried, it was going to spill out.

And I didn't know what to do. Because Lily was gay, which meant it was possible. But we were friends, and I didn't want to ruin that. And my life here was working, and I didn't want to ruin that.

Falling for a girl wasn't part of my survival strategy. I had two more years of changing in the PE locker room. Two more years of classmates who left awful comments on a girl's Instagram because they thought she needed a bikini wax. Two more years in a house where conservative news anchors blared their nightly reports.

And yet, here I was, dancing with this incredible girl, the curves of her hips bumping against mine. We weren't doing anything friends wouldn't do, but I couldn't tell if we were doing it as friends.

Lily was beautiful. Was it queer of me to notice, or just normal? Or was the queer part that I kept noticing all the dozens of tiny ways she was beautiful? That I never stopped noticing, because as long as she was around, I couldn't look away? I could close my eyes and picture her, the smooth, soft expanse of skin, the shape of her eyes, the unevenness of her front teeth when she smiled. The beauty mark above her mouth, the way her hair came to a point at the nape of her neck. The soft mauve of her lips. The woodsy silage of her perfume.

I'd never known I could like a girl like this. It was how I liked boys, but it was also completely different. I liked the way boys' arms felt around me, and how confident they were, how loud and boisterous. How being around them could make me feel like such a girl, instead of such a misfit.

It would be so much easier if you just got a letter, like in Harry Potter. *You're a wizard, Harry. You're bisexual, Sasha.*

But I didn't know that for sure. Maybe there wasn't a label for what I was, other than weird and different. Maybe plenty of straight girls imagined what it would be like to kiss their friends.

Then Lily smiled at me, and in that moment, I knew that it didn't matter how hard I pushed it down, or locked it up or tried to explain it as nothing. My feelings weren't going away. And least, not while Lily was around.

So we danced, because we were teenage girls at a concert, and it was the most natural thing in the world.

"Yes! You guys look sooooo hot," Friya said, coming over to dance with us.

Lily rolled her eyes as Friya bumped her hips against ours, glancing thirstily toward the stage.

"Come on," Cole groaned. "All three of you now?"

"Stay back," Lily warned him. "None of your bullshit is allowed up in here."

"It's a conspiracy," Ryland shouted, accidentally sloshing his Coke. "I'm sure of it."

And then he stiffened, grabbing my arm.

"Look—Mabel's here," he said dramatically.

I swiveled around, and sure enough, she'd come with

a group of drama kids. Her dress was amazing, black and gauzy and sheer. Her lips were deep red and her eyelids sparkled with glitter. But most important, Adrian was nowhere in sight.

"Go say hi!" Lily and I urged.

Ryland protested, but Lily literally shoved him over there. And then we watched as he danced with Mabel and her drama crowd friends, who seemed to totally get what was going on, and more than that, to encourage it.

It was barely nine thirty when Lily and I got back home. Our friends' band had gone on laughably early, and they'd kicked out everyone who didn't have a twenty-one-plus wristband at nine.

I didn't have to be home for another hour, and I fought the disappointment that the night was over.

"Want to come in?" Lily asked.

"Sure," I said. "That would be great, I mean, I have like an hour until my curfew, so."

God. I hated how awkward and in my own head I was being. It was like one moment we were talking about nothing, and the next I was babbling.

Lily's parents were in the kitchen, splitting a bottle of wine. Well, Lily's mom and Adam's dad. Lily's mom was gorgeous, even in an oversized Berkeley sweatshirt and yoga pants. Adam's dad was completely bald, with the kindest smile on the planet and Adam's chin exactly. And then there was Gracie, in her Star Wars pajamas, lying on the rug, playing on an iPad.

"This must be the infamous Sasha," Mr. Ziegler said, beaming.

"Unless there are two of us,'" I joked, returning his handshake and inwardly cringing, even though he laughed politely.

"You girls hungry?" Mrs. Chen asked. "I can make scrambled eggs and tomato."

My heart twisted at the offer.

"No thanks," Lily said.

And then we were faced with a barrage of parent questions. When we finally went to make our escape to the backyard, Gracie reached out and grabbed my ankle.

"Hi," she said, rolling over on the carpet and staring up at me with wide dark eyes. Her hair was brown like Adam's and wavy like Lily's. "Are you Lily's girlfriend?"

Everyone laughed. But Gracie was completely serious.

I wish, I wanted to say.

Instead, I shook my head. "Just her friend. And your neighbor. I live with my grandparents two doors down."

Gracie sat up, blinking at me.

"You do?" she said. "They have the best dog! We take care of her when they're out of town. I taught her how to play find the ball. It's a game where you hide the ball and—"

"She gets it, Grace Kelly," Lily said. "Isn't it your bedtime?"

"Baba said I could play five more minutes."

"That was ten minutes ago," Mr. Ziegler called, coming over and swooping her up. "Say good night, Gracie." Gracie giggled as her dad spun her around, and I felt this stab of sadness at the thought of my own dad. I glanced at Lily, and I could tell she felt it too.

"Glad that's over," Lily said when we stepped into the backyard. "My family can be a lot."

"I think it's nice," I said. "I almost died when Gracie asked if I was your girlfriend." The words slipped out, and my cheeks burned.

"Oh god," Lily groaned. "She asks if *everyone* is my girlfriend. Even our cousins. My mom accidentally overdid it with the whole 'girls can have girlfriends' talk."

"Oh," I said, trying not to let my disappointment show.

"She's the most woke six-year-old on the planet," said Lily.

The grass felt soft and wet under my sneakers. It was strange being here, realizing how close my grandparents' house was, just a couple hundred feet, just two fences. Strange how it felt like so much more usually, but tonight, how it felt like so much less.

Lily's house didn't have a pool, like my grandparents' did. Instead, there was a pergola overlooking the ocean and the enormous trampoline. Lily scrambled onto it, and I joined her, surprised at the coldness of the fabric. It was easy to forget how much of California was a desert, and how after the sun went down, it didn't matter how warm it had been during the day. The nights were always chilly.

Inside her house, the downstairs lights snapped off. The night air draped around us, salty and cool.

"Which one's your room again?" Lily asked as we sat cross-legged on the trampoline.

I pointed.

"Mine's on the other side," she said, disappointed.

"I know," I said, a little too quickly, and then reminded her, "I've been there before."

"Oh." Lily laughed. "Right."

She lay down on the trampoline, her hair fanning around her face. I lay down, too, next to her. It felt achingly intimate, the two of us there, staring up at the sky.

"The stars here are terrible," I said. They were much better where I was from. In Bayport, they were dulled and blurry, barely anything.

"Good thing we're not here for the stars," Lily said, her smile stretching wide. Her head was turned toward me in the dark, and I shivered, from the cold but also from something else.

"Do you know about the airplane curfew?" Lily asked, which I wasn't expecting.

"All the teenage airplanes have to be home before midnight?" I joked.

"Terrible, but no. Orange County has this curfew where flights can't land after ten p.m. If they come in late, they have to reroute up to Los Angeles."

"Weird," I said. "Why?"

"Rich people complained about the noise." Lily shrugged. "Anyway, when my mom and I moved here, I had trouble falling asleep somewhere new, so I made up this game. You wait until just before ten o'clock, which it is right now. And then you guess which is going to be the last plane allowed to land. And you see if you're right. But you only get one try."

"I'll play you," I said.

We stretched back on the trampoline. Our shoulders were so close. My right arm, her left, a matching set.

High above us, I saw the blinking light of an airplane.

"Last plane," I said.

"We'll see." Lily grinned.

We lay there a moment, breathing quietly in the darkness, waiting. And then another plane angled across the sky.

"You lose. Last plane," Lily called.

We waited a minute, and then another.

Lily held up her phone. It was 10:01.

"I win," she said, propping herself up on her elbow.

She was facing me, and she was so close, and so happy, and I don't know what came over me in that moment, but I leaned toward her and brushed my lips against hers.

It was the kiss I'd wished for as we danced beneath the stage. It was the kiss that had been threatening to spill out, and now it had, pure and sweet and terrifying.

I expected the earth to shift, the ocean to rise up, the stars to drop like ripe plums into the soft grass. And for a moment, it felt as though they might. Because Lily was kissing me back. Her warm lips, her wicked tongue, and mine. Oh god. Mine.

The whole world started to spin, and then Lily pulled away, her face asking a question that I wasn't ready to answer.

"That was unexpected," she whispered.

"Yeah," I gasped. "I—sorry."

"Don't be sorry," Lily said, grabbing the front of my shirt in her fist and pulling me back for another.

We kissed under the blurred stars, on that cold trampoline. I reached up and ran a hand through her hair, and it was in that moment that I remembered—I was kissing a girl.

I pulled away. My heart was hammering, and I was the good kind of dizzy, and I didn't want it to stop, but I needed it to stop.

Everything was overwhelming all of a sudden, and I realized that I was hyperventilating.

"I have to go," I said.

I hopped off the trampoline and ran through her backyard, toward the safety of my grandparents' house. Toward the safety of being someone I wasn't, which of course wasn't safety at all.

CHAPTER 22

UNTIL THE KISS, THERE HAD BEEN a possibility that I was wrong. That I'd made a mistake, calculating my feelings all wrong. That I had multiplied instead of divided. But now? There was no denying it.

Kissing Lily was an earthquake, and now I didn't know how to put everything back, or if I even wanted to. The ground had shifted. Plates had collided. Or maybe that was just our mouths.

Later that night, I lay across my bed, staring up at the ceiling, my heart racing and my lips tingling.

Lily, I thought. *Lily, Lily, Lily.* Her name was a symphony, a novel, a sculpture.

It was a forbidden thing, off-limits, beyond the path I'd promised myself I'd never stray from, in this house that wasn't mine, in this town that wasn't mine, in this life that was never supposed to be mine.

My mom had died, and my world had shattered, and

putting the pieces back together was supposed to be hard. It was supposed to be lonely and miserable. It wasn't supposed to be *Kintsugi,* because I wasn't supposed to be transformed into something more than I'd been. And I definitely wasn't supposed to burst with happiness as I pressed my lips against another girl's. As I kissed her, and she kissed me back, revealing the truth I'd tried to push down for so long.

I was queer. Definitively, for sure, no longer wondering and questioning.

I'd been convinced I could keep it inside for a while longer, something to deal with when I didn't live here, in Bayport, with my grandparents. But there was no turning back now. Because that hadn't been a nothing of a kiss.

Our kiss had been a masterpiece.

And I wanted to go on making art with Lily forever, tracing the curves of her hips, sketching my fingers through her hair, painting her lips with mine.

But I was terrified of what came next. Of my grandparents finding out, which would be a nightmare. They wouldn't understand. Just like they wouldn't understand about quitting Mock Trial, or why I'd stopped hanging out with Cole's crowd.

For my whole life, I'd thought adults were rational. I'd thought they would understand, and that they could be trusted, my dad notwithstanding. But then they'd started wearing MAGA hats, and actual Nazis were marching in the streets, and grown-ups were screaming at strangers on social media. *Give teachers guns. Build a wall. Grab 'em by the pussy. Yes all women.* Kids getting shot for wearing hoodies. The active shooter drills we practiced in school. *Teen Vogue* was reporting politics, and the president was insulting people on Twitter.

I didn't know what was safe anymore, or who was safe.

My mom had been safe. I'd known that, but I hadn't truly appreciated it. My life with her had been a soft place to land. No matter what, it would all be okay.

And now I wasn't sure if it would be. My grandfather had been so surprised that his dental hygienist had a wife. My grandmother kept asking me about Cole with that knowing smile, as though she was already planning our wedding. There was no question in her mind that one day I would marry a man and have kids.

They had visualized my future a certain way, where any deviation from the path was a failure, not a choice. And they'd done the same thing with my mom.

I imagined telling them that I was queer, that I liked Lily. But all I could picture was my mom wrapping me in a hug and telling me how much she loved me, no matter what. I couldn't picture my grandparents reacting the same way.

So what if she's a lesbian, my grandmother had said of that dental hygienist. *It isn't as though she lives next door.* Next door was the worst place my grandmother could think of.

Parents sometimes kicked their own children out for being gay. And Eleanor and Joel weren't even my parents. They were grandparents who barely knew me, who I'd seen twice a year for dinner up until they became my guardians.

But I wasn't gay. I might kick up an enormous fuss only to fall madly in love with a boy in ten years and live a life indistinguishable from what they pictured.

I was Schrödinger's box, containing two possibilities at once. It was too much, and I didn't know what to do about any of it. Kissing someone shouldn't be so stressful, so frantic, so terrifying.

There weren't a lot of safe spaces here. There were definitely less now than there had been a year ago. And yet Lily held her chin high every day, with her rainbow pin on her bag, not being loud about it, but not hiding either.

Were my grandparents safe? I couldn't tell. They looked at me, and I knew what they saw. A girl who wore makeup and dresses and liked to read books. A girl who did well in school and was shy around boys and had a baby face that inspired strangers to call her sweetheart. I passed the test. And so I didn't tell anyone that their test was wrong.

They'd gotten stuck with me, on top of losing their daughter, and I barely knew them, and I wanted them to like me. So I had pretended there was no Schrödinger's box.

And now that the box was open, I was all alone, with no one to tell what I'd found inside. I wanted my mom. I needed her, more than ever.

I looked around at this bedroom that had been hers, at the desk still scuffed with her pen marks, the closet still containing her clothes, at all of the things she'd left behind and had never meant for me to have.

"Tell me about this girl," she would have said. Or maybe she'd know Lily. Maybe she would have already guessed.

But now she'd never know. I'd thought I had the rest of my life to find the courage, but it turned out I only had the rest of hers.

And now she was gone, and I was alone with my panic and my questions, and downstairs the television was saying trans people shouldn't serve in the military, and my grandparents were listening as calmly as if it were a traffic report.

I took out my computer, searching for the video I'd watched far too many times on YouTube. I followed maybe ten beauty and fashion vloggers religiously. Alone in my room, I watched their videos, desperate for girls like that to be my friends, to be as nice to me as they were being when they talked to a camera. Except they never were. And I knew that I wasn't like them. That something inside me didn't match.

I drank in their secrets. What they ate for breakfast. Their morning routines, and where they shopped, and what their bedrooms looked like. It didn't help. I still wasn't like them.

But then I found one girl who felt different than the rest. I watched her talk frankly about acne and period cramps and dandruff. She joked about being a broke college student and how awkward she was at parties, and it felt so revolutionary. So honest.

I remembered the day she posted a coming-out video. Remembered sitting in our living room on a Saturday afternoon, my earbuds in, shocked as she explained not about toner or beach waves, but about being bisexual.

It was a revelation.

I hadn't known that queer could look like her. I'd thought girls who liked other girls wore flannel and had short hair. I'd thought that because I loved fashion, because I wore makeup, because I was feminine, I couldn't be queer. That I was just weird or wrong or my own brand of awkward. I'd watched her coming-out video more times than I cared to admit, looking for clues that would help me solve the mystery of what I was.

Now, with Lily's kiss fresh on my lips and my heart beating fast, I watched the video again. It seemed old now. The quality wasn't great. But the words, the message, they were still the same punch to the gut. The same truth that I'd thought was a broken piece of me, not a shared piece of what it meant to be queer.

I closed my laptop and climbed into the shower, wishing

the hot water would solve all my problems. Except hot water never does. You get about three seconds of clarity, and then it's just you, naked, with a bunch of slimy plastic bottles at your feet, and instead of working out any answers, you wind up wasting water before you reach guiltily for the shampoo.

CHAPTER 23

WHEN LILY TEXTED ME THE NEXT evening, asking if I could meet her outside, I said yes. I'd been wanting to text her all day, I'd even picked up my phone and started composing my message in notes, so she wouldn't see the typing dots, but in the end, I hadn't found the courage.

I was glad Lily had. Because I didn't want to face her again for the first time on our Monday carpool, with Adam riding shotgun and me in the back seat, trying not to make it awkward, but inevitably doing that anyway.

"Where are you going?" my grandmother asked when I came downstairs.

"Just meeting a friend," I said.

"Which one?"

"Um, Lily Chen."

"Oh." My grandmother sounded disappointed.

I figured it was easier not to ask why. Once she started on one of her tirades, she kept going, until she had picked apart every speck of a person. I'd heard her do it recently with Marion from her book club, and from the amount of vitriol she was spewing, I was shocked when, two days later, she mentioned their going out for coffee together after yoga.

"Well, see you," I said awkwardly.

"Wait," my grandmother said, and I turned around, my heart pounding. "When are you going to ask Cole to dinner?"

Oh god.

"Um, probably in a few weeks," I said. "Now isn't really a good time. Because of soccer."

I felt terrible lying to her, but I didn't want her to say I couldn't meet Lily.

"Make sure to find out what he doesn't eat," my grandmother said.

"Will do," I promised, grabbing my keys.

Pearl trotted over to the door, looking hopeful, like she might get a walk, even though my grandfather had literally just taken her on one.

"You can't come," I told her, and she huffed before trotting away to play with her green ball.

Lily was standing at the curb, wearing a sweater and jeans, her hair back in a braid. When I saw her, my heart sped up.

Lily, Lily, Lily, it sang.

It was like my blood remembered kissing her. I felt it

rush to my cheeks, warming them.

"Hey," Lily said. "I thought we might walk down to the beach or something."

"Sure," I said. I was tiptoeing around her, waiting for her to bring up what had happened.

Except she didn't, not right away. She started walking, and I followed. The sun was just beginning to set, and the sky glowed pink. Golden hour, it was called. The best lighting for taking photos, because it makes everything appear more perfect than it is.

I wondered if it would help me. If, when Lily looked at me, I'd appear better.

"I've never been down here before," I said as Lily led me toward a small private beach at the end of the block.

"Seriously?" Lily's eyebrows shot up. "You need to get out more. Go exploring."

"I'll pack a sled with provisions and make Pearl pull it," I joked. Lily smiled, shaking her head slightly.

It never failed to shock me how close we were to the ocean here, how just at the end of the block, it was the end of the entire continent. We were standing on the edge of something, always. But how easy it was to forget.

There was a small kids' playground down by the water, as though the ocean wasn't enough.

"Fake sand," Lily said, her smile crooked as she stared at the sandbox. "Isn't that amazing?"

"Wait," I said.

I ran across the short strip of grass to the beach, bending down until my cupped hands were filled with sand, and then I brought it back to the playground, letting it sift through my fingers.

"Now it's real sand," I said.

"Just tell me," Lily blurted. "Did last night mean anything to you, or were you just playing around?"

She winced after she said it, leaning back against the orange plastic of the jungle gym. And I realized that, despite her brave face, she was as rattled as I was by what had happened.

"Of course I wasn't playing around," I said, wondering how she could think that.

Lily's shoulders sagged in relief.

"Okay. Good," she said. "Because when I told you I was gay—" She stopped, steeling herself. "You acted really cool about it, and really supportive—and really straight."

I was going to have to say it.

But if the first person I told was Lily Chen, here, on this golden beach full of real and fake sand, I thought it could be okay.

"Well, I'm not," I whispered, and then I took a deep breath. There was no turning back now. "I've never told this to anyone before, but . . . I'm bisexual."

I expected silence after I said it. For the world to screech to a stop, but it didn't even slow down.

"That's awesome," Lily said, relieved.

"It's awesome?" I said. I didn't think I'd heard her correctly.

"I can't believe I'm the first person you told," she said, smiling at me.

"Also the first girl I ever kissed," I said, since I was pretty sure middle school games of truth or dare didn't count.

"Wow," Lily said. "Your v-card. I'll treasure it."

"Moderate sunlight," I instructed. "Water it once a week."

"I'll text you updates," Lily joked. And then she took a deep breath and admitted, "You have no idea how relieved I am. I mean, that night on the beach when you pulled the spaghetti out of my hair. And at the museum. And last night at the Den. I thought I was looking for something that wasn't there."

"It was there," I admitted. And then I asked, "Why were you looking?"

"Because I have the biggest crush on you," she admitted.

"Impossible," I said.

Lily raised an eyebrow.

"Because I have the biggest crush on you," I finished.

It felt so right, confessing my feelings to Lily. With boys, it always felt so precarious. Like at any moment they might declare that actually, they were just joking, that of course they didn't like you. With boys, I was always waiting for them to make the first move, to set the tone.

Here, it was just us. Just Lily and me. And we could be

whatever we wanted. It was that easy. And also, that hard.

"And I've never," I went on. "I mean. It's all really new."

"We're sixteen," Lily reminded me gently. "It's allowed to be new."

"You're right," I said.

"So, speaking of new things, would you maybe want to go on a date?" Lily asked, her eyes shining. She looked so hopeful and so beautiful in the fading golden light.

Oh my god, a date.

Lily Chen had just asked me out.

"Um, I'd like that," I said. "A lot."

Lily's smile was luminous in the sunset, and I could feel myself glittering, too.

But the moment I agreed, the logical part of my brain kicked in, reminding me of the million reasons we couldn't. The million reasons I couldn't.

"Except," I said, my voice hitching. "I, um, I don't want to tell my grandparents yet. About being bi. I don't—I don't really know how they'll react."

Lily bit her lip, considering.

"Oh, Sasha," she said. "I didn't even think. And I want you to be in a safe space, and to come out if—and when—you're ready. So if you need it to be a secret date, I understand."

"Really?" I said.

It hadn't even occurred to me that we could just . . . not tell anyone.

"Of course," Lily said seriously. "I'm super lucky with my family. But my grandparents—they're old-school PRC."

"PRC?"

"People's Republic of China," Lily clarified. "My aunt lied to them for years about living with her boyfriend before they got married. It was ridiculous."

"So about this secret date," I reminded her.

"It would be very secret," she promised. "We might not even know that we were on it."

"As in, we might even be on it now?" I asked.

"Anything's possible," Lily said, smiling.

And then we climbed up onto the plastic jungle gym and watched the sun set over the ocean. The moon was already out, which my mom always said was a good omen.

"There's the rabbit," Lily said.

"Where?" I glanced around the grass.

"In the moon," Lily said.

"I thought it was a face," I said.

"Rabbit," Lily said. "With a pestle, mixing the elixir of life."

"You're making that up."

"It's from an old folktale," she said. "Look at the moon and tell me you don't see a rabbit."

She pointed, and I squinted, and sure enough.

"How have I gone my entire life not knowing that there's a rabbit in the moon and we're all made from dinosaur pee?" I said.

Lily shrugged.

"What can I say?" She grinned. "You were missing out."

"You know what else I was missing out on?" I asked.

"Cheeseburgers with chopped chiles?"

"Close," I said, and then I kissed her.

CHAPTER 24

THE NEXT WEEK WAS TORTURE.

Lily was true to her word about keeping everything a secret. She behaved just as she always did around our friends. But occasionally her hand or her leg would brush against mine, and she'd wait a beat too long before moving it away.

Our eyes would meet at lunch, or in Art Club, or the locker room during Phys Ed, and I'd see the wicked twist to her smile as she glanced away first. And feel the flush in my cheeks as I didn't.

"Secret date this weekend," she told me as I was switching my books at my locker on Tuesday after school.

"I'm all yours," I promised.

"Obviously," she said. And then she made an excuse to touch my shoulder. I shivered involuntarily, and Lily clocked it, pleased. "I love your top. Where'd you get it?"

"I can't remember," I said, my cheeks flushed. Oh god,

she knew exactly what she was up to. And I knew my shirt was Forever 21. But that would ruin the game. So I cleared my throat and said, "You should check the label."

I twisted around, lifting my hair off the back of my neck, stiffening as I felt the soft brush of her fingers at the top of my spine.

"Today sucks," Adam declared loudly, interrupting us.

Lily and I sprang apart guiltily.

"Spanish test?" she asked, sounding surprisingly normal.

"I got an eighty-seven," Adam moaned, and Lily made a face. "It was one verb conjugation. But every time I used it in the essay, Ms. Gonzales took a point off. I stayed after and tried to argue about it, but she was like, 'Too bad about your future, you forgot the transitive form of *esperar* for *usted*.'"

"Bright side?" I said. "You'll never forget it again."

"It's *esperando*," Adam said miserably. "Not *esperanto*."

"Isn't Esperanto that made-up language that was supposed to be the universal standard?" Lily asked.

"Yep," Adam said. "We were learning about it in AP Gov last month. How can I be expected to learn *esperando* and Esperanto and not confuse them?"

"The one with the E is for government," Lily said without hesitating.

"Shit." Adam shook his head. "I should have thought of that."

I glanced over at Lily, impressed by how quickly she'd

come up with the study trick.

It was fascinating to watch when they smart peopled like this. No wonder their homework was always perfect; if they ever had a question, they could just ask each other.

We climbed into the car, and Lily turned right out of the parking lot, instead of left. I frowned.

"We're not going home?" I asked.

"We're going to cheer up Adam," she said.

"Impossible," he said.

"Also, for one afternoon only, we can listen to your stupid podcasts," she said, passing him the auxiliary cable.

We merged onto the freeway, listening to two dudes banter about James Bond movies, which was predictably uninteresting.

"Is it far?" I asked.

"I can't tell you that," Lily said seriously. "Because then Adam will know where we're going."

"I already know it's the frozen cookie dough place," he said.

"Wrong." Lily grinned.

And then she took the exit for a giant luxury mall. I stared out the window at the Bloomingdales and Neiman Marcus, realizing with a sinking feeling that I had like a dollar on me.

Thankfully, we weren't going to the mall, but to a small cluster of restaurants just across the street.

"Cauldron!" Adam exclaimed, cheering immediately as

we walked toward an ice-cream shop I'd never heard of before.

The walls were covered with steampunk clocks, and smoke billowed from behind the counter, where they were mixing ice cream with liquid nitrogen. Everyone there was eating ice cream shaped like roses, wrapped in fluffy, still-warm waffles. Instead of the grid shape I was used to, these waffles looked like bubble wrap.

"Wow," I said.

And then I remembered that I didn't have any cash.

"Um, can I pay you back?" I asked Lily.

"Don't even worry about it," she said, taking out a debit card.

Lily had me hold up my cone next to hers, for an Instagram. I stared down at my phone, with the tag notification, getting a little thrill out of making it onto her feed. There was a secret meaning to the photo that only we knew about—everyone else would just think we'd gone for ice cream.

The ice cream tasted even better than it looked. Lily caught my eye and nodded at Adam, who was happily demolishing his sea salt caramel crunch.

I loved Lily when she was like this. I loved her loyalty, and her fierceness, and the way you could always count on her to sense when something was wrong and to know just how to make you feel better, even if she couldn't fix it.

"I'm going to pee," Lily said, standing up. "Want to come with?"

Lily had this mischievous expression, and I wondered what was up.

"Um, sure," I said.

Adam rolled his eyes and took out his phone.

Lily opened the door to the bathroom, and there was just the single toilet.

"I'll wait outside?" I said, wondering if I'd misread the whole thing.

"I'm just putting on lip gloss," she said, dragging me inside with her.

I wasn't even sure how it happened, but suddenly we were kissing. Her fingers were in my hair, and mine were on her waist, and I realized that in my stack-heeled boots, I was a few inches taller. It was disorienting, being the larger one, but I didn't mind, oh god, I really didn't, because her lips were ice-cream sweet and her tongue was cold, and we were all alone, with a lock on the door.

We finally pulled apart, and Lily was like, *well*. And I was like, *I know.*

"So lip gloss, huh?" I teased.

Lily shrugged. And then she took the little tube out of her pocket, redid her lips, and passed it over to me.

It smelled like birthday cake, was decorated to look like a frowning cartoon bear, and was somehow the most Lily thing I'd ever seen.

"Wow, I love this," I said.

"Keep it," she told me.

"Really?" I asked, surprised.

"You'll never be able to stop thinking about kissing me now," she said with a wicked smile.

She was right.

I spent the rest of the week counting down until my secret date with Lily. Whenever I'd think about it, my heart would pound faster, and the hours would feel endless, but somehow they managed to tick past.

The best part was how my grandparents didn't suspect a thing. How in their minds it was Cole whose texts made my phone buzz during dinner, to the point that I was asked to leave my phone in a different room. How they still thought that, when I came home late from school, it was because of Mock Trial.

"She seems happier," I overheard my grandfather telling my grandmother one night. "Haven't you noticed?"

I *was* happier. Lily and I texted every night before bed, sometimes watching the same TV shows at the same time and sending each other commentary, and sometimes talking about more important things than *Schitt's Creek* or *The Marvelous Mrs. Maisel.*

I'd never felt this way about anyone. Giddy and terrified and so obsessed with the tiniest things about her, the brand of mascara she used, the websites she liked, the bands she listened to.

My grandparents had no idea. And neither did our friends. Lily was true to her word about it being private, about letting me figure things out on my own terms.

Which meant I could just not think about what I was going to tell my grandparents, or when.

So I didn't.

Instead, I kept Lily's lip gloss in my pocket, taking it out and reapplying it far too often. I'd never known a tube of lip gloss could make me feel giddy and warm inside, but then, there were so many things I didn't know about dating girls. It was the same world I'd always lived in, but slightly different, an alternate reality.

In PE, we had assigned lockers, and mine was in a different row from Lily's. But that Friday, she wandered over anyway, asking if I had an extra hair tie.

My shirt was off, and I stiffened, embarrassed. My bra wasn't very cute, and I had a pimple on my chest, and I was bloated from my period, my muffin top spilling over the waistband of my jeans.

"I think so," I said, digging through my bag.

Lily leaned back against the locker. I could feel her eyes on my back, my chest, my belly. I could feel her drinking me in, in that wicked, silent way of hers.

I took my time, letting her look, because I liked that she wanted to. Even if it did make me feel self-conscious.

"Found one," I said, passing it over.

"Thanks."

Lily flipped her head over, gathering her hair into a blobby bun.

"I hope we're not doing badminton again today," she said, unbuttoning her own shirt, letting the center of a lacy white bra peek out, and revealing the tight, tanned stretch of her stomach.

She was teasing me. Her eyes met mine, and her lips tugged into a smile.

"It's the worst," I agreed.

"Hey, you're not supposed to change here," a girl in my row said, scowling.

She was covering herself with her sweatshirt and glaring at Lily.

Lily rolled her eyes and didn't even glance over.

"Hi, Natasha," she said. "Am I bothering you?"

"Actually, yeah," the girl said, being openly hostile about it.

I felt terrible. And I waited for the fire to burn in Lily's eyes, for her to tell Natasha exactly where she could shove it. But instead of fire, all I saw was pain.

Lily's smile went tight, and her shoulders hunched forward, just a little.

"No problem," Lily said calmly. "I was just leaving."

After Lily left, Natasha whispered loudly, "*She's a lesbian.*"

I realized belatedly she was talking to me.

"So?" I said.

"So, it's *gross,*" Natasha said, making a face. "I mean, we're changing our clothes. I don't want her looking at me."

I had a flash of middle school. Of Tara's cruel accusation in the locker room, and how the girls who followed her lead had made me feel. It wasn't okay. Lily hadn't stuck up for herself, had taken it in stride, and that made me so *angry*.

"Speaking of looking," I said, "you should probably get that homophobia looked at."

Natasha's jaw hit the floor. So did mine. I couldn't believe what had come out of my mouth.

Now that I'd said it, I couldn't just stay there. So I picked up my stuff and finished changing with Lily and Mabel.

"That was badass," Mabel said approvingly.

"I didn't know you had it in you," Lily said, looking proud.

"Yeah." I shook my head, still in shock. "Me neither."

When Lily picked me up on Saturday, I was so nervous, fluttering around and changing outfits about a million times. She refused to tell me where I was going, but had told me to dress "like Anna Karina in that scene in *Band of Outsiders*, when they run through the Louvre."

It was an absurdly specific request. So I'd tied a ribbon around my ponytail and worn a baby-doll dress with a collar. And then I'd stared in the mirror, appraising whether or not I looked cute enough. For a boy, it was easy. Show some skin, wear something tight. Break the dress code. But I doubted Lily would be impressed by a low-cut top.

Pearl went crazy when I opened the front door, practically leaping into Lily's arms.

"Hiya, little dog," she said, making a face and twisting away as Pearl's tongue came out.

My grandfather was out with his hiking club, thank god, but my grandmother, who was in the living room, came to see what the fuss was about.

"Oh, Lily. What a lovely blouse," my grandmother said.

It *was* nice. Black with lace sleeves. She'd worn it for me, I realized, and I felt my cheeks heat up.

"Thank you," Lily said.

They chatted a moment, and I held my breath, waiting for some lie to spill out, about Mock Trial or Art Club or Cole, but of course nothing did.

"So where are you girls going?" Eleanor asked.

"The movies," said Lily.

I frowned, because I was pretty sure she was lying.

"Well, have fun," my grandmother said.

"Will do," I promised.

When Lily and I climbed into the car, I was like, "Did you really tell me to dress like a character out of a Jean-Luc Godard film just so we could go to the movies?"

Lily snorted.

"Of course not," she said. "But I didn't want to ruin the surprise, so the lie was necessary. If you feel bad about it, we can see one after."

"That's okay," I said.

"You look really pretty with your hair like that, by the way," Lily said, smiling.

"You look really pretty always," I said.

She looked especially great today, in that black lacy top and a long, fluttering wrap skirt and a leather jacket.

"Well, I feel gross," Lily said. "Got my period this morning."

It shocked me that we could talk about something like this, but I tried to cover my surprise.

"I've had mine since Thursday," I admitted.

"Oh my god," Lily said. "You *gave* it to me."

"I did *not*," I said.

But Lily just shook her head and turned on some music.

"Who is this?" I asked.

I was always asking. Lily's knowledge of music was extensive. I had the impression she was playing songs for me, testing to see what I liked, and she always smiled when I asked her one I didn't know.

"Phoebe Bridgers," she said. "I'll make you a playlist."

We turned onto Ocean Avenue and drove north, past the sparkling private beaches and the marina, past the dingier public beach with its boardwalk cafés, and even farther still. The beach was just a narrow strip here, along the highway.

Lily stopped the car in a lot labeled "scenic viewpoint parking" and then grinned.

"Where are we?" I asked, frowning.

"Really?" Lily's grin stretched wider. "I was worried you'd already been here."

Lily pointed down the edge of the parking lot, toward a small brown building on the side of the highway.

When we got closer, there were signs.

"It's a camera obscura!" I said, delighted. "I've read about these!"

Lily's smile was a beautiful thing. She bought both of our tickets from the man behind the counter, even though I protested that we could split it.

"You can buy lunch," Lily said, holding open the door.

There was a little hallway with black-and-white photos displaying the history of the building and explaining about the camera, how it was a projection of what was happening outside, cleverly rendered through light and mirrors. How the pinhole camera was created from natural phenomena in the seventeenth century, and how its invention led to modern photography.

The place was deserted. A family with a young child had been leaving when we walked in, so we had the room to ourselves.

"Shall we?" Lily asked, holding back the curtain.

I stepped inside.

The room was dark and round, with an enormous disc at its center the size of our dining table. And projected on the disk was a flickering, moving image of the Pacific Ocean.

"Wow," I said, stepping closer.

"I thought you'd like it," Lily said.

And I did. Because it wasn't an image of the past. It was a projection of now. We were seeing the present as art.

Everything was flattened, circular, warped. But it was still recognizable. It was still Bayport.

Lily was standing so close to me. Her hand brushing against mine. And then she reached out and clasped my hand in hers.

She smiled at me, her face lit up in the glow from the camera obscura, and I felt myself shimmering with happiness.

And then a loud family of tourists in Pismo Beach sweatshirts thundered in, ruining the whole thing.

"Guess we should go," Lily said.

And I realized we weren't holding hands anymore, or standing quite so close together. That subconsciously we'd stopped what we were doing for fear of someone noticing.

I'd never had to do that before. It was all so new, not just being on a date with a girl, but being on a date where we had to be cautious.

We slipped outside, taking a seat on one of the benches along the beachfront hiking path. The plants were a wild tangle, and you could hear the ocean crashing onto the rocks below, and everywhere the sunlight was soft and warm and perfect.

"Well?" Lily asked. "You going to sit next to me, or are we leaving room for the Holy Spirit?"

I snorted and scooted closer, briefly resting my head on her shoulder.

"Thank you," I said seriously. "For bringing me here."

"You're a photographer; it's a giant camera," Lily said. "It seemed like a safe bet."

"But I'm not," I confessed. "A photographer, I mean. I haven't taken a photo since my mom died."

Lily turned toward me, frowning.

It was so easy to tell Lily things. And so I explained about how she'd bought me the camera, and how difficult it was to bring myself to capture a world without her in it, and to take pictures she'd never see.

"So Mr. Saldana's been giving me these photography books," I said.

"He does that," Lily said. "Means he likes you."

"He does not," I protested, uncomfortable with the compliment. "But he gave me one by John Berger. And it explained how our relationship to the subject defines what we see. So, if you looked at a picture of my mom, it would conjure up her presence. But if I took one, it would define her absence. And that's the trouble. Every photo I take defines her absence."

"But maybe it's better to define things," Lily said, considering. "So you know exactly what you've lost, and what you still have left."

She stared out at the ocean for a moment, and I stared out, too, wondering what she saw in it.

"Losing a parent is awful," Lily went on. "But you can't let it hold you back from pursuing the things you love. Because a life without beauty and art isn't a life worth living."

Lily smiled at me, her soft warm hand reaching for mine, and her fingers stroking my palm. She was right, I realized. I'd been letting so many things hold me back. Maybe it was time I started pushing myself forward.

"How did I get so lucky?" I asked, leaning into her.

"Not that I'm advocating for this at all," Lily said, "but you *did* show me topless photos."

I stared at her in surprise, but she was laughing, and I realized I was too. With Lily, somehow that horrible night had become bearable. And that was no small thing.

"I'm going to kiss you now," Lily said solemnly, "because if I kiss you after lunch, we'll both have onion breath."

"Spoiler," I accused. But then her soft lips pressed against mine, and I didn't say anything at all. She tasted like lip gloss and happiness, like trips to museums and cookies fresh from the oven and cheeseburgers on the beach.

Being here, being together, felt surreal, like all of it was an elaborate dream, the good kind that kept all of my problems at bay. And I didn't ever want to wake up.

We got lunch from a taco truck in the parking lot of a gas station. It didn't look like anything special, but there was such a long line that it had to be. When we finally got to the front, the smell of spit-roasted meat was amazing, and I'd mentally upped my order from three tacos to four. We got plates of al pastor and Mexican Cokes and took them over to the curb.

"What's the difference?" I asked.

"Cane sugar," Lily said. "There's no high fructose corn syrup."

"I didn't know it was possible to be a nerd about soda," I teased, balancing my plate of tacos on my lap.

"Oh, it's possible." Lily assured me, squeezing more lime onto her tacos. "God, I could eat a dozen of these."

Lily was right, we did have onion breath. It was also so, so worth it.

When we pulled up to the curb on our block, I didn't want it to end. I wanted to lose myself in Lily, to spend the rest of the evening with her and then tomorrow and tomorrow and tomorrow, locked in our own private world where nothing else mattered except us.

"Getting out?" she asked.

And I realize we'd been stopped there a while.

Because this was where the kiss was supposed to be. Except there wasn't going to be one. Because of me.

"Nope. I live here now, in this car," I announced, scrunching down.

Lily laughed.

"I really like you, Sasha Bloom, even if you did give me your period."

"I really like you, Lily Chen, even if you do have onion breath," I returned.

"Hey, yours is worse!" she teased.

And I wanted so badly to kiss her goodbye. To take her face in my hands and press my lips against hers. To feel the flutter of her eyelashes, the curve of her cheek, the soft slick of her lip gloss against mine.

But my grandmother was out front, pruning her rosebushes, so I just said goodbye instead.

CHAPTER 25

I TURNED SEVENTEEN ON THURSDAY.

I didn't want to be seventeen, because my mom had never known me as a seventeen-year-old, and she never would. The rituals I was used to, the small personal ways the two of us always celebrated things, were gone.

No silly plastic tiara hung on my doorknob for me to wear to breakfast. And there weren't going to be pancakes in the kitchen, studded with chocolate chips spelling out my age.

I wondered if my grandparents had forgotten my birthday altogether. Or if we were going to ignore it. But then, either of those was better than making a big deal of it.

When I came down to breakfast, there was a card on the kitchen island, alongside a yogurt and a banana.

"There's the birthday girl!" my grandfather said, pouring coffee into his travel thermos. Pearl danced at his feet, begging for coffee. "All right, all right, you little monster," he told her, and then he bent down, letting her lick the spoon he'd used to stir in creamer.

My grandmother took that exact moment to come in, and she wasn't amused.

"Coffee, Joel? She's a *dog*."

"It won't hurt her," my grandfather said, gazing lovingly at the little fluffball.

They were *so* weird about their dog.

"Sasha, sit down and open your card," she scolded.

When I did, they stared at me, as though waiting for something. I stared back, confused. I'd opened it. There wasn't a check inside.

"Well, aren't you going to read it out loud?" she asked.

It was a grocery store card, which my grandmother had signed for the both of them, "Love, Grandma and Grandpa," no personal message included.

"Oh, sure," I said, and then I did, while my grandparents looked on and beamed.

"We got you a little something," my grandfather said, taking a bright blue Tiffany & Co. box from his suit pocket.

It was a silver necklace with a heart-shaped charm. The kind of nice, generic thing I'd seen on plenty of pretty, popular girls. The kind of necklace the granddaughter they wanted would have loved. So I pretended I loved it.

They'd also made dinner reservations for tonight, at this "fun Italian place," according to my grandfather.

"I asked Cole to join us," my grandmother said, taking a sip of her coffee.

I stared at her with a dull sense of horror.

"What?" I said, confused. "*How?*"

"Facebook," she said proudly. "How else?"

Oh god. This was awful. She'd kept asking when he was coming to dinner, and instead of telling the truth, I'd made excuses. And now he was coming whether I'd invited him or not.

"I just figured," she went on, "he can't be too busy to celebrate your birthday dinner."

"Uh-huh," I said weakly.

It was fine, I tried to convince myself. I'd just make Cole say he was sick or had something come up. Because no way was I sitting through a dinner with him and my grandparents.

So I ate my fruit and yogurt and pretended to be cheerful, even though this was by far starting off to be the worst birthday I'd had in a while.

Lily's car was full of balloons. There were even streamers tied to the headrests. And a box of donuts sat on the cup holder. Rainbow sprinkle, because of course.

"Happy You're Old Day!" Adam said as I climbed in. He helpfully pelted me with one of the balloons. I loved how oblivious he was to what was really going on between Lily and me. It made it so much easier to pretend, but so much harder to be alone.

"Wow, you guys went all out." I glanced down at the donuts, and then up at Lily, who grinned.

"Every birthday should start with sprinkles," she said.

It was the opposite philosophy from my grandmother, who apparently believed that every birthday should start with fat-free Greek yogurt and the realization that she was quietly messaging my friends' moms on the internet.

I ate a donut, trying not to think about it. I mostly wanted to pretend it wasn't happening.

When we got to school, I mumbled an excuse about needing to print something in the library, and then made a beeline for Cole's locker.

Thankfully, he was alone that day, instead of chatting with his sporty boy friends who were always sipping on protein drinks. He looked exhausted, and like he'd lost weight. He was staring at nothing, just some distant point inside his open locker, and I was almost embarrassed to interrupt.

"Cole!" I called, giving him some warning.

"Oh, hey," he said. The transformation was instant. He ran a hand through his hair and leaned against his locker with a smirk. Just like that, he was back to picture-perfect. "Happy birthday, Freshman."

"I'm so sorry," I said. "You don't have to come to dinner."

"First of all, your grandmother messaged my mom on Facebook to invite me, so yeah, I kind of do," Cole said, his eyes crinkling around the corners.

"It's not funny," I said.

"It's *hilarious*," he said. "Also it's a free Italian dinner on a random Thursday. I'm so down."

"You're so down," I repeated.

"Better than eating Postmates by myself," he said, with a rare flash of vulnerability. And then he coughed and acted embarrassed, like he'd confessed something he shouldn't.

And I realized I had no idea what his life was like. There'd been hints of it: the dark comments about his brother, the asides about his dad being on top of his grades, the way his mom never seemed to stop working.

"Your parents aren't home?" I asked, confused.

"No, they are," Cole said, and then he paused, as though mentally debating how much he wanted to say. "It's just . . . complicated."

"Fine," I relented. "But if you come, you have to be on your best behavior."

"Scout's honor."

"You were never a Boy Scout," I accused.

"Shows what you know, Freshman."

Cole leaned one arm against his locker, looming over me. It felt very boy of him, and all of a sudden, it felt so strange, the two of us standing there together.

He was flirting. And it was so disorienting, because I couldn't tell if I was flirting back, or if I was just talking. Oh god, was it possible I did nothing *but* flirt? Looking back, half of the conversations I'd had with Lily had been total flirtations, little nudges of *hey, I like you, you're cute,* even if I wasn't aware of them at the time.

More important, did *Cole* think I was flirting back? Because I wasn't.

The bell rang, and I realized I was halfway across campus from my first period.

The Italian place was a terrible idea. I knew it the moment we arrived, Cole holding open the door of my grandfather's car for me so everyone could see what a gentleman he was. I wanted to kill him for it, and for dressing up and combing his hair and bringing me flowers.

My grandmother had melted over the flowers, and she talked nonstop about how thoughtful they were, and how she had the perfect vase for them. Cole caught my eye and tried not to laugh.

The restaurant was down one of the little streets just off Ocean, which was filled with older boutiques and businesses, all done up in clapboard for a nautical vibe. Out front, a large sign boasted that it was "Family Owned and Operated Since 1978." The front porch was crammed with families waiting for their tables to open up, and inside, most tables had booster seats or kids coloring in their menus with crayons. There weren't any seats left on the porch, so the four of us stood around awkwardly.

And that was before I saw the magician. He couldn't have been older than fifteen, swimming in his polyester suit. He was going around asking people to pick a card or keep their eye on the foam ball as he made it pass through a plastic cup.

I hated close-up magic. Mostly, I hated the moment

during the trick when I knew that I was being duped, that I was being forced to look at one thing so I wouldn't see something else. Misdirection, it was called. A diversion from the truth.

I was never awed by the trick, in the end. I was always just frustrated I'd been so easy to deceive. But my grandfather loved the magician. The loud, happy boom of his laugh made more than a few heads turn in our direction as the kid produced my grandfather's three of clubs from inside his wallet.

I suppose I should have been relieved that my grandfather was such an easy mark, all things considered.

My phone buzzed in my purse, and I dug it out one-handed.

Hey, I still need to give you your birthday present! Lily texted. **You home?**

No, at bday dinner with my grandparents ughhh, I wrote back.

Anywhere good? she asked.

Will report back. There's a magician, and my grandfather is into it.

There were three dots while Lily was typing.

"Sasha, put that away," my grandmother scolded. "Honestly."

"Sorry," I said, tucking my phone back into my bag.

Finally, our table was ready.

"The menu's yours to take home," our server said. "You can color it in, if you'd like."

He offered Cole and me a cup full of crayons and winked, which was a little weird.

"All yours, kiddo," Cole said, pushing me the cup.

I shot him a dark look.

"Your mom used to go crazy for this place," my grandfather said, which I doubted, unless she was eight. "Every time we came, she ordered the spumoni. Loved that stuff."

So that's why we were here. I'd been wondering.

"It must be really hard for you all to celebrate without her," Cole said sincerely.

"Thank you," my grandmother said, reaching out and patting his hand. Coming from her, a hand pat was basically the same thing as a full-body hug.

"But it's been wonderful getting to spend so much time with our granddaughter," my grandfather added, acting surprisingly sincere. "Silver linings."

It was strange to hear him say that, and to hear my grandparents being sentimental.

"We're lucky we didn't lose you, too," my grandfather went on.

I stared at him in surprise. That hadn't even occurred to me. I'd always thought their taking me in was a burden, not a relief.

And then I felt a soft elbow in my side.

"What's he talking about?" Cole whispered. "Were you in a car accident or something?"

He looked so concerned, and the strange part was that he wasn't faking.

"Earthquake," I whispered back.

"Whoa. You never told me that," he accused, his concerned expression deepening.

I shrugged, busying myself with folding a little zigzag out of my straw wrapper. Of course I hadn't told him. We'd never talked about anything important.

"So, Cole, I hear you're the one to watch on the soccer team this year," my grandfather put in.

"I wouldn't say that," Cole said. "There are lots of great players. Do you know Ethan Barnsdale at all? He's one of our best forwards."

Cole chatted with my grandparents about soccer, draining his second glass of Coke. I was so bored that I actually took out some of the crayons and started coloring in the menu.

When the waiter took our order, Cole added on "a basket of garlic knots, if that's okay?" looking to my grandfather for approval. He ate practically all of them, plus three slices of pizza.

"Wow, you sure can put it away," my grandfather said, shaking his head and laughing. "I played football when I was your age, and you're not going to believe this, but I could polish off an entire pizza."

"I believe it, sir," Cole said politely.

It was so strange, watching my grandfather bro around with Cole. He'd never done that with my dad. But then, he'd never liked my father, who was always talking about how all he needed was to get discovered off one gig, and picked up by a manager, and then it would happen for him. The way my dad told it, he was always two steps away from becoming the next Lenny Kravitz, and if we didn't believe that, it was because we didn't have vision.

I'd gotten a birthday email from him, which I hadn't deleted, but hadn't opened either. I reached for another slice of pizza, and my grandmother frowned at me in warning.

"Sasha, you already had one."

I hesitated, pulling my hand back. And then Cole dropped the slice onto my plate with a wink.

"Come on, Sash, you gotta keep up," he teased. "I've lapped you twice at least."

I was weirdly touched.

Still, that didn't mean I was having a good time. This was my mom's birthday restaurant. And Cole wasn't my boyfriend. No one had bothered to ask me what I wanted, or where I wanted to eat, or how much, or who I wanted to invite. Everything had been chosen for me. And I hated that.

I wished I could choose for myself. And then I realized I had: Lily.

My grandmother made a comment about Mock Trial that I half missed.

"Didn't you quit?" Cole asked.

I swear my heart stopped beating.

"No," I said, hoping he got the message. "I thought about quitting, but I went back to it."

"Oh," he said. "Right. Right. I remember."

And then I felt his foot nudge mine under the table, like, *I gotcha, we're lying about this.*

He cleverly swerved the conversation back to my grandmother, and how his mom was thinking about starting her own book club, and I smiled at him, grateful. I got that he realized he'd messed things up with me, and then made a disaster of the apology, but I didn't see why it mattered to him.

Somehow, without our noticing, my grandfather had ordered the spumoni.

It went down in front of me in an agonizing display of clapping servers, with a trick birthday candle stuck in, so that no matter how many times I blew it out, it kept flickering back to life, drawing out my impossibly awkward birthday dinner even longer.

CHAPTER 26

"I STILL CAN'T FIGURE OUT HOW he did that trick with the red ball," my grandfather said, shaking his head as he pulled into the garage. "That was neat."

"It sure was," Cole said, nudging my shoe with the toe of his sneaker. "Well, thank you for dinner."

"Anytime," my grandmother purred. "I'm just so thrilled to see you kids spending time together."

"Come on, Elle," my grandfather said. "Let's give them a moment alone."

Before I could say anything, they'd gone inside.

I stared at Cole, in my grandparents' garage, standing amid all the clutter from someone else's life. An old baseball glove dangled from a half-open storage bin, poised to catch a ball that was never coming.

Was that my mother's? Had she played softball as a kid? I'd never asked. It had never seemed important. And now it was just another conversation we'd never have.

"So," Cole said, stretching. "How'd I do on the Boy Scout part?"

"Acceptable." I hefted the bouquet of flowers, pink and orange roses from Trader Joe's. "These were a nice touch."

"Those are for real. You only turn seventeen once," he said.

"Well, thanks," I said. "All right, this is the part where you go home. I'll, uh, walk you to your car."

"Such a gentleman," Cole teased, and I rolled my eyes.

At the curb, Cole leaned against the side of his Land Rover, smiling down at me.

"Don't I get a birthday kiss?" he asked.

"It's *my* birthday," I protested.

"Oh, right," Cole said, his eyes glittering with mischief. "I guess that means *I* owe *you* a kiss."

"Don't even think about it," I warned, just as he was about to lean in.

"That's just making me think about it more," he complained, but he held his hands up and backed away.

I waited as he climbed into his car. He rolled down the passenger side window.

"See you tomorrow, Freshman," he called. And then he drove away so quickly that his tires squealed against the asphalt.

I turned back to the house, and that's when I saw Lily sitting on our front steps, a homemade birthday cake on her lap.

Oh no.

Oh no, oh no, oh no.

This couldn't be happening. Because I knew what it looked like, and it looked bad. Very bad.

"Hi," I said guiltily.

"What the hell, Sasha?" she fumed.

I'd never seen her so furious.

"Can I just explain—"

"—Explain what?" she retorted. "You said you were at dinner with your grandparents, so I baked a cake to surprise you. And then I saw the car and thought, huh, that's weird, that looks like Cole's car. And then I saw *you*. With *him*."

"It's not—"

"Did he give you *flowers*?"

We both stared down at the bouquet I was holding.

"Yes, but—" I started.

"Which is it, Sasha?" she demanded. "Are you *his* girlfriend or mine?"

"I'm not—it's not." I tried again. "There's nothing between Cole and me."

"Which is why he was at your birthday dinner," she said sarcastically. "A dinner you conveniently didn't want me to know about. So thanks for that." And then her eyes went wide. "Oh my god. That night at the concert. I had to *drag* you away from him."

"You did *not*," I protested.

"He was *all* over you," Lily said. "And then you fed me that bullshit about keeping us a secret? I should have known! I thought you wanted to tiptoe around because you're still in the closet, not because you're a cheat and a liar."

Lily let out a cross between a sob and a gasp. Her shoulders were shaking, and her fists were clenched, and the cake sat forgotten behind her on the steps.

I was close to tears myself. They were threatening to pour out, hot and angry, but I wasn't going to cry. Not now. Not yet.

"Cole's just a friend," I promised.

"Does *he* know that?" Lily asked. And then, without waiting for an answer, she added, "Yeah. I didn't think so."

"I just—I didn't want anyone to get hurt," I said, my voice small and watery.

"Lie," Lily accused. "Because you, Sasha Bloom, are a coward. You're so terrified of people not liking you that you tell them whatever they want to hear. But you know what? Hurting the people you care about is worse than not being liked."

She was tearing me apart. I was in ribbons. Shreds. I was soggy confetti, stuck to the sidewalk. I was a spill, a stain, an absolutely terrible excuse for a human being.

It was the worst thing anyone had ever said to me. I felt small and worthless and horrible. And I hated it. This time, when the tears bubbled up, I didn't stop them.

"No, it's not like that," I said.

"It's *exactly* like that," Lily corrected. "You didn't want to hurt anyone? Bullshit. You lied because it was easier. Because the truth is always hard. Because being queer is hard, and coming out is hard, and it never stops being hard. The world keeps shoving into you. But you stand tall anyway. You take up space anyway. At least, I've tried to. And I thought you were with me. But then you shoved into me, too."

"Lily, I'm so sorry," I said.

"I know you are," she said. "But you hurt me. So right now, I don't really care about your feelings."

She stormed out of there, leaving me on my lawn with the sickening aftertaste of what I'd done.

And I deserved it. Oh god, I deserved it. I'd ruined everything.

I started up the front steps, tremendously upset, shaking, feeling the bile rise in my throat. My birthday cake was still sitting on the steps. Chocolate frosting, with white candles arranged in a grid, like the lamppost forest.

I crouched down to rescue it, but in a grand stroke of irony, I couldn't carry both the cake and the flowers. So I left the flowers on the porch.

They'd live. Although I wasn't sure I wanted to.

What I wanted was to scramble onto Lily's backyard trampoline with my birthday cake and cup my hands around hers as a shield while she struck a match. I wanted to blow out the lamppost forest of candles. When she told me to make a wish, I wanted to lean forward and kiss her instead, because that was better than making a wish that would never come true.

I wanted us to eat as many slices as we wanted, or maybe just stick our forks straight into the cake. And I wanted us to lie back and stare up at the terrible stars and the blinking lights of the airplanes trying to make their curfew.

I wanted us to talk for hours. About what it was like to celebrate a birthday without a parent, and how hard it felt to lose your traditions, and how grateful I was for the way she'd decorated her car, because I'd never had a friend, or a boyfriend—or a girlfriend—who would go to that kind of trouble for me before. I wanted us to talk about silly things, like which Hogwarts houses we'd sort the contestants on this season of *Great British Bake Off* into, and what was the deal with that fish-shaped ice cream cone on her Instagram, and did she think I'd look good with bangs?

But I'd messed up, and I couldn't do any of that. I couldn't have any of that. All I could do was march inside, holding her beautiful cake, which was tainted beyond repair.

My grandmother was waiting in the foyer. So desperate to hear how it had gone with her precious friend's perfect grandson. To know everything about me without actually knowing *anything* about me.

"Sasha, what's going on?" she asked, frowning. "I heard yelling."

"We broke up," I blubbered. "We broke up, and it's all my fault."

I was talking about Lily, not Cole, but she didn't know that.

"What happened? What did you do? Sasha, talk to me."

"I just want to be alone," I said. "Please throw this away."

I handed her the cake, and then I bolted for the stairs. Pearl followed worriedly at my heels, whining.

"You can come," I told her.

I scooped her into my arms, hugging her tight.

And then I slammed the door to my dead mother's room and lay on the bed with someone else's dog, my eyes heavy with tears.

School the next day was predictably terrible. I wondered if Lily would wait at the curb for our carpool, or if that was over.

And then I realized that I didn't want to find out. So I left early, walking to school with my headphones on, listening to gloomy breakup music, figuring that if anyone ever made a movie of my life, I might as well help them out by choosing the soundtrack.

Even with my headphones, I still felt Lily's car drive up behind me, as if by magic. I knew it was her even before she sped past, windows down, Tegan and Sara blasting. I caught a glimpse of Adam's face in the passenger seat, staring out at me with concern.

And then it was gone, and I was left alone with my sad music and my impractical shoes that would almost certainly give me blisters.

"What's going on?" Adam asked at the lockers. "Are you guys fighting? Lily won't talk to me about it."

"Yeah," I said with a sad smile. "We're fighting."

"So apologize," Adam said.

I sighed.

"I wish I knew how."

But I barely knew how to get through the day, much less repair the damage I'd caused. I saw Lily between classes, just for a moment. She glared at me in the crowded humanities courtyard, angling to march straight past, with her chin jutting stubbornly.

And then some hulking football dudes started fake shoving into each other, and everyone skirted around, and for one moment, Lily and I were so close, our shoulders inches apart. But the energy radiating off her was so hostile.

Weirdly, while Lily wanted nothing to do with me, Cole was the exact opposite. He was waiting by my locker at lunch to ask me why I'd never told him about the earthquake.

"Why do you even care?" I asked.

"Because we're friends," he insisted, frowning.

Were we friends? I wasn't sure. I knew Lily couldn't stand him, because of what he'd done when they were fourteen. And even though I was still upset with him over the photos he'd taken, and his lackluster apology, I couldn't bring myself to write him off completely.

The forlorn way he looked, sitting at his lunch table sandwiched between two couples. His comment about eating delivery dinner by himself, and his allusions to everything at home being complicated. How his drinking and smoking seemed to be an escape from something. His soccer injuries that Ethan never seemed to have, even though they were both on the team. His flashes of insight, and the way, when he teased me about being a weirdo, it was never mean, only delighted.

He'd had my back at my birthday dinner, defending me to my grandmother about the pizza and lying for me about Mock Trial. There was more beneath the surface than I'd initially thought. And I wasn't sure if anyone else noticed. Which had to be hard, being so obviously someone else than the person everyone else saw.

"Yeah, I guess we're friends," I agreed.

"For now," Cole added cockily, making me wince.

I was about to correct him, but then some soccer bro came past, shouting "Colon!" and jumping all over him, and Cole laughed, transforming into a deep-voiced jock, and I slipped away while he was distracted.

•••

I pretended to have a migraine to get out of Phys Ed. I hadn't been to the nurse's office since Lily had taken me with my sprained ankle, the day she'd first offered to drive me home, and it felt fitting to be back here again now that that was over.

I didn't know what to do. How I was supposed to face her at lunch or in class, or pretty much ever, especially since our friends had no idea what was wrong. Dating in secret had seemed like a good plan at first, but now it meant having to carry around this enormous amount of pain and to lie about it.

Now I'd broken Lily's heart, and she couldn't tell anyone, which was like hurting her all over again.

It was a mess. My mess.

And I hated it so much. I wanted to hide from it forever. To crawl under the covers and wait for it to pass.

I didn't know how to talk to Adam or Ryland or Mabel. Or anyone. Lily got to keep everything she'd loaned me, while I lost almost everything that made life in Bayport bearable.

I had the house to myself that afternoon. My grandmother was putting the finishing touches on a pet adoption fund-raiser, and Pearl was at the groomer's, and my grandfather was at the office.

The emptiness felt bigger without the dog. Or maybe the sum of my own emptiness and the huge, echoing house that was empty in a different way was just too much to bear. It was Friday, and the weekend stretched in front of me, long and lonely.

I didn't know what to do about Lily. How to make her listen. How to explain. Because it wasn't what she thought, and because I was sorry, and because I didn't know what else to do.

I picked up my phone.

Can we please, please talk? I texted.

But she didn't reply. And I didn't blame her.

I knew what it had looked like. How hurtful it must have been for her to see that. To see me with him, of all people.

Cole was just a friend. Nothing more.

Does he know that? Lily had asked.

I wasn't sure.

I went into the kitchen and got myself a snack. Unlike after my mom died, when I'd lost my appetite entirely, this disaster with Lily had left me starving. I ate a bagel, which I was surprised we even had in the house, and then some of my grandfather's stash of chocolate-covered almonds, which he kept at the very top of the pantry.

Lily still hadn't texted me back. I wondered what she was doing, and if she was thinking about me.

The seconds trickled by in agony.

Was it really only three o'clock?

I couldn't concentrate on anything. It was hot outside, the sun blazing stubbornly, despite it being halfway through

November. So I changed into my bathing suit and grabbed a book I'd read a dozen times, taking it into the backyard.

The pool is calming because our bodies are seventy percent water.

Actually, they're seventy percent dinosaur pee.

I tried to concentrate on my book, but it was no use. Lily was everywhere. In the blank space between the paragraphs, I found myself thinking about the smell of her perfume. In the margins of the page, the way it felt to press my lips against hers. My broken heart was a bookmark, marking the place where she was supposed to text me back, and where I checked my phone again to see that she hadn't.

I closed my eyes, feeling the pressure of uncried tears against my eyelids. Even with the sun warm against my face, even with the pool and my bathing suit and a book, I couldn't do it. I couldn't numb myself to the world and lose track of time the way I had over the summer.

Instead, I was all too aware of each painful moment. I wondered if Lily was home, if she was standing at some window staring out at my yard, at me. If she missed me the way I missed her.

And then I worried she didn't. That, without me, she was fine. With Adam and Ryland and Mabel, with Art Club and her awesome accepting family and her fancy house and fancy car.

Without her, I was nothing. A sketch of a person I didn't want to be, all shadows and imperfections. I wanted to crumple it up and start again, the way Mr. Saldana let us in class.

I left my book on the chair, closed my eyes, and started walking.

It only took a few steps before there was nothing beneath my feet except air. Before I plunged into the freezing water.

I let myself sink to the bottom of my grandparents' pool, and then I stared up at the wavy surface, far above my head. At the pale, anemic sunlight. At the world that kept fracturing around me, no matter what I did.

Maybe I was a fault line, and that's why no one around me was safe. I was made of broken pieces, and it was only a matter of time before they shifted and everyone I loved got hurt.

The pool hadn't been heated, and the cold was almost unbearable. But I deserved it, I told myself. I hurt her. I ruined it. I screwed up.

I needed air. Needed to breathe. My lungs screamed, but I forced myself to stay under, to endure it for a few seconds longer, because at least the pain of frigid water and empty lungs was a pain that didn't have to do with my mother dying, or Lily hating me.

I crashed to the surface, gulping for air.

Wanting to live. Needing to keep going. But the worst part was, no matter where I went or what I did, I still felt so alone. I was shedding the people I cared about like ballast, no matter how much I tried to hold on.

CHAPTER 27

"SO TODAY'S THE DAY," MY GRANDFATHER said at breakfast the next morning. I had no idea what he was talking about. Or why we were eating bagels, instead of something healthier.

I nodded, my mouth full, and mumbled an approximation of "yep."

Lily still hadn't texted me back, and I was miserable. I'd wanted to wallow in bed forever, but my grandmother had insisted I wake up so we could all have breakfast and "get going."

"Are you all ready?" she asked, reaching for the cream cheese.

"Ready?" I echoed.

"For the big event," my grandmother said.

I stared at her, confused.

"What are you talking about?" I asked.

"The Mock Trial match against St. Stephens," my grandmother said. "I saw it on the school Facebook page."

My chest clenched as I tried not to panic. This couldn't be happening.

"Really, Sasha, you should have said something," my grandmother went on. "If I hadn't looked . . . well."

"I had to cancel a round of golf at the last minute, so I didn't miss it," my grandfather put in.

I wanted to die.

I wanted the ground to open up beneath me, for an earthquake to happen right at that moment, for any disaster, natural or man-made, to divert their attention so I could make my escape.

"Oh, um, you guys don't need to come to that," I said. "I don't even think it's allowed, actually."

"Nonsense," my grandmother said. "It was right there on the event, friends and family welcome."

She took out her iPad and showed me the Facebook page, the font blown up huge.

Mock Trial head-to-head: Baycrest vs. St. Stephens, friends and family welcome! the event read.

"How early do you need to be there, sweetheart?" my grandfather asked me.

Shit. I was going to have to tell them.

I took a deep breath, my heart hammering.

"Um, Grandma? Grandpa?" I said. "I actually quit Mock Trial. I'm really sorry."

The room went deathly silent. The burble of the coffee pot seemed too loud all of a sudden.

"You quit," my grandmother repeated flatly.

"Even after we discussed it?" my grandfather added.

"I tried to tell you it wasn't for me, but you didn't listen."

"When?" my grandmother demanded. "When did you quit?"

"Maybe a month ago?" I said. It came out like a question.

"Right after we told you it was a bad idea," my grandfather said, not missing a beat. Of course not. He was a lawyer, which meant he only asked questions when he already knew the answer.

"I was only a timekeeper," I said, babbling nervously. "You were supposed to start as a freshman and work your way up, and because I didn't they were punishing me. I had to make photocopies—"

"Photocopies?" my grandmother interrupted. "You quit because someone asked you to make *photocopies*?"

"No, I—" I said, realizing the conversation had already derailed. No matter what I said, I couldn't make them listen. And I hated that. "You don't get it!"

I didn't know how I'd started yelling, but it had happened, somehow.

"What don't we get?" my grandmother demanded angrily. "That you quit when something got hard? You made a promise, and you broke it, and you lied to us! And god knows where you've been going after school if it wasn't to Mock Trial!"

"Art Club!" I shouted back. "I was going to Art Club, okay?"

My fists were clenched at my sides, and my chest was heaving, and I didn't know whether to cry or to scream. Everything was turning into a complete mess and it didn't matter what I did, the mess kept growing.

"We need to know where you are!" my grandmother shouted. "What if something *happens*?"

"Like what? An EARTHQUAKE?" I was really going now. "Because I knew exactly where Mom was and she still *died*. And now she's gone, and I am NOT OKAY! And you're making it worse! All you've done is to make everything WORSE!" I screamed.

"All we've done is love you and do what's best for you," my grandmother retorted. "You're the one who doesn't come to us! You never ask for anything!"

"I'm not supposed to ask! Mom never made me ask!"

"Well, I'm trying," Eleanor shouted.

"No, you're not," I said. "You're punishing me for her mistakes!"

"I'm making sure you don't repeat them! But no one *ever* listens to me. If Alice listened to me, she'd still be alive!"

"And I wouldn't!" I shot back. "That's what you want, isn't it? For my mom to be some fancy lawyer with some fancy husband you can have dinner with at the club!"

"No one's saying that, sweetheart," my grandfather said, trying to step in.

"She literally just said that!" I accused.

"I don't want to hear this!" my grandmother roared back. "Go to your room!"

"You mean HER ROOM!" I shouted.

As I barricaded myself inside, my heart was pounding, and my eyes prickled with tears, all too ready to spill out.

I couldn't stop them, and I didn't want to. Everything was terrible. So I cried into my pillow until I felt shivery from the shame. What had I been thinking? That I could lie to them forever? Of course they were going to find out I'd quit Mock Trial. It was only a matter of time.

I'd never shouted like that in my life. I didn't even know I could. And some of the things we'd said had been horrendous. I'd accused my grandparents of wishing I didn't exist.

I really was a fault line. A harbinger of disaster and ruin and disappointment.

At least they'd only found out about Mock Trial, and not about me and Lily.

Lily.

I wanted to talk to her so badly. To explain what had happened so she could tell me how to fix it. But I couldn't. She didn't want to hear from me right now. Especially about Mock Trial.

There had to be someone I could talk to.

And then it came to me: *Cole.*

I called him before I could change my mind, and I stared down at my ringing phone, breathless. There was no turning back. If I hung up now, he'd still see a missed call from me.

"Hey," he said, sounding surprised. His voice was gravelly, and I heard him yawn and stretch. "What's up? It's crazy early."

He was lying in bed, I knew. He was certainly being loud about it. Probably wearing nothing but his boxer shorts. I tried not to think about them, Calvin Klein and black, which of course meant that I did.

"My grandparents found out I quit Mock Trial and have been lying about it for like a month," I said, sniffling.

"Shit," he said. "And they let you keep your phone?"

"Yep. Old people," I said, which made him laugh. His laugh made me snort, and for a tiny moment, I didn't feel so terrible. "They're really pissed, though."

"I'll bet," Cole said, and then he was silent for a long moment before saying, "You know, sometimes adults are wrong. And they get really angry about it, and you think they're angry at you. But really they're pissed because the world is changing and they can't keep up."

I was playing with my earbuds, wrapping and rewrapping the cord around my fingers. But after Cole said that, I let the cord dangle, surprised.

He was so right. They weren't mad at me—they were upset at being wrong.

"Wow," I said.

"Nailed it, right?" Cole sounded far too pleased with himself.

"Completely," I said, surprised by his insight.

"Anyway," he went on, "don't let it get you down. If you know you made the right call, stand by it. Make 'em see your side."

"I guess," I said.

Maybe that would work for Cole Edwards, with his golden hair and his golden touch, but I didn't think I could stand up to my grandparents like that. To convince them that they were wrong and I was right.

"You all good?" Cole asked. "'Cause I really have to pee."

"Then pee," I told him, rolling my eyes and hanging up.

CHAPTER 28

IN A MOVE EVERYONE SAW COMING, I was grounded. And to fill the emptiness on my résumé where Mock Trial should have gone, my grandparents decided I'd start helping out at my grandpa's firm two afternoons a week.

It sounded awful, but I knew I was in no position to protest. Especially after the fight we'd had. I hated that they were upset with me. That I had let them down. But then, I'd been doing that a lot lately.

Sasha Bloom: Most Likely to Disappoint.

And the disappointments kept on coming. Mr. Saldana reminded us all in Studio Art that we had two weeks before our submissions were due for the gallery show.

"Remember, if you're more comfortable in a medium we're not exploring this semester, you're welcome to hand in outside work," he said in class on Monday, his gaze resting on mine for just a moment. "Just so long as it fits through the door and doesn't require food, water, or sunlight."

I sank down in my seat. I knew he was expecting me to turn in photographs, but I didn't have any new ones. And he'd already seen all of my old work.

"While you're not receiving a grade for the work you submit," Mr. Saldana went on, "you'll be required to attend and write up half a page about one piece that spoke to you. Your grade will come from that."

A couple of students groaned.

"The grammar of criticism." He beamed. "I did warn you. If you wanted that easy A, you should have taken ceramics."

And then he passed out flyers for us to give to our friends and families, inviting them. I took one because it was the thing to do, not because I was planning on inviting my grandparents. Especially the way things were between us right now.

I spent that week adrift in a sea of high school students. The days felt sour, like expired milk. I wanted to pour them down the drain. I ate lunch alone in the library. I didn't go to Art Club. I walked to and from school, and then went to my room and did my homework and hugged the dog and checked my phone for a response from Lily that was never coming.

Dinner every night was tense and awful. My grandparents acted like I was a search engine, asking me question after question about school in a monotone, which I answered as blandly as possible. None of us knew how to fix what had broken between us. And so we tiptoed through the wreckage, pretending it wasn't there.

There were no overtures of apology, just awkward, stilted moments when everyone was chewing, and I wished desperately I were anywhere else. Pearl cried and sobbed, throwing a fit while we ate, until my grandfather pushed back his chair with alarming force and shouted at her, and my grandmother shouted at him for yelling at the dog, and I raced to put my half-finished plate into the dishwasher so I could go upstairs.

Except my hands were shaking, and somehow I missed the counter. I watched in horror as the plate smashed onto the floor.

"Shit," I swore, staring down at the fractured pieces.

"Sasha!" my grandfather boomed. "You need to be careful!"

"I know!" I said, feeling awful. "I'm sorry."

"Don't be sorry, be better," my grandmother scolded.

"I will," I said, bending down to pick up the pieces.

My grandfather scooped up Pearl before she could get into the mix of pesto and smashed porcelain. I couldn't believe I'd dropped the plate. It was so stupid of me.

Everything I touched, I ruined.

"Sasha, move," my grandmother said, coming up behind me with a Swiffer.

I backed away, letting her take care of it.

•••

Thanksgiving was on Thursday. The school week ended early, and somehow, in all the chaos of essays and midterms, I didn't see it coming until it blindsided me:

My first Thanksgiving without my mom.

Everything about it felt wrong. Instead of driving down to Bayport, I was already here. But there was nowhere else to go. We certainly weren't flying to Quebec to see my great-aunt Gail and her third husband, Ronny. Now, Thanksgiving was just a fancy meal in the house where we all lived. It made the whole thing feel like there wasn't much of a point.

Especially since everything was still so tense and awful.

My grandfather barricaded himself in his office, watching football with the volume turned up all the way. And I could hear my grandmother banging around in the kitchen. There was a loud clang, of something dropping, and then a curse.

I waited for my grandfather to shout and see if everything was okay, but he didn't. My grandmother cursed again, and then I heard the sink turn on and stay on.

My curiosity got the better of me. I felt ridiculous hiding upstairs, listening. So I wandered down to the kitchen to make sure everything was okay.

I stopped in the doorway. There was an enormous raw turkey in the sink, and my grandmother stood over it, crying. She was still in her pajamas. Her shoulders trembled, and her hand was over her mouth, and she didn't look even the tiniest bit okay.

"Grandma?" I asked.

"Oh, Sasha." She straightened up, wiping her eyes.

"Do you need any help?" I asked.

My mom and I had never helped in the kitchen. Eleanor had insisted on doing it all, deputizing us to bring ourselves, and maybe a dessert, and then telling us that she'd have a backup in case ours wasn't good. It made my mother furious.

"Oh no, no, sweetheart. I'm fine," my grandmother said.

She turned off the sink and gave me a thin smile.

"I can help," I insisted. "I want to."

I picked up a package of cranberries and tore it open.

My grandmother didn't protest. She just watched as I gathered a saucepan and a measuring cup, and then took out my phone, googling a recipe.

I stirred the berries. and it was oddly cathartic, watching as they started out separate but came together. My grandmother got to work on the turkey, and after a while, I felt her over my shoulder, checking on me.

"What are those seeds?" she asked, frowning.

"I found a recipe that said to use orange zest and whole grain mustard."

"Mustard?" Her frown deepened. "I've never heard of that in my life."

She took the spoon and lifted it to her lips as though expecting the worst. And then her expression brightened.

"You know," she said. "That's delicious."

She rested a hand on my shoulder, very softly, for the briefest moment, before pulling away and reaching for a dishcloth.

"We still have to make mashed potatoes, and rolls, and dessert," she said.

And then she got out the family recipe card and put me to work making rolls. As I mixed the dough, I noticed my grandfather hovering in the doorway, holding the dog.

"Didn't realize it was so crowded in here," he said. Something passed between the two of them that I didn't quite understand, but I pretended not to notice.

After my grandfather left, I kneaded the sticky, stretchy dough. I was glad I'd come down and offered to help. It was too much for my grandmother to do on her own, and somehow, my being in the kitchen made everything feel new, instead of highlighting how my mom was missing.

Suddenly I was blinking back tears.

"Sasha," my grandmother said, surprised. "Sweetheart, are you crying?"

"No," I croaked, swiping my nose with the back of my arm.

"I miss her too," my grandmother said. "But it's nice to have help in the kitchen again. Alice used to make those rolls."

"She did?" I asked, and then I felt foolish, because of course she had.

Here I was again, stuck in a skipped-forward repeat of my mother's childhood.

"Until she almost burned the house down," Eleanor said with a sigh. "The phone rang, and she completely forgot they were in the oven."

That sounded like my mom.

"I told her she was permanently off kitchen duty after that," my grandmother said, and I could hear the regret in her voice, the yearning for all of those lost holidays, all of those long hours she'd spent alone in the kitchen because she didn't know how to admit she'd been wrong about not wanting help.

We both stared at the skillet. And I thought, it's like she was just here. "She's supposed to be here."

I didn't realize I'd spoken that last part aloud until my grandmother said, "I know, honey. I know she is."

And somehow that made me feel better, remembering I wasn't the only one who'd lost her. I felt a tear roll down my cheek, and I realized my grandmother was sniffling too.

"Come here," she said, opening her arms.

It was an awkward hug. Her skin was cold, and she smelled of expensive creams and coffee, and she seemed as light and hollow as a bird. But I closed my eyes and held on anyway, because it was the first time I'd ever felt close to her.

Later that evening, my grandfather gave a toast about how thankful he was for his family, and everyone agreed that cranberry sauce tasted better with mustard seeds. And somehow, the frost between us seemed to thaw.

•••

I still hadn't heard from Lily by Saturday, even though I'd texted her more times than I probably should have. I pictured her up in Fairfield with her family, staring down at her phone and seeing it was me, and deciding to ignore it. Again and again and again.

Each time I picked up my phone, hoping for a missed text and finding none, it was like a small piece of my soul withered. Did she really hate me this much? Would she ever forgive me? Or even just talk to me again?

Of course, my grandparents were under the impression things had gone south between me and Cole. And while I felt extraordinarily guilty for letting them believe that, I also went along with it. It was easier than explaining the truth about my moping, or the fight my grandmother had half overheard, or the mysterious cake that I'd insisted she throw away.

It had barely been a week since we'd broken up, since the morning Lily had decorated her car for me. And I missed her so much.

I missed her in this desperate, aching way because she wasn't gone the way my mother was. She was just angry.

And I couldn't tell if her anger was permanent or temporary. If I would go on missing her forever, because she was lost to me, or if this was only a blip of misery in the middle of something bigger.

I was out walking Pearl on Saturday when I saw them come home. Lily and their parents were unloading suitcases, and Adam was running around the driveway with

Gracie while she shrieked and giggled.

"Hi!" Gracie said, spotting me. "Oh! It's the dog! Can I pet her?"

"Um, sure," I said.

My eyes searched for Lily's. They met for the briefest moment, and then Lily marched inside and didn't come out again. Gracie patted and cooed over Pearl, who was a perfectly behaved marshmallow, although her expression seemed to say, *I better be getting a treat, stat*.

"If you keep petting her like that, she'll go bald," Adam said, coming over.

"You're lying," Gracie said.

"What do you think happened to Dad's hair?" Adam shot back, and Gracie's jaw dropped. "Go ask him if you don't believe me."

Gracie shot off into the house, screaming for their dad, and I tried not to laugh.

"He'll corroborate anything," Adam said, shrugging. "How was your Thanksgiving?"

"My grandpa got a new iPhone," I said, making a face. I'd had to spend forever setting it up for him.

"That's like a six-word horror story." Adam shuddered.

"How was yours?"

"My dad and I hid out and watched *Star Trek* in the guest room," Adam said. "Also, Lily's cousins gave me shit for liking cranberry sauce."

"It's the most Thanksgiving part of Thanksgiving," I said.

"Exactly," Adam said. And then he shoved his hands into his pockets, suddenly serious. "So, um, question. What did you do to make Lil so mad?"

I shook my head, sighing.

"'Cause I'm assuming the worst," he told me. "Murder. Grand theft arson."

"It's grand theft *auto*," I told him. "You can't steal fire."

"You can *totally* steal fire," he said. "Like, the Olympic Torch? What do you think you'd get charged for if you ran off with that?" He raised an eyebrow. "Grand theft arson."

I couldn't help it, I snorted.

"Whatever you did," he went on, "can't be as bad as that."

"Worse," I said. "And now things are . . . over."

"It's not like you two were dating," Adam scoffed.

I stiffened. And then I could sense the gears turning in that freakishly smart brain of his.

"Noooo," he said. "How did I miss it? You were totally dating!"

"We were not," I protested. But I could tell he didn't believe me.

Screw it, I thought. What did it matter if Adam knew?

"Okay, yes, we were dating," I admitted. "And then I messed up."

"Shit," Adam said seriously. "Am I going to have to beat you up for hurting my sister?"

"Or you could help us get back together?"

Adam grinned.

"I like that so much better."

Now that Adam was willing to help, all I had to do was come up with a plan. Everything seemed either too grand or not enough. I wasn't looking for a huge romantic gesture, but I was hoping for a meaningful one.

And then I remembered the conversation we'd had about *Kintsugi*. About reconstructing broken pottery with gold, and how the scars from being repaired were the most beautiful part.

Lily had said it reminded her of me, and when I'd pointed out how the objects were only beautiful after they were put back together, she'd promised to hold on to me until I was whole again.

It was the best thing anyone had ever said to me, because it was about brokenness, but it was also about hope.

I went down to the garage and dug through the trash until I found the pieces of the plate I'd shattered. They looked so small and jagged. Like they weren't anything anymore. Like no matter what you did, you'd never be able to reassemble them in any meaningful way.

"Breakage is just part of the history," I reminded myself.

I washed them off and mixed together a concoction of glue and gold nail polish. And then I sat there, holding the plate until I could feel the glue drying, until there was nothing left to do but let go and hope.

And so I did. Miraculously, it held. Before, the plate had been plain. Now, with the gold cracks running through it, it was worth noticing. It was special.

I cut out a little square of paper and wrote: *PORTKEY. Leads to lifeguard stand on chopped chiles beach at 7 p.m. If Portkey doesn't work, come anyway.*

And then I texted Adam.

"Hey," he said, meeting me outside. "So what's the plan?"

"I need you to deliver this to Lily," I told him, handing over the plate.

"A broken plate?" Adam said skeptically, staring down at it.

"It's *Kintsugi,*" I told him. "And it's not broken."

"It's weird," he said.

"Your face is weird," I told him.

"Acceptable," he pronounced, and then he nodded slowly. "Okay, fine, I'll give her this exceptionally ugly ashtray, but only because riding to school in her cloud of gloom is seriously harshing my vibe."

"Trust me," I told him. "You don't have a vibe."

I changed my outfit and redid my hair about a million times that night before heading down to the beach. I didn't know what to wear that simultaneously screamed, *I'm sorry, take me back,* and *look how cute I am,* but in the end, I was pretty sure it wasn't a striped sweater, my army jacket, and skinny jeans, which is what I went with.

"Sasha?" my grandfather asked, poking his head out of the den. He was playing a game on his new phone with the volume all the way up. "Going somewhere?"

"Just walking down to the water," I said, "if that's okay?"

I didn't quite know the boundaries of what it meant to be grounded here.

"Don't forget your jacket. Or your phone," my grandfather said, and I breathed a sigh of relief.

"Got both," I told him.

"Damn!" He grimaced at his phone. "Missed again. I've been trying to get that gold coin for half an hour."

"Um, if you're really stuck, maybe google it?" I suggested.

He stared at me in surprise.

"That's so smart," he said.

"Well, see you later," I said, and then I slipped out the front door.

I didn't know what I was going to say to Lily. Just that it had to be good. And honest.

The sun was fading fast as I walked toward the white Cape Cod–style house. Whoever lived there was home, and the whole house was lit up like a beacon, or a lighthouse.

I doubted it would help me find my way.

Lily was waiting for me at the top of the lifeguard stand. I'd pictured it differently, imagining how I would get there first, and how I'd see her small figure coming toward me, across the beach. How her hair would whip in the wind, and how she'd wave.

Except I was the one doing that.

Lily didn't wave back.

"Hi," she said when I got there.

"Hi," I said, out of breath.

I climbed up and sat next to her, and we were both silent for a moment as we stared out at the dark churn of the ocean. This was it. The end of everything. Or the beginning of everything, depending on your perspective. The total and complete edge of Bayport, of California, of the continental United States, and hopefully, *hopefully,* not of us.

"I'm glad you came," I said, smiling.

"I felt like I tortured you enough," Lily said. "You're right, we do need to talk about what happened."

"Okay, good," I said.

"But I don't think you're going to like what I have to say," Lily said.

"Before you do, can I please say something?" I asked.

"Sure. It was your Portkey," Lily said, shrugging.

I took a deep breath. My heart was pounding, and I felt so nervous that I could barely sit still.

"I've known for a while I was attracted to girls," I said. "But it scared me, so I set it aside. And then I met you and I didn't want to ignore it anymore. I literally couldn't. You're amazing, and I screwed up. I lied because it was easy, and because I didn't think I'd get caught. But I did, and I made a mess. I've been trying to fix it. I *want* to fix it. Just—tell me how I can fix it."

Lily gave me a sad smile.

"I'm sorry," she said. "But I don't want to sneak around with you again. I'm not ashamed of myself, and I'm not going to hide who I am, or who I'm dating."

She stared down at her lap for a moment, and just when I thought she wasn't going to say anything else, she said, in a rush, "You need to accept yourself, Sasha. You need to live your truth, whatever that means for you. But what that means for me is that I can't be with someone who's willing to live a fake life."

"Oh," I said, feeling awful.

I'd thought—I don't know what I'd thought. That Lily would take me back, that an apology would be enough if it came with a handmade gift and a little bit of fanfare.

"I deserve better than this," she went on. "I know you didn't mean to treat me badly, but you did. I understand why, and I get that you're sorry, but that doesn't make it okay."

It hadn't worked. My medium romantic gesture hadn't been enough.

I stared out at the ocean, blinking back tears. I didn't know what else to do.

"Okay," I said, my voice thin and nothing, barely even a whisper. "Sorry."

"Me too," Lily said.

I glanced over at her, the stubborn set of her jaw, the defeated cast of her shoulders, the way the ocean breeze was rippling through her hair. And I thought, I want to kiss you here, on this lifeguard stand that feels like ours. I want to press my lips against yours and pretend the force of it is what controls the tides, the ocean, everything. Except I couldn't. Lily was right there, by my side, but that was only because she was willing to hear my apology, not because she'd forgiven me. She'd made that clear. And as much as I wished I'd been able to fix everything, I also knew that she was right.

I didn't deserve to get her back. Not like this, in secret, with the fresh-churned wake of my lies still trailing behind us.

If I gathered up every decent part of myself, Lily still deserved more. I wanted to give her the universe and then all the parallel universes alongside it. Except I was too late: It was the game we'd played the night of our first kiss, where we watched the last airplanes land.

Here we were, and it was 10:01 and now I had to keep going, even though I didn't want to. Even though I was so close that I could see the lights twinkling from the runway. There wasn't going to be an exception for me. At least, not tonight.

Lily wanted to keep the distance between us. She wanted me to know that it wasn't her job to lead me out of the closet, or to fix my brokenness. That those things were up to me. She was right. Of course she was. Just like she was right about deserving better.

So I said goodbye, and that I was sorry, and I left her there, atop the lifeguard stand in the fading twilight.

CHAPTER 29

MY GRANDPARENTS DRAGGED ME TO THE club for Sunday brunch. Apparently being grounded wasn't a get-out-of-jail-free card when it came to that kind of thing. So I ate my egg white and veggie omelet with a side of fruit, and smiled dutifully, and said hello to their friends.

Whatever fragile okayness had knitted itself back together between us was still intact, and I wasn't going to ruin it. I hadn't realized how hard this holiday was for them, too. How maybe the way they'd blown up at me over Mock Trial was part of a bigger anger.

Not that that excused anything. I couldn't stop thinking about what Lily had said to me on the beach, how she deserved better than the way I'd treated her.

The worst part was, she was right. In all of my most awful moments, Lily had been there, offering so much of herself. And what I'd offered back wasn't nearly enough. Dating in secret, and breaking her heart with a boy who had hurt both of us, and leaving her in the ruinous aftermath of my lies.

I picked at my omelet, which had gone cold and unappetizing. And then I went back to the buffet, loaded up a plate with pastries, and brought them back to our table without comment. My grandmother pursed her lips in disapproval, but my grandfather took one, mumbling that they looked good.

And I thought: I get it now. Different people expect different things from me. And you can't please everyone all of the time.

When we were finally about to leave, Cole came over to our table, smiling sheepishly. The golden swoop of his hair was less swoopy, and there were purple smudges under his eyes. He looked exhausted.

My grandparents, predictably, were thrilled to see him. I narrowed my eyes, wondering what was going on, since his family was on the opposite side of the banquet hall.

"Hey, Sasha," he said. Not, *Hey, Freshman.*

"Hi," I replied warily.

"Is there any chance I could take you to dinner tonight?" he asked.

"Um," I said, confused. Was he still doing this? Pretending for our grandparents? I'd thought we had stopped. Or maybe *I* had stopped. I couldn't remember. "I can't, because I'm grounded. But thanks for asking."

"Right," Cole said, looking disappointed. "I forgot."

"Actually—" my grandmother said. "I suppose it would be all right if you went, just for dinner."

I stared at her, surprised.

"Wait—" I said.

"Great," Cole said. "I'll pick you up at seven."

And before I could protest, he was gone.

"What happened to being grounded?" I asked.

My grandmother shrugged and took a sip of her coffee, her lipstick stamping the rim.

"We want you kids to work things out," she said.

And my heart felt heavy, because I knew she was only saying that since it was Cole.

I didn't know why Cole had asked me to dinner, but I'd told enough lies already, and I was done. So I decided not to pretend it was any kind of special occasion. But when I came downstairs in jeans and Lily's *Shakespeare on the Hill* hoodie, my hair in a messy bun, my grandmother was like, "Absolutely not, Sasha."

"It's just dinner," I said.

"Your grandma's right," my grandfather said, padding into the room with the dog tucked under his arm. "Put on some makeup and a nice dress. Boys like that."

So do girls, I thought.

"It's rude to be underdressed," my grandmother put in.

I could tell I wasn't getting out of this one, so I said fine and then went upstairs, putting on my floral dress and some mascara.

"Much better," my grandmother said when I came back down.

Cole even rang the bell, instead of idling at the curb and texting. He came inside, chatted with my grandparents for a couple of minutes, and petted Pearl so enthusiastically that the dog actually sobbed when he put her down.

"Sorry, tiny dog," he said, "but we'd better go if we don't want to miss our dinner reservation."

"Reservation?" I asked as we walked down the front steps.

"Did you think I was taking you to In-N-Out?" he asked.

"Um, yes?" I said, like it was obvious.

And then he held open the car door for me.

"Can you trust me and go with it? Please?"

So I did. Because being friends meant trusting each other. And because I could see how hard he was trying.

He took me to one of those hipster farm-to-table restaurants on the main stretch, the kind where the servers wear denim aprons and the appetizers are all flatbreads with truffle oil and cost like fourteen dollars.

"Seriously?" I said when we sat down.

"What?" Cole asked, like it wasn't weird, and like everyone in the restaurant wasn't twice our age.

It was the kind of place I might have expected Lily to choose, but not Cole. I took a deep breath, suddenly overwhelmed by the thought of how Lily and I might never eat together again. Lily, who'd had so many places she'd wanted to share with me. Now, it wasn't Lily sitting across the table, but Cole. He leaned back in his chair, his button-down shirt freshly ironed, and smiled at me.

"You down for spicy?" he asked. "Because they have this bomb chorizo flatbread we could split as an app."

"Sure," I said, wondering which alternate universe Cole had come from.

The server came over, and Cole ordered the flatbread, and two Mexican Cokes.

"They're different from the regular ones—" he started to explain.

"Because they have real cane sugar instead of corn syrup," I finished. "Yeah. I know."

The Cokes came out right away, and I took a sip of mine, trying not to think of Lily. Cole gulped his down. God. He was such a boy.

"What are we doing here?" I asked.

"Full disclosure? I needed to get the hell out of the house," Cole admitted. "This Thanksgiving break has been brutal."

"Archer?" I guessed, since his brother seemed to be the constant source of Cole's misery.

"You have no idea," he muttered.

"Yeah, because you never tell me," I said.

Cole chewed his lip for a moment before admitting, "He was my bad spotter. All of those times when I told you I got hurt during soccer. It was—well. He'd get into these dark moods, and he'd lash out. And he'd do shit like that on purpose."

"Cole," I said. "That's serious. You have to tell someone."

His face clouded.

"I thought about it," he said. "But I didn't. And now it's too late."

"It's not too late," I said, trying to be encouraging.

"Yeah, it is." Cole let out a short, angry laugh. "He's in a shit ton of trouble at school. He was dating this girl. And, uh, he got really drunk after his team lost a game, and he—fuck, I can't believe this—he sexually assaulted her."

"Oh my god," I said, staring at him in surprise.

"I know," he said. "It's so bad. My whole family's losing their mind over it. He might be expelled, and he's already been kicked off the football team. And my dad was like, 'He doesn't deserve to lose his spot,' and I said that actually he does, and there was a lot of yelling."

And then our server came over and was like, "Have you decided yet?"

Cole gave the guy a look like, bro, come on. But the server just stood there, his pencil poised over his pad.

"Um, I'll have the pork belly banh mi," Cole said, not even glancing at the menu. "Side of charred Brussels sprouts."

"Same," I said.

"Excellent choice. Your flatbread will be right up," the server said, disappearing.

"Is the girl okay?" I asked, worried.

"I think she will be," Cole said. "She might press charges. And while all of this has been going on, it made me think.

And I realized that I owe you a big apology. How I behaved at my homecoming party was messed up."

"Oh," I said, surprised. That wasn't what I was expecting him to say at all.

"Yeah," Cole went on. "I'm really sorry, Sash. I acted just like him. And then I asked you to be quiet about it. I just—I really screwed up, and I feel like shit."

He stared at me across the table, through his eyelashes, and I didn't know what to say. I'd thought we were here as a joke, or a dumb promise to his parents. I hadn't realized he'd asked me out to dinner for real.

He was still staring at me, waiting for me to say something, to acknowledge his apology.

"Well, yeah," I said. "You did screw things up. You can't treat people like that. It isn't okay."

"I know," Cole said seriously. "Believe me, I know. My brother was this hero to me as a kid. I wanted to be just like him. And then, I didn't. But it was too fucking late. When Lily pulled you away from me at that concert, it hurt. She acted like I was unsafe. And the worst part was, she wasn't wrong."

The server was back.

"Here's that flatbread you were waiting on," he said, sliding an enormous wooden cutting board onto the table and promising our entrees would be out shortly.

"Taste test," Cole said, passing me a slice of flatbread and watching me take a bite.

It was spicy and gooey and really, really good.

"Wow," I said.

"My mom loves this place," Cole admitted. "I figured it was more your speed than the Italian."

"Little bit," I said.

"Besides, I couldn't eat a whole flatbread by myself," Cole said.

"I've seen you take down an entire basket of garlic knots and three slices of pizza," I argued. "So nice try."

We lapsed into momentary silence, eating.

"Thanks, by the way," I said, reaching for another piece. "For bringing me here."

Cole looked up hopefully.

"Does this mean you forgive me?" he asked.

"I accept your apology," I amended. "How about that?"

"Just so long as you don't think I'm a garbage person."

"You're not a garbage person," I told him. "But you've done some shitty things. And you need to own that. And be better."

"I'm trying," Cole promised, fiddling with his napkin. "I swear."

"And you should talk to someone about Archer. It doesn't have to be your parents, but, like, if there's an adult who can help?" I said, realizing I didn't know if there was anyone. "Like you said earlier, it's not okay. And if your parents are having a hard time with processing what's going on, they should know that he's been treating people badly for a while. That it's a pattern."

Cole nodded, considering. And then he looked up at me, his green eyes blazing. "Do you ever feel like high school is this huge performance, and everyone's watching and criticizing if you get it wrong, but no one's helping you get it right?"

"Totally," I admitted, shocked that someone like Cole had those thoughts too.

"Okay, good," he said. "Because I just—I'm feeling really lost right now. And I like you, a lot. And I was hoping you could help me."

He was staring at me as though I was the answer to all his problems, instead of a girl who had too many problems of her own.

"Cole," I said, and he could tell that it was bad news, because his expression crumpled. "I *can't*. I'm not some manic pixie dream girl who can swoop in and magically fix your life. I appreciate the apology, and the dinner. But the only way I see things going between us is friends."

"You're sure?" he asked, dejected.

"One hundred percent. And you've got to stop trying to make it more than that. Because I'll be honest, I'm into someone else."

"It's Adam Ziegler, isn't it?" Cole said mournfully.

"Adam?" I actually burst out laughing.

"You're *always* with that dude," he accused.

I took a deep breath. For some reason, I felt like he

would get this.

"Actually, it's Lily," I said.

Cole dropped his piece of flatbread.

"No *way*," he said. "That's like the hottest thing ever. Are you two, like, *dating*?"

"We were, but now it's over, and she hates me," I said.

"Nah. No one could ever hate you," he said. "So, whoa, hold up. You're *gay*?"

He frowned at me, confused.

"No. I'm actually bi," I admitted.

I winced, waiting for his reaction. For him to make fun of me, or act uncomfortable. But he didn't do any of those things. Instead, he grinned, shaking his head.

"That is *so* hot." Cole moaned, sinking down in his seat. "So a threesome—"

"—is a really rude question," I told him.

"Ahh. Right. Sorry," he said, shaking his head. "See? I don't know what I'm doing."

"Neither does anyone," I promised. "You have to figure it out as you go. And you have to help yourself get it right."

And I realized that I needed to take my own advice.

Because this conversation was giving me déjà vu. It was eerily similar to what had happened with Lily. It was too little too late. It was asking the person you hurt to do the work, instead of working on improving yourself.

Oh god. I was her *Cole*.

I'd never thought of being straight-passing as a privilege

before, but of course it was. When people looked at me, they saw someone who didn't exist. Someone who had it easy.

And choosing to walk out from under that privilege was terrifying. Sure, I could keep on hiding forever, if I wanted to, but the only person I'd be hurting was myself.

I didn't want to live as half of myself. I knew that now. I'd already lost so much—my mom, my old life. Choosing to lose even more when I didn't have to seemed foolish.

I'd been shaving off pieces of myself for years, pretending they didn't exist. Pretending I wasn't miserable or scared or unhappy. Pretending I didn't like girls because I also liked boys.

I'd spent years brushing my fingers over the things I truly wanted, then selecting whatever was safe and plain and boring. But I deserved to try on any identity I thought might fit. I deserved to let myself *have* instead of *want*.

I'd been acting like I didn't live here. Like this was someone else's life. But it wasn't—it was mine, and every day that I sacrificed toward making other people happy was a day that I'd never get back.

Bayport would always carry the history of my mom in it, but I'd been wrong to think of this town as solely hers.

It was ours.

I hadn't been dropped into a repeat of someone else's life. I'd started a new chapter of mine.

I hadn't understood that for a long time, but I saw it

now. And I also saw what I had to do. If I wanted my grandparents to truly understand me, then I had to show them who I was. And that meant I had to tell them who I wasn't. Just like I had wanted to do in yearbook the day of the earthquake, my small first step toward honesty, in six-point font.

Our server appeared with our entrees.

"Actually," I said, as he reached to put mine down, "can we get those to go? And the check?"

"No problem," the guy said, hustling our sandwiches away.

"What's going on?" Cole asked, frowning.

"I'm really sorry," I said, "but there's something I have to do."

"Right now?" he asked.

"Yes," I said firmly. I was sure of it. "Right now."

CHAPTER 30

THE SECOND I GOT HOME, I did something I should have done a long time ago. I took out my camera. And then I went to my bedroom window and lined up a shot.

The shutter clicked softly as I took the photo. The image flashed across my screen: the ocean, dark and churning. The same view that my mom must have seen when she stood at this window. It wasn't a picture of her absence. It was a photo that existed because of her.

My ISO was too high, making the picture grainy. But it didn't matter if the picture was good. It just mattered that I'd taken one.

The next one would be easier, and the one after that, and the one after that. Doing this wasn't nearly as hard as I'd thought. But then, most things that you build up so much in your head never are.

By picking up my camera again, by reclaiming the idea that I was a girl who took pictures, the world didn't end.

And by telling Lily and Adam and Cole that I was bi, the ground hadn't fallen out from under me. If anything, the earth felt even more solid, and I'd begun to feel even more tethered to this place.

I wrenched open the window. Outside, a cricket chimed in the soft grass, and the waves pounded faintly in the distance. I could smell the deep, salty rush of the ocean, and feel the balmy air against my skin.

And I was here. Living in this world. And that was worth capturing.

I stared down at my photo again, realizing it wasn't nothing. It was the permission I'd been looking for to keep going with something that I couldn't remember why I'd stopped.

You can't always bring your comfort zone with you. Sometimes you need to walk toward something terrifying, until you're close enough to see that it isn't scary at all, that it's actually just hard.

And hard things are doable.

All of the important things that had happened to me this year had actually happened. They weren't excuses, or things I'd experienced by standing in the corner with my camera, watching them happen to other people. They weren't captions in a yearbook, with my name as the only proof that I'd ever been there.

And after that conversation at dinner, I knew exactly what I was going to submit for the art gallery.

•••

I brought my camera to school on Monday to work on my submission for the gallery show. It seemed so obvious in retrospect, but then, the best ideas usually do.

Mr. Saldana had given me all of those essays and books to read about art, and they all said the same thing: that art is a mirror, a political act, a confession.

I was trading some books at my locker when I heard Adam announce very loudly, "Wow, a library! I suddenly have to go in there immediately." I didn't think much of it, but when I glanced up again, Lily was standing next to me.

She'd cut her hair shorter, the blunt ends swishing just below her ears. It suited her.

"Hi," I said, surprised.

"Hi," she said, raising a hand self-consciously to her hair.

"I love the cut," I said.

"I've been working up the courage to go short for a while," she confessed, playing with it. It made her look older and more serious, like one of those college students who are very into houseplants and sustainable fashion.

"You should come back to Art Club," Lily said. "I don't want you to quit something you obviously love just because of me."

I stared at her, confused. And then I realized she didn't know what had happened. We'd never talked about it.

"It's not because of you," I said, spinning the combination on my locker. "My grandparents found out I wasn't doing Mock Trial. And then they found out where I'd been instead. So I'm grounded."

"Oh," Lily said. "Wow, that sucks."

"Yeah."

We let the silence hang there for a moment, because we both knew whose idea the lie had been.

"When did this happen?" Lily finally asked.

"Couple days after my birthday?"

"I wish you'd told me," Lily said.

I wished I'd been able to.

"I thought you wanted space," I said, wondering which it was.

"Right," Lily said, as though she'd forgotten. And then she fiddled with the strap of her backpack for a moment.

I opened my locker, grabbing my chem textbook and putting my camera inside. I felt Lily notice it.

"You're taking photos again?" she asked, surprised.

"Well, someone told Mr. Saldana that I'm a photographer. So he's expecting them." I shrugged.

"I thought you'd stopped," Lily said.

"I thought so too," I said. "But it turns out photography's like riding a bicycle. Actually, no, it's not. Sorry. I don't know why I said that."

"Because everything's like riding a bicycle and everything tastes like chicken?" Lily suggested.

"Well, except for chicken. Which tastes like riding a bicycle."

Lily snorted. And then I saw her remember that she wasn't supposed to be laughing with me. Her dark eyes turned serious.

"I didn't think you cared," she said. "About the gallery show."

"I always cared," I confessed. "I was just scared of not having anything worthy."

I was ready to be honest. I'd spent such a long time putting so little of myself out there. Playing it safe. But disasters happen whether you're being safe or taking a risk.

I wanted to tell her that. I wanted to say so many things. But Mabel came by then, having a complete meltdown over a lab write-up that was due in thirty minutes, and before I could say another word, Lily was gone.

"How does next week sound?" my grandmother asked at dinner that night, handing me the salad bowl.

"For what?" I asked, confused.

"For you to start helping at your grandfather's firm after school," she said.

"We were thinking two afternoons a week," my grandfather said.

They were both staring at me. Expecting me to say, "Sure, sounds great," because that was what I always said. Even when it wasn't true. Especially when it wasn't true.

It was now or never.

And so I chose now.

"Actually," I said. "That's not going to work."

"Your grandmother can drop you off after school," my grandfather said, as though transportation was the issue.

"Okay, but that isn't the problem," I said. My heart was hammering, and I felt faintly ill, but I pushed through, because I knew I would feel even worse later if I backed down. "You told me I should join a school club. And I'd rather do that than waste my time at an internship I don't care about. I want to go back to Art Club. It's important to me."

"You didn't even want to take an art class," my grandmother said. "You wanted yearbook."

"Well, I was wrong," I said. "I only did yearbook so I could take the photos. That's what I like—photography! And I got to do that in Art Club, and I made friends there, and I was happy there, and you took it away."

My grandparents were frowning.

"Why am I just hearing about this now?" my grandfather asked.

"Because I didn't want you to be upset with me, so I tried to act like it wasn't a big deal," I confessed.

It all came out in a rush, about how awful Todd was, and how miserable I'd been, and how all I'd wanted was to join the Art Club instead, and I hadn't meant to lie. That it had just happened. And that when faced with the choice between miserable and happy, I wanted to choose happy, and I hoped they'd understand.

After I was finished, my grandparents stared at me.

"Sasha, honey, you have to tell us things," my grandfather said. "We can't be here for you if we don't know what's going on."

"I know," I mumbled, feeling terrible. "I'm sorry."

"For the record, none of this excuses the way you behaved," my grandmother said. "Trust goes both ways. Your mom did the same thing. Always kept her distance. If she had a problem, she dealt with it herself. We kept waiting for her to reach out, but she never did."

My grandmother looked so sad, thinking of my mom. It was like her permafrost had thawed, finally. I hoped this wasn't a herald of impending global warming.

"She was really stubborn," I offered.

"The women in our family always are," Eleanor said.

She smiled thinly, and I wondered for the first time what she saw when she looked at me. I'd always thought it was my mother, but now I realized she must have also seen herself.

"So what does one do in this Art Club?" my grandfather asked.

"Lots of things," I said. "We watch documentaries, and we visit museums."

"I didn't know you liked museums," my grandfather said.

"Well, I used to work in one," I said.

"That's right," my grandfather said. "Eleanor, she used

to work in a museum. You know, I like the sound of this Art Club. It certainly seems more enriching than doing filing in my office."

"Really?" I said, hardly daring to believe my luck. "I can go back?"

"Well—" my grandmother began.

"Yes," my grandfather said firmly.

"Joel," my grandmother said, her voice tinged with warning.

"She should be around other kids her age, doing what makes her happy," he said firmly. "Not sitting around some stuffy law office."

My grandmother clearly didn't agree. I could tell from the twist of her mouth and the way she'd folded her arms.

"Thank you, Grandpa," I said, giving him a hug.

"You're all we have left, kiddo," he said.

I'd never thought of it like that before. I knew we'd all lost my mom, but I'd never considered the negative space. I'd never considered what it was that we all had left. Or rather, who.

"So, there's one more thing," I said, taking the flyer out of my pocket. "My art class is having a show next weekend. I hope you'll come."

CHAPTER 31

I WENT BACK TO ART CLUB on Wednesday. Lily had said she didn't mind, and anyway, I missed everyone.

Ryland wrapped me in a hug and was like, "I'm Switzerland, I'm neutral about whatever went down between you and Lily, but I still missed you."

Mabel showed me pictures of the cat her little sister had rescued over Thanksgiving and named Applesauce, which she thought was one of the worst cat names ever.

"It's totally a horse name," I told her.

"Thank you!" Mabel said. "That's exactly what I said."

Even Adrian was overjoyed to see me. He'd made a pinhole camera out of a box of mac 'n' cheese and wanted someone to geek out over it with him. Although he kept annoying everyone by telling them to "say cheese," and then asking if they got it.

Lily gave me a nod. She was putting on a documentary about Ai Weiwei, and she crept over after it started to sit next to me.

"You came," she whispered.

"I came," I said.

"Do your grandparents know?" she asked nervously.

"Yeah," I said, and then clarified, "I mean, they know about Art Club."

"That's great," Lily said.

"I know," I whispered back.

And then Danica and her friends very loudly shushed us, and Lily rolled her eyes. But she didn't leave. She sat next to me for the rest of the movie. It was agony, having her so close, having this cautious friendship between us, which was better than nothing, but wasn't at all what I wanted. It was what *she* wanted, though.

I didn't go back to sitting with Lily at lunch the next day. I wasn't sure I was invited, and I didn't want to push. Besides, I'd already learned that things don't snap back into what they've been.

I sat with Cole for the rest of the week, the two of us decamping onto a slope of grass behind the math-sci courtyard. Without the constant presence of Friya and Whitney, Cole seemed more relaxed. He told me about computer programming, and some of the apps he wanted to design, and he confessed to being overly competitive at board games.

"We should get a game night going over winter break," he said, getting really excited about the idea.

I knew it was a distraction. And he knew that I knew. It

was so much easier to talk about real things now that we weren't trying to figure out what we were to each other, or what anyone expected us to be.

"You tell your parents about Archer?" I asked one afternoon.

He nodded, his expression unreadable behind his sunglasses as he gave me the bullet points. It sounded rough. I nudged his shoe with mine, and he nudged back.

"You tell your grandparents that you're into Harry *and* Hermione?" he asked.

"Working on it," I said. "I have a plan."

And I did. I'd turned in my submission for the art gallery. I didn't want anyone to see it early, so I wrapped it in brown paper bags and left it in the pile. It was the best thing I'd ever made, because it was the most personal thing I'd ever made.

I'd hidden behind photography before, but now I was revealing myself through it.

This piece was my insurance policy.

If I didn't tell my grandparents before they saw it, they'd find out anyway.

In a way, it felt poetic. You're supposed to count down before you take a photo. Three, two, one . . .

I counted down the days left for me to come out.

I felt jittery and a little sick as I sat down to breakfast the morning of the gallery show. I watched my grandmother bustle around as I stirred my yogurt and made small talk with my grandfather.

It all felt unbearably normal.

How can you not know? I wanted to scream at them.

But then, we never know when the earth's about to fall out from under us. Even when we're the ones causing the shift.

My hands were shaking so badly that I was afraid I'd spill my yogurt if I tried to eat any. I could hear the tremendous thump of my heartbeat in my ears, and I wondered how no one else heard it too. How my grandparents could sit there calmly discussing the latest food recall on romaine lettuce.

My grandmother got up to refill her coffee cup, and I realized that if I didn't tell them now, I'd miss my chance.

"So, um, there's something I want to tell you," I said.

"What's on your mind, sweetheart?" my grandfather asked, setting down his phone. He really was addicted to that jewel-collecting game.

This was so much harder than I'd thought it would be.

I took a deep breath, my heart pounding so loudly that it felt like my own heartbeat was rising up around me, ticking, a clock to mark this particular moment in time. This was it. I was telling them.

This was the timestamp on the photograph. The spike on the seismograph. The end of the world as I knew it.

"First of all, I love you," I said.

"We love you too," my grandfather said. "Very much. Now what's going on?"

"Okay, so there's no easy way to say this, and I guess I've wanted to tell you for a while. And just. Well. What I wanted to tell you is that I'm bisexual."

Judging from the looks on my grandparents' faces, the word had tumbled from my lips, gained corporeal form as a dancing bear, and was doing high kicks all over the breakfast table.

"That can't be true," my grandmother said. "It's so confusing being young and—"

"I'm not confused," I said. "Not anymore. I like boys and girls. I just thought you should know."

"But you have a boyfriend," my grandmother said, as though reassuring herself. "You're dating Cole."

"No," I said gently. "We're just friends."

"But you were dating someone," my grandmother said. "On your birthday, you were so upset over breaking up with . . ."

I saw her pause, realizing.

"Lily," I supplied.

The room got very quiet and very cold as a frost of displeasure crossed my grandmother's face. My grandfather was frowning, as if confused.

"I didn't tell you because I wasn't sure how you'd react," I went on. "And that's partially why we broke up. Because it wasn't fair that we had to lie and hide it." I took a deep breath. "So I wanted to tell you now, because if I feel that way about someone, I want to be able to date them. And not hide it."

"I'm not sure I understand," my grandfather said. "Are you saying that you're gay?"

"No," I said. "I still like boys. But I also like girls."

"But even if you 'date' a girl, you're eventually going to marry a boy and have children," my grandmother interrupted.

"I'm not going to make that promise," I said. "That's not how it works."

"Well, maybe it should be," my grandmother said.

"Eleanor," my grandfather growled.

"What?" my grandmother snapped. "Are you telling me you're okay with this? With our granddaughter saying she might marry a woman?"

"It's not like it was in our day," my grandfather said. "The world is changing."

"Just because the world is doesn't mean I have to," my grandmother said. "I don't care what other people do, but that doesn't mean I want my own granddaughter doing it."

"Doing what?" my grandfather asked. "Finding someone who makes her happy?"

My grandmother's mouth twisted.

"If she can be happy with a boy, then I think she should try that," she said.

"I did," I cut in, refusing to let them have this conversation about me like I wasn't in the room. It was time to take charge of my own life. "I tried so hard. But then I met Lily and I—I just, no one else compared. And it didn't seem right to ignore the way I felt."

I stared down at my napkin, which I'd somehow torn into ribbons. "I'm sick of hiding things and lying. I want to know that we can be honest with each other, and that I can share important parts of my life with you."

"We want that too," my grandfather said. "We're just very surprised, sweetheart. You're such a pretty girl. You could date anyone."

And I realized that he didn't get it. That they didn't get it.

"I know," I said. "And I'm telling you that's what I want. To date anyone."

"But if you date a girl, it's going to be so hard for you," my grandmother said, her voice small. "I don't want your life to be hard."

"I think it's going to be harder on me if that's something I want and I tell myself I can't," I admitted. "I'm just—I think the hardest thing is that I've known for a while, and I was never brave enough to tell my mom. And now she'll never know."

My grandmother had never been at a loss for words before, but she certainly was now. I stared at her, willing her to say something. But it was my grandfather who spoke.

"Sweetheart, she knew *you,*" my grandfather said. "And

she loved you more than anything. And so do we." He shot a look at my grandmother. "Right, Eleanor?"

My grandmother was very quiet, and I realized she was crying.

"Grandma?" I said.

"I don't want it to be hard for you," she said. "We just wanted to give you a good life. To make things easier for you. And being . . . bisexual . . . isn't easy."

"No," I said. "It's not. And it's actually been really hard not being able to say anything about it."

"Sweetheart," my grandfather said, wrapping me in a hug that felt fierce and protective.

My grandmother's hug was brief and perfunctory, but as she reached out to offer one, I realized that the thing I was most afraid of had already happened. That I'd told them my truth, and that they'd listened and tried to understand, and that, somehow, even though it wasn't okay yet, I felt like it was going to be eventually.

My grandparents were never going to hate me for being the person I was instead of the person they wanted me to be. I hadn't understood that because I hadn't tried to understand them.

We were three people who had been broken by a loss and then thrown together, and we were learning how to fit ourselves into a family. And that want was the glue that bonded our broken pieces together, instead of individually. I hadn't realized the pieces were connected.

I had felt like a stranger here, ghosting through someone else's life. My real life, I'd been convinced, was the one I'd lived with my mom, full of quiet desperation. We'd both spent years pretending to be happy, pretending for each other, because each other was all we had.

But then I lost my mom, and found myself. And it turned out there was more to me than I'd ever known. I'd stood on the sidelines for so many years, capturing other people's best moments. Telling myself it didn't matter that I was missing my own. And then, when I got them, I told myself it didn't matter that they felt wrong. Because it turned out I hadn't wanted to fit in after all. That what I'd really wanted was to be seen.

When we got to the high school, we followed chalk arrows that someone had drawn from the parking lot. Mr. Saldana had reserved the black box theater, and twinkle lights were strung across the lobby, along with flyers for our show. It looked beautiful. And somehow, I knew it was Lily's doing. Although I couldn't spot her anywhere.

The theater was surprisingly crowded. The music playing was familiar, and it took me a moment before I realized the song was from Whitney and Ethan's band.

I watched as my grandparents looked around politely, taking in the art. There were more than a few mediocre seascapes and painfully precise bananas. But there were also a lot of wonderful things.

The panels from Ryland's graphic novel. Cakes frosted out of plaster, which I knew immediately were Lily's. Adrian had hung photographs from the ceiling on fishing wire. On one side were black-and-white snapshots, and on the other, colored photos of the sky stamped with the date.

Mr. Saldana spotted us and hurried over.

"Welcome," he said. "You must be Sasha's . . ." He trailed off, frowning. I could see him realizing that, despite my grandmother's regimen of face creams and Zumba, she was too old to be my mom.

"Grandparents," I supplied.

"You must be so proud," he said. "She has quite an eye for photography."

"We're fans," my grandfather said.

My grandmother looked confused, as though she couldn't figure out how she'd missed this. As though she was just beginning to piece together who I truly was.

"It's been a pleasure having her in Art Club this semester," Mr. Saldana went on, chatting politely in that teacher-parent way.

After Mr. Saldana got pulled away, my grandfather smiled.

"I like him," he said. "So, where's your work?"

"It's interactive," I warned. "You're going to need your phones."

"Interactive?" My grandmother frowned.

"You'll see," I promised, steering them over and hovering

nervously, waiting for their thoughts. I'd taken four portraits of my classmates, in the style of a page of yearbook superlatives. I'd even done the layout. Across the bottom of each, I'd written their names and the titles that immediately came to mind when I thought about them. *Cole Edwards: Most Likely to Succeed. Whitney Jackson: Most Likely to Become Famous. Todd Burnham: Most Likely to Become Your Boss.* It was only when you saw the note, off to the side, inviting you to take a picture of the art with your phone, that you realized what the art was really about.

The captions were a deception. Over them, I'd used IR-spectra paint, which was invisible unless seen through a camera lens.

When you held up your phone or your camera, you saw the true captions on my photographs. *Cole Edwards: Most Improved Human. Whitney Jackson: Best at Taking Selfies. Todd Burnham: Biggest Ego.*

In the bottom right was one of Adrian's pictures of Lily and me. *Best Friends,* the caption read. But when you held up your phone, it changed to: *Cutest Couple.*

She'd told me that I needed to want to stop hiding. And now I did.

Just because I was terrified of doing it didn't mean I shouldn't. It just meant that I had to push through the fear.

So here I was, showing my truth. Bearing my soul. And hoping that she'd see it. That she'd understand what she'd meant to me, and how much I wanted another chance to do it all right.

I watched as my grandparents held up their phones to each picture, as they saw that when they did, the images changed.

"This is neat!" my grandfather said, shaking his head over it. "How'd you do it?"

"Invisible paint," I said. "It's supposed to show how the overall idea of someone isn't actually the truth. How sometimes, who we truly are is hidden."

"Sasha!" Ryland said, coming over and sweeping me into a hug. "The photos are amazing!"

"Thank you," I said.

"Best at taking selfies." He cackled. "I died."

"Ryland!" my grandmother said, spotting him. "How's your grandmother doing? Does she still need help with that silent auction?"

"I can find out," he said, chatting with them politely.

My grandfather was frowning at his phone.

"Everything okay, Grandpa?" I asked.

"Just trying to save these pics," he said, looking lost. "How do I get them in my cloud?"

I tried not to laugh.

"I think it's automatic," I told him. And then I waited a moment before asking, "So, do you like them?"

"You blow me away, sweetheart," he said. "So creative."

"Thanks," I said.

"You look so happy there," he said, pointing at the picture of Lily and me. "Elle, did you see this one?" A shadow flickered across my grandmother's face. "Have you ever seen her look so happy?"

"No," my grandmother said, gritting her teeth. "I haven't."

I got that she was trying. That they both were.

But I kept twisting around, looking, hoping, waiting for Lily.

Except she wasn't there.

So many other people were, though. They kept coming up to me. Telling me how much they liked it, how they were choosing my piece for their write-up. These were art kids, after all. They knew what it was like to be different. They didn't even blink at what my art had revealed. And I wished I'd realized that sooner.

I don't know what I had expected.

For Lily to come. For her to see my yearbook portraits and rush into my arms. For the smashed pieces of what we were to magically float into the air and stitch themselves back together.

But she hadn't shown up.

I waited and waited, until far after my grandparents were ready to leave, and then I slunk into their back seat and smiled faintly as they politely assured me that they'd enjoyed themselves.

Even though I knew it had made them uncomfortable,

seeing the picture of us with its innocent caption and then holding up their phones and seeing the truth.

Even though I knew I made them uncomfortable now, every moment they realized how much they'd misunderstood me. So I'd told them that I was tired, and I'd gone up to my room and collapsed onto my bed and put on some music that was in no way helping me to feel better.

I'd failed. Not at the most important thing, but at something that was important to me. At *someone* who was important to me.

But I could do this without her. I didn't need to define myself in the negative space of other people. I could trace my outlines and sketch in the shadows and darken the lines without being afraid of messing up.

There was a knock at the door.

"Sasha?" It was my grandfather. "Someone's here to see you."

Oh god. I hoped it wasn't Cole.

It was Lily.

I sat up, startled at the sight of her. She was in her Quidditch sweatshirt and leggings, and her hair was a mess, and she didn't have any makeup on. She looked beautiful.

"Hey," she said.

"Well, you girls have a nice . . . chat," my grandfather said, making to close the door. And then he stopped halfway, realizing, and mumbled something about leaving the door open after all.

"You told them," Lily said. It wasn't a question.

"Yeah."

"How did that go?"

"I'm not sure, actually," I said. "They're dealing with it. They're trying. I think they need time."

"Time helps," Lily said. "It did with my grandparents."

"Where were you?" I blurted.

"Oh god," she said, collapsing onto my bed with a groan. "My sister broke her ankle playing soccer. We rushed straight to the ER from her game, and we had to wait forever, and Adam made some dumb joke about amputation, and she freaked out, and I couldn't leave."

"Holy shit," I said.

No wonder Lily was wearing a sweatshirt and leggings.

"Is she okay?"

"My parents granted her unlimited screen time while she's on crutches, so it's like Christmas came early." Lily rolled her eyes fondly. "Yeah, so I only got to the gallery show for like the last ten minutes. I had to take an Uber. And the driver was an aspiring DJ who swears by his keto diet."

"Woof."

Lily sighed.

"How does nothing ever go the way it's supposed to?" she asked, half to herself.

"I loved your plaster cakes," I blurted.

"They were just an amusement." Lily shrugged. "Nothing like what you made."

I stiffened.

"You saw it?" I asked.

"The real art is the photo you take of the art, not the piece hanging on the wall," she said. "Clever."

"I wanted to play with the idea of how we curate versions of ourselves that are rarely honest. And how easy it is to forget that we don't really know each other, but we live in this social structure that presumes we do," I explained.

"And are you scared?" Lily breathed. "For people to know who you really are?"

"I was," I said. "But not anymore. There was this really great girl who taught me how to live my truth."

"So tell me about her," Lily said, stretching back on my bed. "Is she cute?"

"Eh, she's okay."

"Sasha!"

"Whatever, you know you're gorgeous," I said. "And brilliant. And brave. And that I really, really like you. And that I want you to be my girlfriend."

I stared at her, completely unsure. I'd created my own safe space, and brought the people I cared about inside of it. I'd confronted what I'd lost by reminding myself what I still had left. I wanted that to be enough. I hoped it was enough.

"I want to say yes," Lily said. "But there's something I need to do first."

"Oh," I said, disappointed. "Okay. Um."

But then Lily leaned forward, holding my face in her

hands, and brought her lips toward mine. Before I knew it, we were kissing.

And I don't know if the stars fell from the sky, or the ocean thundered in applause, or the books on my shelf felt a tingle run up their spines, but I hope they did.

I read somewhere that everyone in California lives less than thirty miles from the nearest fault line. That we're all constantly at risk of our lives falling apart. And yet no one seems to notice. *Somewhere else,* we all think. *It'll happen somewhere else.* Which means that what happened to me could have happened to anyone.

It's much easier to avoid these kinds of things. To build houses on top of fault lines and hope that no one ever realizes it could all crumble away at any moment. To think about dinner or homework instead of how it's not a matter of if but when.

But the thing is, the idea of impending disaster doesn't scare people away. Not to the extent that you'd think. Instead, we bolt our bookcases to the wall and stick our breakables to the shelves with putty. We go about our lives, and most days we forget.

Most days we *want* to forget. But sometimes we need to remember.

I used to be afraid of brokenness. I was terrified that if people saw the real me, they'd pack their bags and leave. That if I let myself follow my heart, it would only lead to regret, and make it that much harder to find my footing.

It wasn't until I lost my mom that I truly learned what it felt like to have the ground pulled out from under me. That I learned what it was like to look around at my life and think, I don't belong here. I don't live here.

Except it turns out I do.

The world shoves into you, but you stand tall anyway.

Which is exactly what I did.

Acknowledgments

This page is basically the mattress tag. Do not remove or else warranty is void, and book might sprout legs and scuttle under your desk, where it will growl at you while building a nest out of bobby pins. I'm not saying this will definitely happen, but, like, it's possible. And so, out of an abundance of caution, the following people are granted a lifetime warranty, tag or no tag: My incredible literary agent, Merrilee Heifetz, my brilliant editor and publisher, Katherine Tegen, my new ride-or-die editor, Sara Schonfeld, and the entire team at HarperCollins. This book owes a lot to the wonderful insights of Amy Spalding and Amy Rose Capetta, as well as the encouragement of Zan Romanoff, Maura Milan, Julie Buxbaum, Alexandra Monir, Emily Wibberly, and Austin Siegemund-Broka. Thank you, so very much, to my parents. And to my husband, Daniel Inkeles, who has been promoted from development to executive producer on this, the third book I've written since we met. Thank you to the many friends with whom I have discussed identity and queerness and art, and who will no doubt find pieces of our conversations stitched into this story. To my book club, who better not suggest we read this, even as a joke. To Ye Olde Cheshire Cheese, where I frantically found myself writing the final pages of this story, because deadlines, what deadlines, oh look, a Netflix. Thank you to all of the queer writers and filmmakers and activists whose work paved the way for stories like this one, and who helped me realize that we have a responsibility to create the world we want to live in. And last, thank you to my readers. However you found my books, through a friend or a bookseller or a school assignment, I'm so glad you did. PS: Maybe check under your desk for stray bobby pins, just to be safe.